Growing Wings

Growing Wings

Anne Christie

PIATKUS

First published in Great Britain in 1993 by
Judy Piatkus (Publishers) Ltd of
5 Windmill Street, London W1

**The moral right of the author
has been asserted**

*A catalogue record for this book is available
from the British Library*

ISBN 0–7499–0203–5

Set in 11/12pt Times by
Phoenix Photosetting, Chatham, Kent
Printed and bound in Great Britain by
Bookcraft (Bath) Ltd

With affectionate thanks to Pamela Gillilan and
Barry Underwood for their help and encouragement.

One

Heat. Pain in head and limbs, his brains on fire. Retching till there seemed nothing more to come, and always the awful nightmares, back to New York and the horror of that filthy basement. Then the relief of cool water, the touch of brown fingers. Arms lovingly propping up his wasted body. Concerned dark eyes and smiles like Ram's when he was saying goodbye, and all the time talk in a language he didn't understand.

Nathan retched again and fell back exhausted. A wet cloth was patted on his face. He sucked at the water like a baby, unable to find the strength to drink from the brass bowl. This time he really thought he would die, but it was different because in a strange way he could accept it. It was as though he was about to float through a dark tunnel of water at the end of which an infinitely seductive light glimmered; he knew that there, where the light was, he would find an end to all the pains: physical, mental and spiritual. He felt certain that there he would at last be free. Floating, he wanted only to reach out to that peace and release himself from everything.

Halfway home that night he had wished that he'd taken a cab from 42nd Street, but he'd needed some air. That part of the walk home was always scary so late at night, especially when he was hampered by the saxophone; the streets were almost empty of people or automobiles and it had felt strange after all the noise. He was still high from the gig which had gone on till after three. It had been some gig: they had flown together, the group and the audience. For the first time since Laura he

1

had felt able fully to express his grief and to forget – forget the guilt etched in his guts by the image of her face and body, and the almost animal sobs of her mother who obviously blamed him entirely: 'Always on the road! That's what started Laura off! How could she possibly be OK with the life you forced on her?'

He hadn't defended himself; there had seemed no point. Laura could not be brought back, the needles had been used, the trips taken. 'I can handle it, I just need to open my doors of perception. I can paint like an angel, I know it. I just need to see further into that world that opens up – to expand – to understand and see the whole damn' drama working all at once, inside and out. I need it, honey. I'll never get hooked . . .'

He'd tried persuasion: he'd raged and cried and they had made love and promises. She'd even tried cold turkey twice, but somehow she'd been magnetised to her own destruction. Would it have helped if he'd stopped touring? He'd begged her to come with him but she wouldn't because of her exhibition. 'I need to be in my studio – you go. I've got to make it in my own right, not just be Mrs Famous Sax-Follower. I'll be here, honey, I'll never let you down.'

And Nathan had been innocent enough to believe her.

It was freezing; he could see the white cloud of his breath as he hurried. There were millions of stars up there, and a little sickle moon; the stars were swinging round as well as the street lights.

'Shit, Laura. God damn you, you stupid bitch! Why? Why? What were you trying to prove?' His sax, his golden angel as he called the horn with its glittering curves and magic buttons, could carry him away to that benign universe which was more liberating and secure than any of his other worlds. Perhaps he had loved the music-making too much? She'd yelled that at him once. Wildly, he stared at the sky, the huge mystery of it. Then, groaning with despair and rage, he lifted the case high above his head and hurled it with all his power – wham! – against a grafittied wall where it bounced, teetered on to some gappy railings and fell into the well of a basement to lie in ghastly silence.

He couldn't drink at that point: like tonight just one or two and he was gone, a lightweight. The fucking horn – packed tight into its two thousand bucks custom-built black coffin that was after all designed to withstand earthquakes and car wrecks – had got to be intact. He was so pissed that he really wasn't quite sure whether he wanted it to be unharmed or not. As he leaned dizzily over the railings, sobbing like a kid, he was aware of a light going on in the basement and a man's angry voice demanding what the fuck was going on.

He stumbled down the steps knee-deep in rustling trash and a door burst open. For a moment he thought his heart would stop when he was met by the slavering Dobermann. He glimpsed a chain and a big black guy hanging on to the animal, then two large young men carrying beer cans. All three had belts jangling with keys and the big-gutted blond one had a knife. Nathan had never felt so scared in his life: he thought he would shit himself.

'I-I'm sorry. I dropped my sax. It fell down there . . .'

'Poor l'il sweetie pie, let's help the man. Lost your instrument, huh? That's just too bad. I guess you'd better just come on in and tell us all about it.'

The knife guy had tattoos, and blond hair gelled into peaks.

'Move, kiddo.' Nathan felt the weapon in his side and almost stopped breathing when the leather of his jacket slit.

'Hey, you cut my coat, man.'

'Get inside.' The black guy, who had picked up the case – which amazingly didn't look too badly damaged – shoved him roughly.

The dog's black fur was standing up in peaks too, all along his back. Nathan stumbled into a mess of an apartment with broken furniture and a TV Western blaring; the guy on the white horse was about to be ambushed. There was a huge unmade double bed in the corner.

'Jesus Christ, what *is* this? I'm real sorry I disturbed you. Please, just let me take my sax and get home. I'm truly sorry – I didn't mean . . .'

His head hit the carpet hard between cigarette butts and empty cans. One of the men knelt beside him, fingers tormenting, forcing Nathan's head towards the light.

He gasped, but got slapped. When he tried to wipe the blood from his nose, the black guy chucked him a filthy rag.

3

'Clean yoself, man.'

He managed to pull off a glove and use the back of his hand, then felt for his wallet. The blond wrenched it from him, pulling out a wad of dollars which he counted fast on to the table.

'Hundred and fifty-five, and a whole l'il stack of gold cards – American Express, Mastercards, Executive cards, Diners cards – enough to have a game of pool. What a rich little boy we are, Nathan, eh?'

His head was jerked back again.

'What have I done to you guys? You can have it all, but please just let me go.'

The black man took the wallet and pulled out Laura's picture, big-eyed, innocent, with a naughty smile. Taken three years ago. Before the heroin.

'Nice.' The big guy nodded and showed it to the third man who had strange eyes, dark, with heavy lids, half-asleep. Skinny almost to emaciation, dressed all in black, he grinned inanely.

'Nice, and you're a nice little boy – well, quite a big boy. Very big, maybe. Let's just have a little look.'

Rough hands rolled him over abruptly, arms pinioned. He yelled again as loud as he could and once more he felt the blade, this time cold at his throat. The blond buy's eyes were staring straight into his. 'Easy, honey child. No more yelling. We don't like noise down here, do we?'

When his belt was hauled off and his zip yanked open, Nathan thought it could not be real. He was twenty-seven years old, trying to get on with his life, and suddenly he was embroiled in this ghastly video mixed up with montage images of Laura as he had found her, slumped across the john, dead as a stone. It was a real live nightmare.

The skinny man kept laughing like some crazy animal until the black one thumped him. 'Cut it out, cuckoo.'

Nathan caught a glimpse of the thin one nursing a bruise, sulking. Aware of arms, feet, he gasped as a boot smashed his ribs and when his legs were upended and his jeans viciously wrenched down, he thought he would lose a foot.

'I'll do it.' Blondie knelt by him and inserted the knife between ankle and trouser.

Nathan shrieked as skin and denim ripped, then lay panting, face pressed into butt ends and dirt, arms bent almost backwards. The dog, growling, was pulled abruptly out of vision.

'On the bed.'

Manhandled like a meat carcase, his sex cold, shrinking; his leg hurt and there were blood streaks on the sheets. Skinny man beat the dog and tied him up. For a moment it looked as though the animal would pull the table over till a swipe made him shut up.

'More.' The black guy gestured imperiously and Skinny handed out new cans of beer.

Nathan groaned as his arms were tied behind him. He was aware of a voice he knew to be his own, sobbing just like in the movies. He heard the cans spurt and sensed the three standing round him. Someone put a foot on his buttock and he felt the pattern of the rubber sole on his flesh.

'Neat little ass. Real pretty. Nice and clean. You a music maker, huh?'

His head was jerked back as he mumbled something unintelligible. The thin man's strange eyes stared stupidly into his. 'You answer me when I ask, see? You a musician?'

He nodded, his mouth full of blood.

'Well, you're gonna play some real nice music for us now.' It was the blond one talking. Then they all laughed, the thin one loudest and longest.

'Let's just tune him up.' From the voice he could tell it was the black guy. There were rustling noises, decisive movements, then a terrible silence before he felt the knife again, this time a glissando all the way from the small of his back down to the bottom of his left leg. He was freezing cold.

'Them's real pretty socks,' whispered the blond man and stroked Nathan's cheek. 'Real nice little musician socks, little pretty red and green stripes – real sweet. Does she like your ass too, your pretty little honey-coloured half-caste ass?' The same man took the picture of Laura and looked at it, snickering, then he took out a lighter and with great deliberation set fire to it. Nathan yelled and they all watched as her smile curled up in the flame. Next thing he knew his head exploded with terrible pain and there were even more stars than the ones he'd seen going round outside so long ago.

5

In the middle of it he had suddenly remembered his long solo of earlier that night: it had been magical. It had grown out of his mourning, a lament for Laura, and the people listening had travelled with him. A girl had come up to him at the end, still crying.

'It was just beautiful, Mr Robson. You moved me so much. Thank you. It was the most beautiful music-making I've ever heard.'

Agony. His own voice yelling, his own head almost slapped off. The steel point was at his throat and Blondie's whisky-beery breath engulfing him. 'No yelling, man. No mouth music or this will cut it out.'

The big black one had hurt him most. Enormously heavy, stinking of sweat, he had seemed to ride him for ever. Skinny had stared again into Nathan's face and tried like a child tormenting a sleeping parent to pry his clenched eyes open. Then Blondie had managed to get going but with much noise. 'Oh my God!' he had shouted. 'Oh my God!' It had made Skinny nearly burst with crazy indrawn yelps of laughter. Then it was his turn.

If only you could choose to die, to quit the body, not with a knife but with a decision – simply turn yourself out like a light. To stop from gagging Nathan tried to pray, but it didn't seem to help a lot; the intrusion on his body was too shocking.

Later, the four men had sat or lain on the carpet. Nathan's abusers were strangely quiet and the dog whined intermittently. Nathan sobbed and shook; somebody had flung a blanket over him and they had drunk more. Skinny, leaning over him grinning, had leisurely poured a can of beer over Nathan's head and the last thing he remembered before he had passed out was watching, appalled, as the black man pulled the horn out of the music-case and forced a squeal or two out of it – farty noises which reduced Skinny to further paroxysms of hysterics. Then, rolling his eyes, the big man had grinned before commencing with a huge claw hammer, coldly and efficiently, to smash the glittering sax to bits.

Two

'Come to India with me,' Nadine had said for years, but Jenni had always been too busy or in some different part of the world. 'I'd love to come,' she always answered, just as she had that first day in France. Now here she was at last, on a freezing winter dawn at Heathrow Airport, waiting for her old friend, filled with misgivings, poised to join a group of dotty yellow-clad strangers on a flight to Delhi.

'If I'm going to be the sort of journalist I intend to be, I must get used to travelling alone,' she had told her mother. 'I'm twenty-three, for goodness' sake. It's only France I'm going to.'

'But it was a French farmer in that same area who murdered that poor English family . . .'

'Mum, it was a farmer near Cheltenham who murdered a whole family last month. I saw the blood, I had to report on it. It can happen anywhere.'

She would always remember that first meeting ten years ago. It had been so hot and glaring that the shadows appeared stronger and more substantial than actual objects in the shimmering landscape. The noise of a car's engine in the distance had made her turn automatically, thumb out, and she had watched hopefully as the little blue Deux Chevaux spluttered to a stop.

'You English?' A woman with well-cut short grey hair leaned out.

Nodding, Jenni said she was heading for the *auberge de jeunesse*. The woman, whose accent was French with an

American overlay, was wearing workmens' blue dungarees, striped tee-shirt, silver earrings and a massive silver bracelet – the effect definitely artistic.

'Hop in.' She opened the passenger door, cursed mildly as she shifted a couple of battered camera bags into the rear, and folded back the seat to make room for Jenni's rucksack.

'You look like you need something to drink.'

Nadine had brought Jenni to a café where they had sat and talked for half the afternoon in the shade of a giant plane tree with camouflage-like bark. It was against those peeling islands of green, beige and brown that Nadine had taken her first picture of Jenni. In it the girl looked all at once mutinous and defensive; it was still the picture of herself that she liked best.

'Do you know a fantastic photographer called Cartier-Bresson?' she had asked soon after the first sip of cold beer.

'Very well; he lives about twenty miles away.'

Jenni tried again 'And Lartigue, do you know his work?'

'Of course.'

Jenni eyed this strange lively woman thoughtfully. 'What did you say your name was again?'

'Nadine.'

Jenni's yelp of delight made the cafe's grey parrot almost topped off his perch in response.

'I know who you are. You're Nadine Mankovitz, aren't you? I saw your exhibition in Avignon.' She looked at her new companion open-mouthed. 'I think you're a genius.'

Nadine had shrugged sardonically, her wide mouth struggling to belie how pleased she was to be acknowledged.

Jenni had been truly awestruck. Nadine's pictures had affirmed all of the girl's deepest ambitions about life and work.

'Those incredible photos of the Bronx, and the Indian ones – I wanted terribly to buy your book but I didn't have the money. I got a poster, though.'

Shyly she looked at Nadine's clever slanting face, with the brilliant blue eyes, and remembered the power of the images.

'Those textured ones of wood and water – the old doors, roots, stones, the cracked dried mud. They were absolutely amazing too . . .'

8

'I did all of those here in Provence. They're recent. I took those mud ones near here.'

Nadine had stood up at this point, her smile mesmeric. She seemed to be both old and young at the same time; erotic, yet of neither sex.

'Why don't we go now to my house? We can have coffee there and a swim in the pool. I think we still have much to talk about.'

The invitation had contained a challenge which Jenni found almost alarming, it being simultaneously both seductive and irresistible. Looking at her new companion, she knew that her mother would have found Nadine entirely dubious.

Jenni had stood up and reached for her rucksack.

'That's very kind of you. I'd love to come.'

Blearily now, she eyed the airport departure screen. Their flight was being called for the second time but where the hell was Nadine? She looked uneasily at the group of devotees that she knew she and Nadine were meant to travel with. Even through her own disguise of dark glasses and yellow garments, the outfits they were all wearing appeared hideous. She hated wearing yellow. It made her look corpselike. Unlike Jenni, as well as yellow, be it lemon, saffron, maize or buttercup, the twenty or so Westerners of mixed ages, plus a few Indians, were all wearing shiny gold dots on their foreheads. It made her want to vomit.

Surely, she had asked, Nadine didn't intend to wear one of those ridiculous things? They looked like Christmas decorations.

Nadine had chuckled throatily. 'It is not for the festive season that they wear the tikka.' She pointed to the middle of her forehead. 'Here is the seat of consciousness.'

Although Jenni, huddling deep into her collar, cringed at the awful possibility of being professionally recognised and classified as part of the group, she found the concept Nadine had hinted at an interesting one. For several days after that particular conversation she had carried the thought, and yesterday, motionless in a traffic jam, en route to her brother and family for Christmas dinner, she had looked towards the oncoming drivers and wondered about their souls. Did they really shine out from their foreheads? It was a fetching idea, but she was relieved to notice when at last an elegant woman wrapped in an assortment of yellow garments made her way towards her that the only thing on Nadine's forehead was her now white fringe, topped jauntily by a bright yellow beret which made for an endearingly clownlike effect.

'I didn't know you!' Nadine exclaimed. 'When did you cut all your hair off? It is like a boy's.' She looked at Jenni appraisingly. 'It's *gamine* – but I miss your lion's mane. You look so different . . .'

'That was the object of the exercise.'

'Ah.' Nadine smiled and nodded understandingly. Always original as well as chic, she had a creative brilliance with all things visual, and today's cleverly combined French trousers, well-cut in mustard yellow with odd buckles and pouches, and rugged matching sweater were well up to standard. Her eyes gleamed as she hugged Jenni. 'At last we go to India together.'

'It must be a decade since you asked me to come.'

Nadine's smile was agelessly beautiful. It shone. 'Ten or twenty years, it doesn't matter. Now we are here and now is life. We go, we see, we be.' She patted her striped woollen bag fondly. 'I have my Leica here and the Nikon too – my beloveds.' She grinned. 'How was Christmas, darling?'

Jenni grunted. 'Not bad. Ma did her usual sherried bleat: why didn't I settle down and produce some grandchildren, and was I sure I wouldn't lose my job because of all the fracas I raised with my interview with the Minister?'

'Any news on the arms programme?'

'Everything closes down at Christmas anyway so it's all gone quiet, but I don't think they'll dare hold it back, though they're still threatening to.'

Nadine's eyes blazed. 'Society here seems to be more and more fascist. What they want to do to your programme is simple censorship, but still the myth continues that this is a free country. It is disgusting.'

'They'll probably lock us all up as dissidents.'

'Ugh!' Nadine's snort held pain and anger. 'All the creative people and lateral thinkers – it will be like America in Macarthy time.' She shivered. 'Or other places . . .'

10

'I think, or hope, that we are too many and too articulate for that to happen.'

Nadine touched Jenni's arm. 'Forget it all for a little. Now you and I are free, at least for a while. Just remember that it is a holiday. Now tell me, most important, the married one? you have seen him?'

'I told you. It's over. *Fini.*'

'Again?' Nadine's smile was ironic.

'This time it's for real. Truly finished. Nothing. I said no meetings, no letters, no calls. I finally got tired of the empty promises, of always coming second best. It was like coming up against a brick wall time and again.'

Nadine sighed. 'How long since you saw him?'

'Months.'

'You miss him.'

'It's the work connection I miss as much as the rest of it – I'm afraid I loved his mind too. But more and more I hated actually being in an adulterous relationship.' She shrugged. 'I just felt bad about it.'

'Love. It is so cruel; an illness.'

'It seems to succeed for some.'

The older woman looked towards the people in yellow who wore their souls on their foreheads. Perhaps these young Travellers were the right ones. They only loved God – the Life Force – but they detached from the bits which brought pain.

'Maybe I should become celibate like them?'

'Or be neutered like a cat.' Nadine laughed her croaky laugh and her face creased all over. Well-baked in the oven of life, she sometimes described herself. 'Then if your lover were neutered too you could just be dear loving friends. So peaceful, la la . . .'

Jenni frowned. Michael's disappearance from her life after all those years of illicit loving still sometimes made her feel as if the cable of her life-support machine had been wrenched, far from being the hard-boiled journalist they had recently called her in Parliament.

'And this Michael – you told me four years ago he had promised to divorce, no?'

Jenni nodded. 'Longer, even, and I went along with it. I

11

really believed it would happen, and that his wife would be relieved to see him go.'

'It is rarely so simple.'

'So I've discovered.'

Nadine took her arm. 'Anyway, the most important thing now is that you become rested. India heals. We don't think or talk work for at least two weeks. A deal, OK?'

'I'll try.' Jenni shuffled.

Nadine was firm. 'I insist that you have two weeks with no work-talk, no work-think. We will decide only to be. To experience. To exist. You agree?'

'Sounds OK to me.' As Jenni bent down to pick up her bag, a slim Indian in gleaming white clothes glided up to them.

'Peace.' He touched his right mid-finger to his forehead and looked at each of them. 'Connect.' He raised his hand, palm outwards, and murmured softly in an American accent: 'Sister Nadine . . . is this your friend Sister Jenni?'

Nadine, who seemed happy to see him, nodded.

The man turned to Jenni. 'I am Brother Ram,' he said, and looked at her with gentle eyes.

Jenni knew that the leaders of the Travellers, who were called 'Enlightened' or 'Liberated Ones', always wore white; Brother Ram, was obviously one of these.

He eyed Jenni as they walked along the corridor. 'I think we have met before – was it at the Hampstead Centre?'

It wasn't anywhere in N.W.Twee, as Michael called it, of that Jenni was sure, except perhaps on his television screen. Sometimes it felt as though almost everybody in Britain thought they had met her.

'I'm afraid I've never been to the Hampstead Centre.'

He nodded, smiled, and did a strange little head wiggle; it was as if his head were working loose in a subtle sort of way. The movement made his gold dot glitter, Christmas tree-like. Very Indian.

Jenni wished she didn't feel so feeble. Yesterday, after the Christmas feast, she had escaped to the sanctuary of her brother's bathroom, where, in an alien landscape of plastic boats and ducks, maudlin from celebratory booze, she had watched her little niece's clockwork porpoise as it swam round and round the basin, whirring relentlessly, spouting

12

water and squeaking every fourth turn. At the time the toy had seemed like a symbol of her own life, except that the white porcelain basin was not a particularly appropriate equivalent for the ghastly images she constantly carried with her; the places of disaster – Croatia, Ireland, and the recent awful explosion at Oxford Circus. Her workaday imagery was so often concerned with horrors: death, drowning, famine, burning, murder, torture. Up till now she had managed to remain objective and as hard-boiled as her image, but recently she seemed to have lost a layer or two in the boiling process and to have turned soggy like potato rather than becoming hard like an egg.

Nadine was still wearing the big silver bracelet on her wrist, although she had warned Jenni that the Spiritual Travellers did not usually wear jewellery. She clutched Jenni's arm as Brother Ram introduced them to the sleepy gathering of yellow people with whom they were to travel. A couple of the female members of the group were quite pretty but none of them was wearing make-up. There was a stark simplicity of presentation all round. Nadine had warned her that all those who went to the ashram were celibate and strictly teetotal. When Jenni had raised her eyebrows at this, Nadine had said emphatically, 'It is good to abstain so you can enjoy it more after a break.' Then, disarmingly: 'Anyway, it helps sometimes to tell the body who is in the driver's seat.'

The journalist part of Jenni was intrigued by the celibacy business, though for once journalism wasn't what had brought her here. She really had come for a break: she felt burnt out, dead inside. The last bombing in Liverpool had been one too many. Seeing all those poor families who were there for a memorial service themselves subjected to another outrage had been impossible to stomach.

Ironically, at thirty-five, she felt almost ready to retire: everything she did at present added to the stress and she yearned only for oblivion. There was also Michael for whom she still cared despite herself. Perhaps these devout youngsters had a point after all: attachment breeds pain, therefore detach. Care also means woe, doesn't it? She hated feeling so sorry for herself, it was out of character.

The Air India jumbo jet had red curves painted above the cabin windows. The hostess, a beautiful girl with a long glossy plait and a sari, had shy welcoming eyes. Already you could smell India: there was an aroma of incense and cardamom, sensual and subtle, as Brother Ram, serene beyond belief, led his Travellers forward. There was no excitement or jabber, no dropped bags or papers or last-minute flurrying. Ram smiled, nodded, barely indicated, and sweetly his group of yellow-clad travellers glided on to the plane, eyes and foreheads wide with hope and expectation.

The young Jenni put down her rucksack and gawped at the whitewashed walls, African sculptures and bouquets of flowers in Nadine's Provençal farmhouse.

'I've never seen a more beautiful place in my life.'

'From the orchard I have a view of the Luberon with Mont Ventoux in the distance. I meditate under the apple tree there sometimes.'

'It's paradise.'

'It is. My paradise.'

Speechless, the girl gazed past the table of dark wood, the pot of basil on the window sill, and beyond to the tangled green vines of the terrace.

Nadine fanned herself. 'It is too hot. You want to go in the pool?'

'Please.' Jenni knelt to search her rucksack as Nadine shuffled out of black espadrilles and went barefoot to another part of the house. She came back with a towel.

'You don't need that,' she said of Jenni's bikini.

For a moment, about to undress, she felt a pang of unease. Did Nadine fancy her? After all artists often were gay and she did look as though she might be a bit that way, and here was Jenni, alone and half-naked in the middle of acres of rampant grapevines. Once more she imagined her mother's face.

Nadine's grin was ironic. 'You are afraid of me, yes?'

'I . . .'

'You are English,' said Nadine firmly. 'That's all. A little inhibited perhaps, but you will be a strong one, a fighter and a creator, I can tell. Try it naked. You will find it good. I take you there and leave you a while. I have things to do.

14

Jenni stripped off and entered in the small pool. She gave herself completely to the cool water and swam, watched by the sphinxlike black cat and a flotilla of butterflies, until Nadine returned holding an earthenware dish filled with tiny cherry tomatoes. She offered one to Jenni. Warm from the sun, the taste thrilled her mouth.

'Good, huh?'

'Wonderful.'

'If I come in now, it won't make you nervous?'

Jenni grinned and shook her head.

For months after the three men attacked him, Nathan had wished that they had finished him off properly. He had come to the next morning to the sound of traffic. He was lying face down on a piece of wasteland by the wharves, aching all over, covered in abrasions, so cold that he could barely move. His leg had stopped bleeding, but he had no pants. He lay half-conscious, groaning, and winced as he remembered his horn, last seen flattened to a voiceless shambles of metal. For a while he hoped that maybe he would die if he lay there, then he became so cold that the pain of it made him try to rise. Wrapping the shreds of his jacket across his thighs, he staggered over the deserted concrete to the side of the road where he tried to catch the attention of the passing motorists, but the sight of his half-clad gesticulations only made the cars move faster. When at last the cops came and picked him up, he had collapsed again.

The law men were not friendly. It was hours before he was given any medical help and the unsympathetic and near-brutal interrogation at the police depot reminded him harshly of the night before. It was obvious that the police had decided he was some pimp or gay who had got what was coming to him. When at last he managed to find a lawyer and was taken to hospital for treatment he had become almost catatonic. The cops and the lawyer made him go over and over the event, then the press got hold of the story: 'SAX PLAYER FOUND NAKED, NATHAN ROBSON IN SEX CRIME.' The story of Laura's overdose was raked up, his parents were driven nearly crazy by pressmen, phone calls, knocks on the door, but even though he was made to look through

15

thousands of photos, the actual men who had attacked him were never found. He only managed to identify one out of the endless staring faces, and when at last the police went to examine the apartment where the incident had taken place it turned out to be abandoned and for a while his story was in doubt.

For three months Nathan saw nobody: he didn't want to talk, play music or do anything. He lay half-asleep mostly or walked for hours through the city, avoiding all the usual places where he might meet somebody he knew. He disconnected the phone and didn't open his mail which was piled up all over his apartment. Sometimes he forgot to eat and quite often he got drunk by himself. The day Ram, a young Indian who worked in a shoe store, came to see him, Nathan had a pretty bad hangover. Ram kept ringing the apartment doorbell and at first Nathan just lay in his unmade bed, sheet over his head, and ignored it. But Ram, sure that Nathan was inside, continued to ring until he was at last rewarded with a shout.

Ram peered through the letterbox and called to his friend. 'Excuse me, please . . . no, I won't, I don't want to go to fuck, Nathan. I've brought some food for you.'

He persisted with such gentleness that at last Nathan allowed him in. If Ram was shocked by Nathan's haggard and unshaven appearance he didn't let him know it. Instead he greeted him tenderly and asked if he might go through to the kitchen.

Naked, wrapped in a blanket, Nathan shrugged and shuffled off towards the bathroom, mumbling to himself.

When at last he emerged, he found Ram with his hands immersed in dirty dishes in the sink. The filthy kitchen already looked clearer, and on the table were fresh vegetables and a huge pack of orange juice.

Nathan watched the young man deftly wiping and creating order in the chaos. He didn't speak until after a while he moved slowly towards the kettle and asked dully if Ram wanted coffee. It wearied him even to turn on the tap.

Ram turned. 'I'll make it. Why don't you go have a shower?' Take your time and when you come out I'll give you some food. You like mushrooms and dhal?'

16

Nathan watched as he expertly made coffee.

'Yeah,' he said after a long time.

Ram looked puzzled.

'I do.'

Ram looked even more puzzled.

'I do like mushrooms.'

'Ah.' Ram smiled.

'And dhal.'

He nodded and they sipped coffee in silence, then Ram started chopping vegetables.

Nathan drained his cup and stood up.

'You want some more?'

He shook his head. 'I'll go shower.'

Ram nodded, a smile flickering in his dark eyes as he continued to chop.

He stayed with Nathan for a few days, took care of the mess, fed him and even washed his clothes and cut his hair. Nathan had worn his curly hair long and tied back for several years but now he asked Ram to cut it really short.

In the daytimes when he wasn't working, Ram could persuade Nathan to come for walks in Central Park and sometimes they would go to a movie. In the evenings they would sit together on the rug and Nathan would listen to Ram as he showed him how to relax.

'Be aware of your body,' Ram would whisper as they sat cross-legged opposite each other, eyes closed. 'Feel aware from your toes . . . up your legs, be aware of your knees, your thighs . . . shoulders, neck, head, eyes.'

Nathan frowned, searching for calm yet somehow unwilling to repossess his body. Gradually the persevering Ram's gently accented voice won through and Nathan found that he could sometimes briefly let go and reach a state in his head where the ghastly thoughts stopped clawing at him and he could gain a sensation of being outside his body so that it felt like something separate – a machine apart from his sense of awareness.

As Jenni watched Nadine's practical and unalarming body, brown and sturdy – bare but for a huge cylinder of silver bracelet which covered much of her left forearm – plunge

17

efficiently into the water of the swimming pool that day, she knew somehow for certain that she could trust her, and from then on experienced no further sensations of fear or shyness. On the contrary, she felt convinced as the two of them talked peacefully side by side, and the evening sky changed to a gentle pink and turned the grey stone skull of Mont Ventoux to an enchanted purple, that her friendship with this sardonic and entertaining artist was something that would become an integral part of her life. The older woman had a courage and independence which had allowed her creativity to flourish, plus a sense of the ridiculous which was totally endearing. Jenni intended to be like that when she was old: vital, but still with a capacity to develop.

Eventually Nathan knew that he must go away. The decision was a sudden one and he told nobody but Ram: he got his jabs and papers as fast as he could, organised what money he had and gave up the apartment. His belongings he gave away or threw out. The ladies in the local thrift shop nearly fainted when he appeared carrying his stereo, video, and all his tapes and discs.

'Don't I know you from somewhere?' one of them asked.

Nathan assured her quietly that he didn't think so and it must have been somebody else.

He set off for Bombay with a small backpack, a few garments, passport, razor, toothbrush, wallet and a notebook to write in. If he thought about music at all it made him wince, just as any passing memory of his marriage and the relationship with Laura made him feel as though his mind had electrically fused. He had shut it all out, the buttons were pressed down and his head couldn't work rationally. His love for Laura and his playing had formed his whole existence. There had been nothing more. The journey to India didn't even feel like an adventure. Part of him hoped that he would die or disappear amongst the teeming millions and become absorbed and swirled away in the river of life, but another tiny part of him hoped that somehow in the process he would find peace when – pale-faced and crop-headed – he set off after hugging the thin shoulders of his one good friend.

'Goodbye, Ram. And thanks, buddy.'

18

'Take care, Nathan. It will be better. You have a lot to give. Maybe you will find somebody there – a nice Indian girl.' He grinned. 'And please write. I will too.' Ram's eyes were dark with feeling. Small, dignified and very still, he stood watching until Nathan passed through the International barrier and out of sight.

Jenni returned from that first visit to France inspired. Meeting Nadine for the first time and seeing the older woman's independence and joy in her profession gave the girl a reference point for her own life. She finished her basic newspaper training and came to London where she worked on various publications. She was working on the *Croydon Gazette* when her big chance came, and it was Michael O'Brien – then a current affairs producer in television – who gave it to her. The interview took place in a grey BBC office near Shepherd's Bush. Jenni arrived feeling sparky, ready to take on the world, but he made it difficult for her.

She was immediately struck by the humour in his long face, the smile that was always hovering. Michael had nicked himself shaving that day and when he asked suddenly why she was looking at the cut, she blushed and to her own subsequent mortification blurted out that she had been wondering if by chance one of the failed candidates had scratched him.

That was that one up the spout. But no, Michael was laughing.

'You did, did you? It was the wife, actually. But I take it that your fantasy means I'd better beware of turning yourself down?'

Jenni opened her mouth but only a gurgle emerged. She wished for instant invisibility, if not death.

'Tell me then, Miss Bartlett. Or – ' he eyed her, his eyes amused, – 'may I call you Jenni?'

She shrugged. She knew and admired Michael's work, wanted the job, but right now felt too nervous to present herself as a sensible, employable journalist.

'Tell me what great assignment you've just come from?' Michael, after offering her one, leaned back and lit a French cigarette. A non-smoker, Jenni inhaled the Provençal reminder and the image of Nadine empowered her.

19

'Yesterday, as it happens, I was sent to do a piece on a dog's cemetery in Kent.' She stared at him deadpan.

Michael nodded encouragingly.

'I found it a little difficult to give it a political slant, I have to confess, but I'm working on an article about landlords. I'm taking mine to court for trying to double the rent.'

'Tell me more.'

She did. The adrenalin flared and she performed in effect a sort of one-woman show, playing in turn herself as innocent wronged tenant, the Pakistani – or was he Welsh? Michael asked urbanely – landlord, plus a series of citizens advice ladies in hats, and as a grand finale an Irish lawyer. When she had finished, she again longed to be able to make herself vanish. Why had she done an Irish accent for this of all men? Michael hadn't laughed at all. He had just watched intently, reacting very little. The other two people interviewing her had laughed loudly.

She sat back in her chair and dared at last to confront Michael fully. He returned her stare, exhaling Gauloise, nodding slowly. A good-looking man but hard to gauge. She wondered if she should apologise for the Irish accent; she had been a little carried away. You would almost have thought she was auditioning for RADA. Maybe she should do. Get out before it was too late. Another few months of dog cemeteries and local government committee meetings would do for her.

'Dear Ram,' wrote Nathan from the Happy Days Hotel, Aurangabad, Maharashtra, two months after he had arrived in India, 'this place is amazing. It's not a very special town, but I spent the last week sleeping in a hut with some poor farmers near Ellora and Ajanta – the places you told me about when we first met. I think they must be one of the wonders of the world. I can't imagine how the guys who carved the temples from the solid granite of the cliffs could have had the faith, energy or imagination to do it. How did they trust or know that the mountain was solid? I would never have envisaged starting such a scheme because I would have expected the stone to be full of flaws. The monks who lived there must have had Mega Faith. They carved into the mountain for hundreds of feet and all by hand. It's like a miracle. Some of the temples must have taken hundreds of years to carve, they're so elaborate. I walked round for a day just crying, those pillars and Buddhas were so beautiful.

'I was lucky, because hardly anybody was there for a lot of the time, so I could sit and stare out across to the west through the trees. I didn't see any tigers or elephants except for painted ones. The old man who showed me round told me some English soldiers on a tiger hunt actually discovered Ellora after nobody had been there for *a thousand years*. Crazy! I sat in one of the original monks' little rock-cut cells for almost half a day, and drank from what must once have been his well. Incredible. And the way the outside rocks are worn smooth from the gushing monsoon waters and there are all those carved steps and pillars. Wow!

'One Buddhist temple was amazing. The old guy who shows you round shone a big shiny sheet of tin so that the gold of the sun reflected inside and lit up the giant Buddha and all the smaller sculptures; apparently they lit the caves like that when they created them, I almost went wild. And the cave – I know they're man-made, but they are kind of like caves – I liked best had a fantastic roof with carved rib-vaults, exactly like a Romanesque church in Europe. There are man-made columns all round and this huge giant Buddha in the middle – so peaceful he was almost smiling, and I just felt real quiet and so full of feeling. I have never experienced anything like it, Ram. And the echoes were fantastic. We must come here together one day and we will meditate in the caves. I sang and hummed "Om" and it went round and echoed and I made a harmony. I wish you had been there with me.

'And the stone *pillars*! They're all carved too – but if you hit them they sing and reverberate like a ghost drum. Half of the sculptures and cells and dormitories (there are twenty-nine caves) are well over a thousand years old and some are about two thousand. It is unbelievable, and that's just Ellora. There's Ajanta just along the cliff and there the temples have incredible paintings of Buddhas, kings, elephants, dancing girls, hunters, animals and birds. You see all of life there, the sensual life that Buddha left behind him and the spiritual life with marvellous angels. I didn't know that there were Indian

21

angels, I always thought they were a Christian concept. There are erotic carvings too, beautiful big-titted girls curling round happy-looking guys. I could go on for pages and almost have. I hope you've got this far.

'I am in love with your country and one day maybe we'll meet up in India somewhere. At the moment I don't ever want to come home, but I only have enough money for another few months. Part of me would quite like just to live in one of the little stone cells in Ellora for ever, but I'm making myself move on and see more.

'What's happening with you? Are your mom and pop still trying to arrange a marriage for you?

Write to me in Delhi. Take care.

Nathan.'

At the end of her interview for the current affairs programme Michael doodled on his desk. 'OK.' He looked up at last. 'Thanks, Jenni. Very nice meeting you. We'll be in touch.' Jenni rose to go, managing to her own mortification as she did so to drop her car-keys and – when they had been retrieved by Michael, with whom she bumped heads – her handbag.

He rubbed his head. 'Well, now you know for sure that you've left your mark on me,' he murmured as she stumbled out backwards.

That night she met a friend and, certain of rejection, drank a large amount of wine, but the next day at work, severely hungover, she received a message to ring Michael O'Brien's office. When she did so she was told that not only had she got the job, but they would like her sometimes to present her stories on screen. She was euphoric, properly on her way at last.

Nathan travelled all over India, up to Nepal, where he walked for hundreds of miles. He stayed on a houseboat in Kashmir where he did little for weeks but watch reflections, his days punctuated by the changing pattern of cloud and water, and later slept on string hammocks, grass, stones, mud and leaves and – occasionally – a clean fresh bed in a Western-style house.

A thousand friendly people must have said 'Please come to have tea in my house', and families who lived seven or ten to a hut had fed him and offered him what little they had. He stayed for a while in a Buddhist monastery where he debated and meditated and learned some tranquillity. For a while the ghastly dreams almost stopped tormenting him. He wandered deep into the south. In eighteen months he saw temples and jungles, fine cities and great rivers. He watched people die and celebrated births and weddings, and grew to love India as though the continent were a living creature.

It was when he had had a spell in Ghandi's own ashram, where he learned about the sage's life and teachings, that Nathan realised with relief that his own version of renunciation of the physical world he had known in New York was a normal and accepted part of the culture here. He saw Ghandi's few possessions – now treasured in a glass case – and was moved by their simplicity. There were the little round spectacles, a pair of sandals the sage had made for himself, and his white hand-woven cotton *dhoti*. These few objects, plus a pencil, paper, a cheap watch and his eating implements, were all except for a Japanese toy – a little clay model of the three monkeys: Speak, Hear and See No Evil. This trinket moved Nathan enormously: he stood before it for a very long time, then he resolved that he must try to live like Ghandi, giving and sharing, asking nothing for himself but those small requirements dictated by his body. He knew that only by doing this would he find peace.

Michael was Jenni's boss for three years until he left the BBC. He was exacting and challenged her as she needed to be challenged; she could not have had a tougher or a better teacher. After his television stint he became a well-respected features writer on a Sunday newspaper. Jenni and he gradually became good friends and often met up on assignments, but in the end neither of them could remember when they actually crossed the boundary between friendship and love, it had become so hazy. Primarily they were colleagues: they travelled and worked together intensively and Jenni admired Michael for his professionalism, and loved him for his humour and brilliance.

For a long time, because he was married, she was reluctant to become emotionally entangled with him though she felt an enormous pull. The domestic set-up that he shared with his wife appeared to be reasonably content if a trifle dull, but in principle a liaison with no sort of future such as she was always advising weaker friends to avoid was the last thing she wanted. But in the end she had succumbed to Michael's Irish charm, and their love affair had lasted for seven years before the break.

Three

A year ago last August Michael had come to the old farmhouse in Provence. Nadine, who was in Paris, had offered the place to Jenni for the Avignon Television Festival. For once Michael had stolen three days for them to be together. His wife was away on a course and it was the first occasion for ages that he and Jenni had time that was not just a snatched drunken evening on a foreign assignment or a couple of hours between their various work commitments. He was researching an article on the state of the nuclear power industry in Europe, and it was extraordinary for them both for once to be able to walk, eat and drink in peace without either of them having to leap up to meet some urgent professional deadline.

The sunflowers were out and seemed to watch them as they walked together.

'They're like a bloody audience the way they all turn at the same time,' said Michael. Eyes filled with vistas of hill villages and distant mountains, they had wandered through fields rich with the scent of wild rosemary and lavender, surrounded by unusual black and yellow butterflies which looked as though their large wings were fixed on back to front.

Jenni remembered a day they had spent at a deserted ochre quarry with yellow walls and bright blue flowers. They had watched dragonflies and swum naked before picnicking on goat's cheese, peaches and local wine. Michael had called her to come and see a praying mantis, elegant and angular, and as they knelt side by side to watch it, he had said – not for the first time – that he wanted them to be together properly. He declared himself ready to leave his marriage and promised he would tell his wife when he got back.

Jenni couldn't remember feeling more content. That night, as they ate seafood, exquisitely arranged and succulent, they had looked at each other across the table until neither of them could maintain the gaze; it had somehow become too intense for public show. She remembered how he had taken her hand when they both turned away. Later, in bed together, listening to the jangling of crickets in a moonlit landscape where the nearby hill village looked like a silver sculpture, they had made love almost till dawn and then again when the birds began to sing. 'Bloody custom-built,' he had murmured later as they breakfasted on the tiled terrace and looked towards the mountains which rose on either side of the house above curling grapevines and golden sunflowers.

Michael was a careful man and voiced his love rarely. He had said it once when she had almost been blown up in Beirut and her cameraman had been killed, a couple of times when he was very drunk, and once again when they had snatched a few illicit hours in an anonymous hotel in Brussels.

'I love you, Jen. I need you. I will leave Nella, I promise. The marriage is really only an exercise in family management these days. I just have to wait till the time feels right . . .'

After almost two years of travelling Nathan became very ill. The tribal people who took him in and looked after him when he collapsed with dysentery had adamantly refused to allow him to cut loose from the heat and pain of life and float off towards the glimmering end of his seductive tunnel. The men and women with gentle brown hands and eyes who had watched over him and tended to his needs for weeks, continued lovingly to do so, slowly luring him back to life. Gradually his stomach became able to accept their offerings of curd, rice and vegetables which nestled on leaf plates. The delirious nightmares slowly fading, he gladly accepted sips of water and buffalo milk from a brass bowl which was polished with mud and sand every day by the woman of the house who squatted in the dust outside the hut where he had lain for so long.

Hens and guinea fowl scrabbled round his *charpoy* bed

26

squawking sleepily, occasionally excitedly if a child or dog chased them. He saw lizards, monkeys and beetles, and watched the villagers resignedly pound, husk and chop the small supplies of food which they unquestioningly shared with him. He was sick for weeks, and three months later, when he was strong enough to walk a little and see where he was, he had begun to understand the dialect of the village and talk with the people who had saved his life.

He knew he was getting better when one day he walked through a field of sugar cane behind the little village. He wanted to be alone; something which is nearly always difficult to achieve in India, and had slipped away when the village was preparing a meal for some important visitors. He was not quite sure who the visitors were, but gathered from the anxious care with which the meal was created from the pathetically sparse food stores available that they had the power to influence the financial future of the place. He understood that it must have something to do with the proposed building of a well which would bring water to about a hundred and fifty people. At present the supply was limited at the best of times, and in times of drought the women had to walk several kilometres to find water. The problem was that wells needed funding, specially if there was a lot of digging to be done and machinery needed to be hired.

Wearing only a ragged pair of shorts round his now scraggy waist, Nathan felt the leaves of the tall cane plants brush against his chest and meet above his head with a feathery rustle as he walked in a state of near-euphoria, aware only of being alive again and no longer overwhelmed by fever or nausea as he had been for so many weeks. When he reached the edge of the field he emerged from the cane and looked back across towards the village with an almost overwhelming surge of affection. These people who possessed almost nothing had offered him everything: their food, their friendship, their way of life.

Gopal, the gentle sleepy-eyed man of the house where Nathan had been nursed, had walked with him down to the dried out river only yesterday and they had sat in the dusk together smoking hand-made cigarettes wrapped in a tobacco leaf and tied with thread.

27

'Nattan *Bhai*,' Gopal had said – 'what will you do now?'

Nathan didn't really have an answer except that he still had no desire to return to the States. Having never felt as happy as during these last few weeks of convalescence, the only strong feeling he had now was a unwillingness to leave. But the Adivasi people were chronically poor. What could he do here but be a burden? He knew that the Adivasis, the 'tribal' people or aboriginals of India, who formed about seven per-cent of the country's population, mostly lived in villages like this one. They were the ones he loved, those who had cared for him and welcomed him.

'I don't know.' He shrugged.

Gopal nodded earnestly. 'You can work with us and stay in my house. You are my brother.'

And so it was. Above him now was a rounded hill topped by two classically perfect palm trees. Beside one of the trees with only the fierce blue sky for background stood a young woman in an orange and pink sari holding a baby. Staring up at her, Nathan found her indescribably beautiful. The landscape, the brilliance of her dress, and the perfect serenity of her gesture embodied everything he loved about this country with its often breathtakingly perverse balance between man and nature.

Conscious of his stare, she turned to smile shyly down at him as a small boy, ragged and breathless, came crashing through the sugar canes, ran to Nathan and grabbed his thin hand.

'Nattan *Bhai, chalo!*' Come now! Excitedly the child pointed back towards the trees by the old well and Nathan saw a white Land-Rover making its way over the stony hill towards the little huddle of mud and thatch huts which he realised with a sudden swelling of tenderness was in fact his home.

It was many months since he had seen another white man, so it was with curiosity and shyness that he allowed the small boy to pull him towards the one who was now climbing out of the vehicle. Nathan joined the waiting group of village elders, and he and each one of the waiting men steepled the fingertips of both hands together beneath their chins in the classic Indian *namaste* to greet the stranger who echoed the

28

beautiful gesture of welcome with the same near-religious action and smiled in return.

It took eight years of working in television before Jenni was given her own show. The Bartlett File was a current affairs programme which dealt with serious issues; Jenni would research her chosen subject and finally present it herself. She was greatly respected in the business for her professionalism and humour; the programme, which was popular, reached a wide audience, and her name was frequently in the media. She was becoming more and more committed as a reporter and was particularly happy with the programme which had been scheduled to be transmitted just after Christmas this year. Called 'British Made', it dealt with the manufacture of chemical weapons in the UK.

The final rift with Michael had coincided with an earlier furore at work. She was doing a live broadcast on the state of the NHS with her least favourite Cabinet Minister, a shrill woman who made Jenni squirm with distaste, political and personal, but who always had an answer.

On screen Jenni pointed to a series of pictures which were brought to the viewers in dramatic close-up.

'These children are in great danger because of the hold-up in treatment. How much longer must their families suffer? Two babies have died in recent weeks, and as we have shown, the medical experts concerned blame the government cutbacks. What, Minister, may I ask, have you to tell these people?'

Jenni did feel concerned and angry, and though she didn't like the Minister in question personally, she prided herself on her professional neutrality, confident that what she was reporting was the plain truth.

The Minister almost had an apoplexy. She puffed up like a great cat and hissed with rage. She shouted that Jenni was biased, that the carefully gathered and edited reports gave an untrue picture. As the end credits rolled across the two women confronting each other and the Bartlett File music ended (two minutes early, a fact which resulted in Jenni's own near apoplexy), the Minister stormed out and refused to go as planned to the hospitality lounge.

Jenni raged to her dressing-room and slammed down her eponymous file. She poured herself a drink and looked up angrily when her producer knocked and entered without waiting.

Roger Norton, somewhat ruffled, bit his lip and gazed mildly at Jenni over his half-spectacles.

'I'm afraid it's trouble, Jenni, and by that I mean for you. I have to tell you that one extremely angry lady Minister has just disappeared in a chauffeur-driven cloud of dust.'

Jenni bristled. 'What do you mean? I can't help it if a politician loses his or her temper on screen. It makes for good viewing. Bet you get sackloads of letters.'

'Jenni, that's not the point.'

'What d'you mean, it's not the point?' She was bewildered. The weekly viewing figures were an obsession with the programme schedulers.

Her producer was embarrassed. 'There have been noises from above. I came to warn you. They're furious about tonight; the gorgon left muttering about bias and misrepresentation, but the main thing I have to warn you about is that they're threatening to put an injunction on the arms programme.'

He winced as Jenni stared at him.

'Please tell me you're joking?'

He shook his head. 'I only wish I could, but I'm afraid it's true.'

She could barely believe him. The programme was her baby. Jenni was convinced both personally and by feedback from people at work that the report and investigation she had done was her best ever – as well as being the most politically outspoken. She alone had made the initial contact, followed up the delicate intricacy of leads, and untangled the story.

She sat down weakly. She had gone from Scotland where the weapons were manufactured to Athens where they arrived en route for Iraq; she had spoken to captains industrial and naval, to little people who packed boxes and filled in addresses and customs forms, and had interviewed the parents and widows of the dead sailors killed by a weapon which originated in their own country. Extraordinarily, the father of one of the seamen blown up on the tanker had actually worked in the factory where they were made. He, poor man, had wept in the interview. Terrible gulping sobs which, though harrowing, had made for brilliant viewing.

He was a courageous man and in the end had given his permission to keep that reel of film in. Jenni felt faint. How dare they now hold back the programme? What it showed was the truth, and a truth that people must be presented with and allowed to judge freely for themselves.

She observed Roger's embarrassed facial twitchings. 'This is censorship. What are we going to do about it?'

He swallowed. 'It's hellish, Jen. I'm as upset as you are, but we can't do anything at present. There will be an inquiry, of course, but meanwhile "British Made" is not going out as scheduled.'

Suddenly almost overwhelmed with exhaustion, she stood up. 'I've had enough. I really have. I'm going home.' All she could think of at that point was that she wanted to phone Michael. She had told him to get out of her life when, after months of prevarication, it became obvious that he would never leave his wife. Despite several months of silence, tonight she really needed him; as a friend if not a lover. Surely he would come over for this?

When she did at last track him down he answered from what was obviously a crowded office; he sounded pissed. He'd ring her back, he promised. But he didn't, and that was it.

The man in the white Land-Rover worked for an American charity organisation called NYAID whose purpose in life was to bring aid to very poor people in rural communities. They would help them build wells, schools and hospitals, but the long-term aim was to enable the recipients of their funds and know-how to become self-sufficient and not to have to rely on NYAID for any longer than was necessary. The aid worker in charge was amazed to find a fellow New Yorker in such a remote location – and one with a supremely useful knowledge of the local dialect. Gradually, over the next few months, the two men became friends and the NYAID man would appear with his vehicle, talk lengthily to Nathan, discuss with him the problems he was dealing with, and use him as an interpreter.

His village was given a grant to build a well and Nathan

became the unofficial organiser of the whole venture and helped to make it happen quickly and efficiently. He had always been practical and welcomed the chance to help create something which so deeply affected the lives of the people he loved. He spent nearly three years in the tribal village living as one of them, and gradually became regarded as a wise man among them – almost godlike. '*Bagwan*' many of the elder people called him.

Four

If pressed Michael would have admitted that it was a bit of a detour to drive past Jenni's Fulham house on his way home from the newspaper office, but he couldn't help it; the silence was wearing him down. Plus he'd had a glass of wine too many on the way over from Sloane Square. He looked at the house for a minute or so, noting hopefully that there was a light on in the upstairs bathroom. He rang the bell but there was no response, so he tried again, more firmly this time. Silence. He bent down and pushed open the letter-box.

'Jen?' he called, but nobody came.

He stood up, frowning, and looked up and down the street. A lone jogger panted by, scarlet-legged, as an old neighbour with a Zimmer frame and a balding spaniel shuffled towards the next-door house. Michael recognised her and nodded.

'Jenni's away,' she told him. 'Don't know where she's off to this time, but she left very early in the morning.'

'Ah.' He smiled. 'I know . . . I – er – saw the light and wondered if she'd changed her plan?'

The old woman grunted and manoeuvred herself with difficulty along the cracked tiles of her front path.

'She – er – asked me to check a couple of things for her,' said Michael suddenly, watching as she heaved first the frame then her wheezing body up the adjoining front steps.

'Oh, yes.' The woman bent towards the dog who wagged its threadbare stump catatonically. 'Who's a hungry Mikey then?'

'I'm sorry?' Michael stared at her blurrily before realising she was addressing her canine Doppelganger.

The old woman shut her door just as Michael eased open

Jenni's. Thank goodness she hadn't changed the lock. He'd never offered her back the precious object – the key of the kingdom, he had called it when she had first given it to him – nor had Jenni asked for it. In his mind the affair had never really ended, he had just needed some time and space to sort out his own pressing problems.

Everything seemed to be as usual in the open-plan room: the patterned kelims, dark blue walls and white-upholstered furniture were all as he remembered them, organised and beautiful like Jen herself. On the far side of the room was her pale wooden desk with the computer and heaps of papers. A couple of files lay on the floor, their insides spilling out. One was titled 'Bosnia' in black felt-tip, the other 'Oil Spills'. It moved him to see her handwriting, but there were no clues as to where she had gone. How about the bedroom? Maybe upstairs would be more enlightening. Realising that before confronting the latter he needed a drink, he found and poured himself a massive Scotch and gulped much of it down in one go. He tried not to remember all the times he had climbed these stairs. Was it, he wondered, only possible in retrospect to recognise true happiness?

The bedroom was immaculate, the bed made. Pinned on the wall near the dressing-table was a photo Jenni had taken of himself in France. He was looking straight into camera with a quizzical smile. He had always secretly liked the picture and enjoyed the fact that it faced her bed. The trouble was that today the image had been slashed across with a large red felt 'X' and there was a drawing pin stuck straight into his left eye. Wincing, he turned to look at the bed where they had so often happily argued, laughed and pleasured each other. God, how he wished he hadn't let her down. It had just all been too much to cope with, and really if he were honest with himself, he had liked having both women.

And now he had neither. Bitterly, he drained the glass and suddenly hurled at the wall where it exploded, spraying the carpet with innumerable shards.

'Fucking useless idiot!' he swore at himself. Groaning, he went back down the stairs to find the brush and shovel he knew Jenni stored under the kitchen sink and returned to sweep up the bits.

34

His finger was bleeding when some minutes later he emerged through the front door. He sucked the wound wearily as he hailed a taxi to take him to his tiny bedsit – new to him and hardly home – where he ate two large bowls of cornflakes washed down with almost half a bottle more of whisky.

Watched by lizards and curious children, Nathan was sitting under a mango tree carefully reading one of Ram's flimsy blue letters, smiling occasionally at the text.

'Dear Nathan,

'Thanks for your news. It sounds good with you, and I am happy for you. One day maybe I'll manage to come and visit you and stay in your village. Meanwhile there are big changes in my life. I have stopped working in the shop since almost a month. I told you in the last letter how I had met a woman called Maya who seems to have a fresh way of looking at life and how to make sense of it. She's a marvellous person, I find her very inspiring and want to learn more from her. She has come to New York to start a meditation centre called the New York School of Spiritual Travel.'

'Sounds kinda zany,' murmured Nathan, and the watching children, squatting on the dusty ground beside him, chortled quietly to each other.

'Anyway, I kept coming to hear her speak and took part in meditations and classes and she has offered me a job in the actual school. I am already liking it a lot. Life seems to have a purpose for me now . . .'

As Nathan wrote back to Ram, a small girl came to him with a beaker of water from the well he had helped to build. The water was cool and sweet. He drank it and smiled at the child, who squatted down beside her brothers to watch him.

'Dear Ram,' he wrote, 'Good to hear that you have started a new lifestyle. It sounds better than selling shoes, but I hope it's not a cranky place you've gotten mixed up with. Some of those sects are really mad. Be careful.

'I told you in my last letter that my US dollars were just about finished and I was worried about what to do. What has happened is really exciting for me. The guy I told you about, Andy who works for NYAID, is due to go back to the States as he's been out here for years. Basically, I'm taking over

35

Andy's job. They reckon the Gandhian ashram training and working here with the villagers has given me enough experience. So like you I am also about to start work. Sadly, it means I have to leave this place, though I'll be able to visit as NYAID has a few projects here. I'll be based in Ahmedabad, but will make field-trips in the Land-Rover for three-quarters of the year. Come and see me some time and you'll be able to travel round with me.'

At the end of the letter he drew a little palm tree with a smiling tiger under it which also made the children smile.

Michael cursed as for the third day running he listened to Jenni's recorded voice sounding unrecognisably prim and professional: 'I'm very sorry that there's nobody here to take your call, but if you leave your name and number, the time and the date, I'll get back to you as soon as possible. Please speak after the dreaded bleep.'

It had become an obsession for him to ring her number, knowing she wasn't there. He left no message, but decided to try The Bartlett File office again.

'I'm afraid she's gone on leave.'

'You told me that before, but where?'

'I'm sorry. We're not allowed to say.'

'It's Michael O'Brien here, for God's sake!'

A pause at the other end.

'Please. I need to get in touch with her. It's urgent.'

More pause. Damn the girl, she was only doing her job, but damn Jenni too for going off into the blue. Uneasily, he remembered how tense she had sounded and the phone call he had not returned.

After a pause the secretary had decided to speak. 'Mr O'Brien . . !'

'Yes, this is me!' He tried not to shout. It didn't help his headache. 'I'm sorry, I've been try all over the bloody place – France, Fulham, her mother's – but there was nobody there either. Can you at least tell me how long she'll be gone?'

'She's away for a month.'

'A month? Is she on holiday for all that time?'

'She took all the leave owing to her and a bit more. Said she needed a break.'

'But you've no idea where she is?'

'I know she had to take malaria pills . . !'

'Africa?'

'Maybe . . . wait a minute now. I think she did say something – hold on, please.'

Michael sighed. It could be anywhere. Pick a pin and stick it on the world map and find her. He closed his eyes as a recurrent image of Jenni, flushed from loving, laughing up at him against a background of sunflowers, tormented him. It was his own bloody Jesuitical fault for taking so long to contact her.

'Mr O'Brien?'

Try a bit of Blarney. 'Still here and hoping.'

'I've spoken to the person I thought might know, but I'm afraid she doesn't. The main problem is that the office is very quiet at the moment because of the Christmas break, nearly everybody's away, but I was trying to find out if I could get a hold of her secretary . . .'

'Good thinking. And?'

The girl's voice faltered. 'I'm afraid she's gone ski-ing.'

'Who has? Jenni?'

A giggle. 'No. The secretary.'

'Shit.'

'I'm awfully sorry.'

'When will she be back?'

'Monday week.'

'OK. Thanks. I'll have to try elsewhere.' He sighed and wearily put down the phone, then abruptly dialled the number of the television centre once more, asked for the same extension and got the same girl. 'Hello, it's Michael O'Brien again. I just wondered – is Jenni not going to be here for the meeting about her programme?'

The girl paused. 'Just hold on a moment, please.'

He did as instructed and grew more angry and bored. She seemed to be taking forever. Then there was a man's voice.

'Roger Norton here, Michael. Can I help?'

'I'm trying to track down Jenni. She seems to have disappeared at rather an odd moment in her career.'

The same crisp voice. 'You can say that again. A law unto herself, that one.'

'Will she not be here for the big meeting?'

'Apparently not. She left me a scribble on the desk saying she'd send a postcard and that she trusted me to handle it.'

'That's not like her.'

'She was due a break: she's been working solidly for two years except for a long weekend in France last year.'

Michael remembered it well.

'How do you feel about the meeting, Roger?'

'Angry with the top brass – and, I may say, our heroine and star performer. It's a bloody good piece of work and she should be here to speak up for it.'

'Knowing Jenni, I expect she reckons that if the programme is any good at all it shouldn't need an explanation.'

'Theoretically speaking she's right.'

What do you reckon will happen? They can't put it on ice for ever.'

'It's got to be transmitted. No transmission and there'll be hell to pay from a lot of us down here.'

'I'll be thinking of you.'

'Thanks.' Jenni's boss still sounded grim, if marginally friendlier.

'Tell me one thing, Roger.'

'If I can I will.'

'This postcard she was going to send you – where would it be from?'

'I have absolutely no idea. All she said was that she was meeting up with a friend.'

Michael bristled like a jealous kid. Who, he mentally demanded, name and number, he wanted then now. And his balls off him.

'A photographer I think – she said she was travelling with a photographer she was going to work with.'

'You don't have a clue as to where?'

'No idea, I'm sorry. She's a secretive one Jen, always was. Sorry I can't help any more.'

'Don't worry.' Michael was firm. 'I'll find her somehow.'

Five

A spontaneous outbreak of applause, which delighted Jenni and Nadine, burst forth from the passengers as the cavernous jumbo jet at last touched down on Indian soil. It was early morning local time, dark and cold, when Brother Ram led his followers through the airport obstacles of baggage reclaim, customs and passport control. Jenni, who hadn't been to India before, was impressed by the almost tangible aura of peace which the group of Travellers carried with them.

As they waited to board the ashram bus Jenni noticed a ragged-looking fellow in a uniform whom she realised after some minutes must be a policeman; there was other people, mostly very thin, muffled in all manner of strange headgear from tall triple pancake jobs to headscarves tied on old lady-style and leather helmets with woollen earflaps. It was murky, and she wondered as she watched whilst a couple of men wrapped in blankets and turbans, who were lying on the road trying to mend an ancient Morris by the wavering light of a single candle, if this was to be the shape of things to come.

At the Gold Dot Depot, as Nadine throatily nicknamed the Centre for Spiritual Travel, the contingent from London unpacked and washed; Jenni, Nadine and several other women were taken to a small dormitory with iron bedsteads, white walls and no decoration but for a large black and white photo of the guru Maya. The picture, which Jenni had already seen discreetly hung in Nadine's house, turned out to be ubiquitous both in the Delhi Centre and the ashram. It showed a strong-faced woman in a white sari. She had a high forehead, large dark eyes and slanting cheekbones, her expression formidable but smiling. She looked slightly familiar, Jenni couldn't think why.

'Would you like to come down to the Power House to Connect?' a tall young American Traveller asked.

'Do you want to come to meditate?' Nadine translated.

Jenni shrugged.

Nadine had taught her to meditate years before, a simple method which involved using a simple mantra which you repeated until you virtually hypnotised yourself into a state of calm. It didn't always work, but Jenni had found it helpful when she got wound up with work and still used it occasionally as a benign sort of tranquilliser. Nadine herself always meditated when she was about to start painting or to take important pictures. She used to say that she needed to clear her mind of all the junk, the knots and tangles, so that she felt 'clean' and uncluttered in her head.

Jenni could do with some such clarification right now: the cutting of her programme had been one too many on top of an Everest of stressful happenings. She still felt enraged by the threat of an injunction; she had only wanted to show the truth, a truth that people must be presented with and allowed to judge freely for themselves. Even now her stomach knotted at the memory.

The Power House of the Delhi Centre for Spiritual Travel was a large plain white room with flowers and candles set on a white-clothed table. There was incense in the air and the floor was covered with a pale hand-blocked Rajasthani cotton print. Jenni's heart sank at the sight of yet another photo of the guru set on the end wall. As they removed their shoes before going into the room she noted that Nadine looked tired, though this was hardly surprising for a jet-lagged woman in her early-seventies.

Settling back on her haunches and crossing her legs, Nadine winked at Jenni, who wondered yet again why on earth she had agreed to come to this crazy place and what the secret of Nadine's fascination with these people was. It was so out of character, Nadine being one of the most original and independent beings Jenni had ever come across. Fond of her wine too. Jenni was sure that her friend didn't really subscribe to the beliefs of the Spiritual Travellers, though she knew that she had paid several visits to the ashram and always returned filled with remarkable energy, akin to that of some of Jenni's more worldly acquaintances who went off to health farms. Maybe the pragmatic Nadine simply used the set-up as a place for personal and mental regeneration; a spiritual gymnasium of sorts. It was obvious that well-applied discipline, be it physical or mental, did make people feel better about themselves.

She closed her eyes for a few moments, determined to relax and enjoy whatever the experience would bring. She wished that she knew what was happening to her programme. What really upset her was her impotence in the matter. She was uneasily aware of the fact that once in the ashram she would have none of her normal contacts with the media which provided the daily rhythm of her life in England, but that of course was all part of Nadine's plan to force her to unwind.

She concentrated on a candle flame and was beginning to ease away from her self-preoccupation when she became aware of a strange moaning. She glanced uneasily sideways to see if she could find out from which would-be Enlightened Traveller, the sound emanated, and decided that it must be the fat American across the room. She hoped he wasn't ill or going to have a fit of some kind, until she realised that he was singing, making an almost feminine noise, wordless, high and sustained. Then to her surprise Nadine, who was sitting next to her, began to sing too, an octave lower but in harmony. Gradually the entire circle of people was singing and humming, and like a glass which is made to ring by running a wet finger round and round the rim, the entire group began to reverberate. It was completely unexpected and Jenni found it both beautiful and extraordinarily liberating, a basic communication without speech that broke through all the normal barriers. She felt compelled to join in too and quickly found herself using subtle rhythms and harmonies, her voice growing like the others stronger and surer as the sound took off.

As she looked at the dimly-lit faces with their glittering gold dots, images of her years of feeding the insatiable television monster surged through Jenni's head. She felt detached and strangely free as her mind seemed to elevate on the uplift of

41

sound like a glider on a thermal. After a time the chanting reached a natural end and the room became deeply silent. Jenni came down from on high with a bump and tried once more to settle her gaze on the candle flame but the disturbing images pressed in on her once more – followed by an especially persistent one of Michael smiling at her in the ochre quarry. She tried to push the memory away – the betrayal of broken promises and unreturned call still hurt, damn him – but irrational though she knew it to be, some vulnerable part of her wished he were here. But was it perhaps not really Michael for whom she longed, but simply love? Somebody for whom she came first. She didn't really know, but she suspected that if another Michael or, preferably, an unattached, intelligent, sensitive man (did they actually exist?) did miraculously come beating on her door, she might be sorely tempted to confound her better nature and get out of this weird set-up as quick as a cricket, meditative thermals notwithstanding.

Across the road from a large detached house in north London a tall dark-haired man with blue eyes stood anxiously watching. It was drizzling and his leather jacket was getting soaked. He waited for several minutes until a group of young people, wearing a preponderance of yellow, emerged laughing together then he watched for several minutes more before moving towards a side street where he stopped at a white car parked on a yellow line. He frowned as he removed a cellophane-wrapped document from beneath the windscreen wiper, stuffed the papers into his jacket pocket, unlocked the vehicle, got in and drove off. Some minutes later the same man could be observed parking on double yellow lines on the steep slope of the nearby high street. Warily, he eyed the crowded pavement up and down before emerging. He slammed the car door and moved quickly towards the nearest shop window, pausing briefly to eye the spotlit display before entering the shop.

An assistant came towards him smiling. 'Can I help you, sir?'

'Please. I'd like one of those.' He pointed to a rack behind her.

'A yellow scarf?'

'Yes. Thanks.' He glanced twitchily out at the street. 'I'm double-parked, they already got me once today.'

The girl put the scarf in a neat black and white bag labelled 'Tie Rack' and laid it on the counter. 'Eight ninety-nine, please.' She rang it up on the till.

He took out a wallet, handed her a card and watched as she stamped it and handed it over for signature.

'The yellow scarves are our fastest selling line.'

'Really? Why's that?'

She responded to his nice Irish voice. 'It's the spiritualists down the road. They mostly wear yellow: socks, ties, scarves. We never have enough. They buy white too – it's apparently to do with the higher up you go. If you're really really good you get to wear white.'

'Sounds like judo belts.'

The girl laughed. 'More like Brownie badges.'

He smiled. 'What are the people like?'

'Very nice mostly. Gentle. They live like monks and all that, they don't drink or have sex.'

Michael raised his eyebrows. 'How do they reproduce?'

'I don't think they want to. They probably imagine the world's coming to an end.'

'They might be right.' Michael took the package and thanked her. He was getting into the car just as a massive termagant of a traffic warden wearing heart-shaped specs approached. He backed up, waved to her and roared off down the hill where once more he parked, this time in a mercifully empty space. Here he unpacked his purchase, carefully took off the price tag and wound the yellow scarf round his neck. Then, thoughtfully, he eyed his leather jacket and touched the hide for a moment before removing it. There was still a thin drizzle outside, but it wasn't too cold to be seen wearing only a sweater. He reached for an umbrella on the back seat, had a quick grimace at himself in the mirror, got out, slammed the door and walked over the road towards the big house.

The woman, in a spotless white sari stood high above the lake in northern Rajasthan. With large dark eyes she was surveying

43

the landscape of palm trees and rocky hills interspersed by greenery where orange and pink blossoms glittered. Far below her, by the lakeside, figures could be seen bathing, and long lines of cloth in various shades of yellow or white were draped on the ground or any available piece of stonework to dry in the winter sun.

The woman had great authority in her bearing, and thick dark hair faintly touched by grey held in a plait. Her eyes, strangely serene as she gazed at her territory, settled at last on a black-faced monkey sitting on a projecting curlicue of roof, nibbling a piece of red fruit. She watched, amused, until a blond young man in yellow collarless shirt and cotton *kurta* trousers, with a yellow shawl across breast and shoulder, entered the room behind her. He quickly touched the gold dot on his forehead with his middle finger before raising his right palm towards the woman and murmuring the standard ashram hello of 'Peace – Connect.'

She smiled at him.

'Connect, brother,' she replied softly. 'Has there been a telex from Delhi?'

'They should arrive on schedule. Ram is with them. We expect them here late-afternoon Thursday.' He paused. 'The two sisters you wanted to know about are with them.'

She nodded. 'Has the apartment been prepared?'

'It's all ready. The girls will put flowers there for them. It looks real nice. Who are they, Maya?'

'Two women. One old, one young. The younger one is not yet an acknowledged Traveller but we hear from the Avignon centre that she has an open, powerful spirit. She is looking for peace.'

The young man sighed. Weren't they all?

'The older of the two is Sister Nadine who has visited us often. She too is a special case, not one of us exactly but a Traveller who has found her own Journey. She is a naturally Enlightened One, truly liberated. A very old friend.'

The young man nodded, his eyes ingenuous. Even in Indian garb he still had the look of the southern Californian lifeguard he used to be.

They noticed simultaneously that the long-tailed monkey had crept up on to the balcony and was bending intently over

44

a platter of fruit. His agile fingers pulled apart an orange ball of *chico* fruit as he darted covert little glances at the humans. The young man shouted, leapt towards the animal, and waved his arms quite violently as the creature bared its teeth and hissed at him, leapt high on to the rooftiles and bounded away with incredible speed.

'They're real crazy characters – aggressive, greedy, thieving. It's all there, isn't it?'

Maya put the fruit dish on to a table and covered it with a white cloth. 'They certainly are. You can see all the mechanisms of the knots and magnets of attachment and desire; it's almost comic, but like humans monkeys can cause an awful lot of destruction in the physical world.' Her accent had an Indian lilt with a definite New York overlay, the timbre of the voice soft but firm.

'Yeah.' The young man turned. 'I've got to go to an Intentions seminar now.'

'Thank you, Peter. Will you say to the others that I shall be alone until sundown? I need to Connect.'

He nodded and gazed at her for a moment as though hypnotised, his large blue eyes unblinking, then touched his forehead and retreated respectfully, palm upraised.

'Contain the light, brother,' murmured Maya, who moved to the balcony and gazed out once more over the wide lake. She reached up towards an overhanging bougainvillaea and touched a magenta bract softly before moving across to a rush floor mat on which she knelt with deliberation. She took a stick of incense from a paper packet, set it in a bronze holder and lit it with a match. She watched intently for a full minute as the smoke curled upwards in slow blue spirals. An aroma of myrrh permeated the space as she settled back on the mat, tucked her legs under her and wrapped the white woollen shawl across her body so that she seemed as smooth as the worn white marble of the palace floor. She was aware of an atavistic disturbance which was almost physical – that which the Scientologists she had once been part of used to call 'Sen'. It was definitely not a guru sensation.

After a while she frowned, rose to her feet and glided across to the door which she locked. Then she went to a cupboard and took out a suitcase which she opened. She

45

frowned again as she looked inside and pulled out a plastic bag; then sighing, she took out a cigarette which she raised to her lips, lit and inhaled deeply.

After a few minutes Maya put out her cigarette, carefully gathered up the ashes and butt and parcelled them up for disposal in the plastic bag. She locked the suitcase, put it away and sat down once more in the meditating position. Her eyes remained open, and for a while there was a self-mocking expression in the strong face with its slanting cheekbones and generous mouth before she succeeded in quieting the jangle of images and emotions which had threatened her usual tranquillity. Her large practical hands, palms upraised, lay one on either knee, until, centred at last, connected by a subtle effort of will which entailed detaching from external reality, she arrived back in that state of peaceful power which the many young Westerners and the few Indians who came to the ashram aspired to emulate, so that they too might become Liberated Ones.

She remained thus immobile on the mat for several hours, viewed only by an occasional chipmunk and one curious little monkey who gazed at her worriedly, brows furrowed, before darting across the marble balustrade to sit high on the roof with his fellows, where a large female immediately busied herself with grooming his silver fur.

In the dormitory of the Delhi School for Spiritual Travel, an appalled, Jenni watched Nadine dress.

'You're not actually going to wear a gold dot? It's too much.' She stared at her friend who wobbled as she stood on one leg to pull on yellow trousers.

'Why not? I think it is funny. It's like a theatre.'

'Well, not for me, but I do realise that I'll have to get some more yellow clothes, I need the camouflage.' Jenni held up her black leather jacket helplessly. 'I wish I'd thought . . .'

'It is wise. You'll be less noticed. Nobody has recognised you yet, have they?'

'Miraculously, no. I've managed to side-step any questions about what I do for a living and the dark glasses and short hair really seem to work.'

'Why do people who have traumas always cut their hair?'

'I guess it's a statement that at least one small part of your life is actually under control.'

'I'm getting used to you. At first I found it harsh. I did love it as it was.'

Jenni shrugged. 'It'll grow.' She looked at Nadine. 'By the way, that musical business where we all sang last night was wonderful. I'll never be able to listen to Philip Glass in the same way after that.'

Nadine nodded. 'I love it. It is so powerful, voices together – intuitive harmony.'

Breakfast was vegetable curry with strange fruits and yoghurt served in the garden under a patchwork marquee. There were noisy birds, mynahs with yellow beaks, pigeons and dozens of sparrows exactly like London sparrows only bolder, hopping fearlessly on to the table and darting in and out under the canvas. High above them soared vultures and one lone kite. At the table Jenni tried to chat to other Travellers but found it hard to make the normal sort of exchange, partly because she didn't want to talk about her work or to lie about what she did. Fortunately the Travellers seemed much more interested in the coming journey to the ashram and the meeting with Maya, who was always referred to with loving adoration. If Nadine or Jenni asked where any of them was from, the answer would inevitably be in terms of which particular school of Spiritual Travel he or she hailed from and how many months or years they had been travelling.

'How long have you been on *Jivan Yatra*, sister?' a pale young woman asked. Awkwardly, Jenni replied that she had barely set out on her spiritual journey.

'Well, you must have come far if you're going to Kundi so soon. You must have been specially chosen.' The girl gazed at Jenni with such awe that it made her uneasy. Knowing that all those who came to Kundi were supposed to have been celibate and free from any stimulant for at least a year, she felt that she was here under false pretences.

'So how come you and I are allowed in? It's like sneaking in to Mecca as an unbeliever,' she asked Nadine.

'I told you. You are invited by Maya.'

Jenni chuckled. 'So what's your pull with her?'

Nadine shrugged. 'Maya is my friend. She trusts my

instinct. I guess she believes that certain people who make their own spiritual journey in the world of creativity are doing something close to what they are trying to do.'

'How long have you known her?'

Nadine didn't answer, but her shrug implied that it was for ever.

'Is she Indian?'

'She had an Indian husband – a film-maker. He left her a lot of money.'

'Was she in show business herself?'

Nadine laughed. 'All this is quite a drama, no?'

'It certainly is. So what did she do?'

'She was in Scientology at one time.'

'You're kidding.' Jenni remembered those perseveringly earnest people who always tried to thrust pamphlets and personality tests at you outside the Scientology Centre in Tottenham Court Road. 'She sounds a real case.'

'She is a very powerful woman who wants to help people to be free in their spirits. In those days even the Scientologists had some innocents in their set-up who searched for truth and genuinely wanted to save the world; I knew one or two people who got involved at the same time as her. Maya stayed in it for about four years and at that time she was very committed.'

'Scientology's full of jargon, isn't it?'

'So's Christianity, also Buddhism. If you have a religion you have jargon. There needs to be a special language for people to be able to make sense of the chaos of living. But Maya could always heal people, she used the techniques as a tool till she got fed up with the set-up and the exclusiveness.'

'Heal them physically?'

'Sometimes, but mostly their heads. She helps ease the angst of living. She is a teacher of positivity and peace.' Nadine smiled. 'I think you will find her interesting.'

'And now she has invented her own jargon?'

'Sure, it's normal. If you become a guru, you need to create a blueprint – a structure – for people to refer to.'

'Will I get to meet her? Maybe I could interview her?'

'Maybe.' Nadine shrugged.

'Does she allow audience with the Unenlightened – the sullied, like me?'

48

'Jenni, you are not sullied. Unclear but not unclean. Tangled, a few knots to unravel, a little lost, but your strength will come back.'

She moaned, 'I feel so utterly pathetic sometimes. Do you think I'm cracking up?'

Nadine looked at her over half-spectacles. 'Is it love, or have I got angina?'

Self-indulgence had a short life in Nadine's company. 'You're not cracking up. No such luck. You are stressed; you've had too many pressures and uncertainties. You'll be OK. You're actually a big tough journalist.'

'Honest?'

'Honest. For heaven's sake, you've even rocked the British Establishment. That takes guts.'

'The big meeting is today.' Jenni frowned.

'You made your decision not to be there. Stick with it. Don't waste energy.'

'I can't help worrying about just leaving something. It will seem so odd that I'm not there when they have the review of the programme.'

'Too late, girl. Leave it.' Nadine took her by the hand. 'Come, we are going to sight-see.'

'I have been on the phone literally all day,' said Michael's secretary. 'Bucket shops, Air India, Scandinavian Air Lines, the lot.' She shook her head. 'It's because of New Year – holiday flights, family reunions and everything. The only possibility is a flight in a week's time via Kuwait to Trivandaram in the south, but I haven't yet got confirmation of any internal flights from there.'

Michael grimaced. 'It's going to cost a fortune.' He frowned. 'With my luck I'll probably arrive there just after her flight home has taken off.'

'The television people did say that she was definitely away for four weeks. Surely she'll spend all of it in India?'

'I expect so. Was there absolutely nothing to Delhi before the sixth?'

'No, but we might get a cancellation. I've got several feelers out – one of them was quite hopeful.'

'OK, Jane, keep with it. I can go as soon as the Sellafield

story is done. It's been scheduled for Saturday week. My God, what's the time?' He looked at his watch, fumbled for papers and document case and grabbed his coat. 'The BBC meeting started a couple of hours ago. I want to be there when they come out to find out what's what.'

Jane watched without comment but was glad to note as he wound a grey scarf round his neck that the canary yellow one seemed merely to have been a one-day aberration, an unwanted Christmas present maybe.

But Michael was muttering, 'I need a yellow shirt – where can I find one?'

The girl tried not to over-react visibly. 'What sort of shirt?' she enquired carefully.

'Any kind. Seat shirt, tee shirt, cuffs, collar – it doesn't matter which just as long as it's yellow. D'you think you might . . . if you just happen to come across one on your travels?' He smiled. 'You're so good at it . . . size sixteen.'

She looked at him expressionlessly. 'That, Mr O'Brien, is good old-fashioned chauvinism. But I just wish I knew why it had to be yellow? Do you really think it's your colour?'

Michael eyed her warningly. 'One of these days I'll tell you the whole story.' He blew her a kiss and left.

'I guess it must be love,' she muttered to herself. 'I hope he'll ask me to the wedding. After the divorce, that is.'

The temple to Lord Krishna was adorned with painted angels and actual people bearing gifts of flowers for the god. Jenni, exalted by the brightly coloured images and the fervour of the Hindus who had come in family groups to worship and admire, was intrigued when a ragged old man carrying a bowl of orange powder called her to him. Many of the Indians had marks on their foreheads as a sign that they had done *puja*, and had worshipped in the temple.

'Come.' His voice was low. Mesmerised, she watched as he dipped his fingers in the powder and leaned forward to draw an orange mark in the middle of her forehead.

Jenni, surprised at her own emotion, felt herself suddenly overflow with tears as she murmured thanks. 'I have no Indian money,' she said apologetically; they had not yet been to the bank.

Smiling, the old man shook his head. 'It is for you. The God of Love,' he whispered huskily. He stared into her eyes. 'It will bring you luck, sister. Love will come to you.'

Nadine's yellow beret and air of dynamism made the people of the city laugh.

'Forrogorra' they would demand, before standing stiffly to be photographed, but Nadine would mime that she didn't like to take posed pictures and show them affectionately and clearly that she wanted them to relax before she pressed the button. She made people of all ages fall a little in love with her. She took such evident pleasure in the white cows, wandering oblivious through the honking traffic, the cars, lorries and bicycles, mixed up with dogs, donkeys, birds, goats, hogs and thousands of bicycle-rickshaws. She loved these extraordinary machines, inventively original, each one built from bits and pieces to an individual design, brightly painted and decorated with tinsel or garlands of flowers. They looked half-human when between fares the drivers dozed on them, heads on saddles, feet on handlebars, backs pre-cariously balanced along the crossbars. Delighted, Nadine took dozens of pictures.

Ram advised the Travellers not to give to the beggars lest they be mobbed, and when once the fat American Traveller who had sung so strangely the night before slipped a few rupees to an old woman who looked ready to drop, they were immediately surrounded by a crowd of outstretched hands and aching eyes. Ram confronted the ring of beggars and told them to go away. He said quietly and firmly that there would be no more money, but it took some minutes before the crowd dissolved.

'I hate to see it.' Nadine frowned. 'We are so spoiled, so rich – the poorest European is a millionaire here.'

Ram shook his head. 'It is impossible to help with a few *paise*. In a way it only makes it worse if you give.'

However desperate the poverty, a sense of beauty seemed to be as organic as breathing. Here even the beggar would make time to braid a flower into a garment, or a man owning nothing but an ancient bicycle would decorate its wheels with flowers or paper streamers. And the women were so visually brilliant and captivating.

51

Nadine smiled at Jenni. 'I love this country – I always feel embraced by India. All life is here.'

Jenni nodded. 'It's like being in a theatre which never stops.'

Nadine waved her arms. 'Yes! A show designed by Rousseau and Gauguin in a visual co-production.' She gripped Jenni's arm, grinning in amazement. 'Look! Can you believe? That man is telling fortunes with his parrot!'

For Jenni too the visual deluge of beauty was almost overwhelming. There were trees everywhere. Bottle palms with tall white stems, and red and pink flowering bushes – alive with grey and white striped chipmunks – made a shimmering background to the hundreds of wheeled and brightly painted market stalls. Fruit and vegetables, always arranged in elaborate and decorative ways, were of such profusion and ripeness that each stall became a cornucopia, though the sellers were often toothless and half-starved. For Jenni to be free for once in her life to absorb quietly, with no compulsion to record or report, was like a miracle of sorts.

The flashes of beauty, as always in India, were contrasted with the horrors: the smells of human piss and excrement, and the tormenting squalor of disease and poverty. Contorted and limbless lepers and beggars were everywhere, along with the old, the blind, the amputees, the hungry mothers and half-starved children. Somehow Jenni felt she could love it all.

But in the middle of the dust and dirt, sellers would lay out their wares on a basket or a piece of coloured cloth, and whether it was a handful of onions or fifty reels of bright cotton, each display of objects would be carefully placed in a pleasing and satisfying pattern which lent dignity and beauty to the meagreness of its contents.

'Each one is like a meditation,' whispered Nadine. 'Peaceful and beautiful in the middle of all the filth and noise.'

Six

Nadine watched the sleeping Jenni as the ashram bus veered round and up the dry mountain road on the last lap of the journey to Kundi. In Delhi they had picked one man from a street of eager tailors who, in the space of only two hours, had made up a couple of suits of *kurta* pyjamas. Dressed as she now was entirely in a subtle barley yellow, hair cropped short, without make-up or jewellery, Jenni reminded Nadine forcibly of the girl she had picked up by the roadside all those years ago; she had had a vivacity and strength about her then which had been enormously appealing. Theirs had become a powerful friendship. Despite Nadine's now being more than double the younger woman's age, they still met up at least once a year. Sometimes Nadine had described Jenni to inquisitive friends as her surrogate daughter. For Jenni it was the same. She felt far closer to Nadine than to her ever-fretting mother or tentative lawyer father who had always eyed his only daughter's exploits with extreme unease – mixed, to be fair, with a giant surge of inarticulate pride when she became well-known on the television screen.

Nadine's eyes gleamed at bullock and camel carts each more brilliantly decorated than the next which rumbled past glittering vistas of white poppies. She nudged Jenni awake when these appeared, the field boundaries marked with red and brown sandstone slabs like gravestones.

'Opium.' She pointed to the white blossoms, large, round and hauntingly beautiful. Jenni blinked and stared, then smiled at the sight of a girl gathering firewood. The girl, sitting high in a tree, brilliantly patterned sari and headcloth

53

spread out in the branches, looked like some marvellous fruit.

Jenni shook her head disbelievingly. 'The females seem to do all the hard work here, look at that lot.'

The bus had slowed down to navigate a sharp bend which gave them time to peer at a group of young women, all wearing silver bracelets, earrings and ankle bands. They were repairing the road, heaving baskets of stone chippings, mixing concrete and battering boulders with pickaxes and mallets. Incongruously elegant, their bodies slender, colours butterfly bright, they stared impassively at the curious tourists.

Hours later the bus crested a hill and the passengers gazed down at a wide blue lake. There was an island in the middle with domes and temples backed by tall palm trees and beyond, on the far side, was a huge complex of buildings of white and pink stone which spread wide and high up the barren hillside, where could be discerned arched windows, balconies and much frondy greenery.

Nadine sighed with satisfaction. 'Kundi.'

'It's fantastic.'

Nadine nodded. 'It was a Maharajah's palace, a ruin inhabited by monkeys and a few very old servants who had been forgotten after the Raj. Then Maya and the Travellers found it.'

'It's like a Mughal miniature.'

'The palace itself is full of sixteenth-century frescoes.'

'I'm surprised they haven't emulsioned them all white and put pictures of Maya everywhere,' whispered Jenni.

Nadine chuckled. 'You are bad. No, much of it has been left or even carefully restored, but I do think there are too many photos.'

'Is it always the same one – the strong staring one?'

Nadine nodded.

'It's an impressive photo, though.' Jenni looked towards the front of the bus where there was the usual picture of the guru staring out in black and white encircled by a halo of golden Christmas tinsel.

'Naturally.'

Jenni looked at her. 'Of course. It's one of yours. I didn't think.'

54

Nadine shrugged, twinkling like tinsel. To Jenni's extreme relief she had abandoned her gold dot after the first day in Delhi.

'Does one meet this Maya personally, or does she only give audiences to massed groups of devotees, like the Pope at Easter?'

Nadine shrugged. 'You'll meet her OK. She likes to talk and make real contact. She is always around, teaching, leading meditations and Harmonic Connections.'

'Harmonic Connections?'

'Like we did in Delhi.'

'I enjoyed that.'

'You can do it lots at Kundi. All day from sunrise to sunset if you want, it can be one long hum-in. It's a wonderful setting; a marble terrace, and the leader of the meditation sits on a marble throne.'

'All this would make a fascinating documentary.'

'No.' Nadine patted her knee hard. 'No. No work-talk, no work-think, remember? Just physical and mental Yoga.'

'OK.' Jenni nodded and looked out of the window as the bus entered through a massive carved stone archway. 'Hey, this is some palace.'

'For me it is still one of the most beautiful places in the world. But can you imagine how it was a hundred or two hundred years ago when the hills and mountains were covered with forest?'

'Mmmmm.'

'You'll see from the old paintings. They show how it was, with lions and tigers, peacocks, jaguars, bears – all in deep jungle. It must have been like Eden.'

'Look.' Jenni pointed to a high wall with cascading scarlet blossoms among which a peacock strutted.

Nadine's smile was ecstatic.

They were met by a smiling circle of young people, Western and Indian, impeccably gold-dotted, dressed in white and many shades of yellow, with shawls of yellow or white. They grouped round the bus when it stopped and moved slowly towards it with upraised palms and garlands of pink or orange flowers, singing open-mouthed or humming in harmony. For a moment Jenni wanted to get up and run, but Nadine was grinning, jaw jutting, yellow beret askew. As the sound died down, Ram stepped down from the steps of the bus to be greeted by a tall blond young man who smilingly placed a garland of marigolds round his neck. They gazed intently at one another for a moment before each touching the middle finger of his right hand to his forehead and then holding up the same hand palm outwards. This salutation was echoed by the entire circle of singers as well as the tired Travellers who were clambering off the bus, and there were many murmurings of 'Peace – Connect' and 'Contain the Light, brothers and sisters'.

Peter motioned to them to follow him from the collonaded courtyard up a steep street of shiny cobbles and through a gate with embattled elephants carved on its stone lintel. They climbed up and up until they arrived at a carved and painted door and entered into a dazzling white courtyard where the marble walls were embellished with detailed and brightly coloured paintings of life as it had once been in the Maharaja's palace.

He showed them to a suite of three rooms, all of which looked on to a balcony from where they could look down through festoons of blossoms and palm trees, past the carved, fretted and domed arabesques of the palace buildings to the glittering lake. Here he poured them cool tumblers of water from a brass pot and left them alone. On a plain wooden table stood a copper dish of nuts and fruit and a vase of flowers. In two of the rooms they found beds made up with fresh linen. To Jenni's relief only one very small print of the ubiquitous photo of Maya was hung above the carved wooden door.

'This is preferential treatment, surely? All the people I've spoken to said they always have to sleep in crowded dormitories in the stable and servant blocks.'

Nadine sat down heavily on one of the beds. 'Maya has always been very kind to me.' She took off her beret and lay back with closed eyes. 'My God, I feel like a real drink now. Phew!'

'Why don't you have some of the Duty Free?'

Nadine fanned herself with the beret. 'Even I can't greet a guru in a teetotal establishment smelling of booze – at least not whisky. If I had thought to bring vodka I just might have, for medicinal purposes.' She yawned. 'Later, maybe.'

Jenni went to peer at the portrait of Maya. 'I still feel as though I'm here under false pretences.'

'I told you, Jenni you are invited. You get what you deserve. It is right for you to be here. Don't be frightened. She's OK, Maya. She's a real person. Special.'

Nadine's voice was quiet and Jenni wondered if she was falling asleep, but within minutes the old photographer had got up, washed and changed so that she once more looked bright and spruce, ready to meet the mysterious leader of this extraordinary organisation of celibate teetotal hummers.

'What would you like to drink, Gordon?'

'Scotch, please. By God, I need it after that lot.'

Carefully, Michael brought two glasses to the table and sat down beside the bearded man who nodded.

'Thanks very much. Welcome stuff.'

'So tell me. How did it go?'

'A noisy day.' The big man wiped his forehead with a spotted hanky. 'It just made me glad yet again that I work from a desk. I couldn't cope with being out in the field any more.'

'Did they reach any decision?'

'No. A lot of pussy-footing. They obviously don't want the programme to go out but there will be big trouble form our end if they cancel it completely.'

'So it remains unresolved?'

'I'm afraid it does. It was very odd to have the whole proceedings without the leading lady as it were.'

'I can imagine.'

'Her name was much mentioned. She's a hell of a girl, our Jen.'

Michael's long face betrayed a flicker of smile.

'So what's next? They'll have to announce something to the press.'

'Och, they'll no doubt invent some anodyne comment about the business still being under debate.'

'Do you think they actually could sit on it?'

'Difficult to say. The Board of Governors which now consists almost entirely of Tory Yes Men – their appointment being individually approved by our dear Prime Minister – are of course lobbying strongly for permanent suffocation. As I said, there was a lot of noise there today.'

Michael eyed him keenly. 'Shouting? Slogans? We want Jenni?'

Gordon chuckled. 'Not quite, but getting on that way. There were a few mutterings about Stalinism and free press. It actually smelt quite nasty for a while. Much angry comment.'

He sighed. 'It made me feel old, Michael, but I've only got another year to go – I'm taking early retirement.' Savouring the whisky he eyed Michael. 'And as for the raid last week. God that was a palaver and a half.'

'Were you there?'

'As it happens I was. Working late, about to go home, when – bang! In they came. Our boys in blue.' A hollow laugh. 'It was bloody unbelievable. The joke was they had a warrant but the Beeb lawyer sent them back with it twice, said it was wrongly addressed.' He laughed again wheezily. 'Not funny though, not funny at all.'

'How long did they stay?'

'Twenty-four hours whilst we just stood round helpless. They took the tapes for six programmes. All Jenni's working stuff about the illicit arms deal and the other nuclear waste one there was such a noise about. I'm telling you, I'll be glad to get out. The world we inhabit is not a bonny one, Michael. It never was, but it's getting less bonny all the time.' A hugh sigh. 'Anyway, enough of that. How about your hunt, have you located the girl?'

Michael drained his glass. 'I have at last. It took a while. Funnily enough it was Jenni's five-year-old niece who gave me the clue I needed. I rang her brother in desperation. Got the five year old whom I happened to have taken to the Zoo with Jen last summer. I asked her straight where Auntie Jenni was and the kid promptly says, "Auntie Jenni's bringin' me a effalent." Where from? I ask, and the kid keeps on giggling and saying, "Dellybelly, Dellybelly" because Daddy says Auntie Jenny'll get Delhi belly if she's not careful. And the penny dropped. I know Nadine is always off to an ashram place in India and guessed that she must be the photographer Jenni had gone with. I checked with the London Centre for Spiritual Travel . . .' He paused to allow Gordon's throaty chuckle to settle. 'And managed to discover with a bit of spiritual baloney that she was heading for the main ashram which is set more or less where the Madhyar Pradeshi, Rajasthani and Gujarati borders meet.

Gordon stared at him. 'I know that area.'

'How come?'

'I have, if you remember, a brother in the Embassy in Delhi. I've been there a few times. He's got friends up in that area so I know it quite well. They're building a big dam there.'

Gordon grinned. 'Trust Jenni. Honestly, I do believe that if you put that girl's head in a paper bag and blindfolded and deafened her she would still automatically find her way to the next hot spot that was about to erupt wherever it was on the globe. She's got an amazing instinct for trouble.'

Michael stood up. 'I have to confess that you've lost me now, Gordon. Let me get you another drink.'

The big man lurched to his feet. 'No. No, it's my turn.' Suddenly he sounded very Scots. 'Same again?'

'Please.'

Gordon returned carefully carrying two doubles and sat down heavily. 'I don't want to be an alarmist but all this is in fact very worrying.'

Michael looked blank. 'All what? I thought for once she might be having a real holiday, a geographically beautiful Third World trip with no major political problems for a change.'

'Heh?' Gordon's rather small eyes twinkled malevolently. 'This is Jenni you're talking about don't forget. For a start you're not even allowed to photograph dams or bridges in India.' He clinked glasses. '*Slainte.*'

'*Slainte.*' Michael's voice was abstracted. 'I fail to understand all this. Is there something sinister about the dam?'

'There certainly would be if you happened to be an Adivasi villager who lived and farmed in the dam area, whose family had been there for generations.'

'Adivasis were the original inhabitants of India, weren't they?'

'Yes. Tribal people, very poor mostly – there's a lot of them, especially in that area. They're about seventy-five percent of the population.'

'And are they being displaced?'

Gordon nodded heavily. 'Thousands of them: many, many village communities and all with no compensation that means anything. It's wholly corrupt. Some of the dam construction workers haven't been paid for over a year, even the pittance they should have had.'

'Sounds like a marvellous story, but how is it dangerous?'

Gordon leant back. 'They are a wild lot up there; they kidnap people and rob them on the road quite often. There are more dacoits than farmers in some parts.'

'Dacoits?'

'The equivalent of highwaymen. It has become a profession, a way of survival.'

Michael laughed. 'You're having me on. What on earth have dacoits have to do with it?'

'It is a mysterious part of the world, Michael – violent too.'

Michael watched as Gordon stood up breathily and heaved on his tweed coat. 'She's a sensible woman, Jenni. Anyway, she's not going for all that. I'm sure it's just for a break that she's there.'

Gordon grunted. 'Sure. Very sensible. But she has an innocence still and an openness which is of course what makes her such a good and honest reporter, but you know and I know that it also makes her vulnerable.'

Michael watched as Gordon fumbled for his diary.

'How about lunch some time next week, Michael? Friday any good?'

'I'm afraid I'm going away next Thursday.'

'Ah. Somewhere hot, I hope?'

Michael grinned. 'Sounds like it. In every sense of the word.'

Nadine and Jenni followed Peter through the main courtyard up a wide curved alabaster stairway to a chamber with mirrored archways and painted images of kings and warriors and voluptuous women in settings of fountains, courtyards and exotic trees. Beyond this was the guru's apartment with its marble balcony, simple bed, sofa and plain cane chairs. After showing the two women where to sit, Peter disappeared into the inner sanctum for a few moments. When he returned he had a glow about him, like one who is in love.

60

'Maya's just coming,' he said with awe. 'She's been Connected nearly all day.'

They waited in silence as the room grew rosy with the reflected light of the setting sun. Peter lit an incense taper which he set in a brass container on a low wooden table and the curling ribbon of smoke spread a sweet strong aroma throughout the space. He stood up. The bright yellow shawl wound round his shoulders made him look like a young Crusader.

'I guess I'll put the lights on,' he murmured, and went to pull an electric switch near the door. The resulting light was so weak and yellow it had almost the effect of gaslight.

At last a curtain on the door to the inner chamber shifted and a woman in a white sari with large dark eyes, black hair going grey, sturdy, not very tall and incredibly alert-looking, came into the room. Nadine and Peter stood up as did Jenni, who now felt almost as nervous as she used to feel at school when summoned before the headmistress.

The guru and Nadine touched fingers to foreheads with the right hand, and raised their palms in greeting, each muttering the ritual 'Peace – Connect' which always made Jenni feel impatient.

She watched as the two women who were more or less the same height looked into each other's faces for a long-held gaze before embracing fondly. She was surprised to see that her friend's eyes were wet.

'Dear Maya.' Nadine drew back and looked at her, smiling. 'We meet again. And here –' she gestured fondly to Jenni, took her firmly by the arm and led her towards the guru '– is Jenni.'

Maya looked at her. 'Like a bloody flame-thrower' she could almost hear Michael say. Somewhat awkwardly she fumbled and, against her own inclination, did the ritual forehead touch and raised palm bit. For a hysterical moment she felt like shouting 'Heil Hitler!' and running out and down the stone stairs and out across the courtyard, then she was engulfed by Maya's power: the flame-thrower had zapped her.

Jenni sensed affinity, warmth, strength, a definite physical frisson. It was bemusing, but she allowed herself to receive it and felt warmed by it just as she had done when first she

61

joined in the humming business. After all she was here for a few days, why not go for it and try to experience it to the full?

She smiled back at Maya and when she felt herself locked in the guru's all-encompassing gaze, tried not to remember that Nadine had told her that Maya means 'Illusion' in Sanskrit, or 'Nothing is what it seems'. This was charisma with a vengeance.

'You are welcome, sister,' said Maya at last. 'You have been called here because it is meant. We have heard much of your strength and honesty.'

Jenni didn't feel too sure about the strength bit just at present and honestly mumbled something to that effect.

Maya looked at her for an embarrassingly long time, then smiled. 'Intensive meditation. Much of it. Then once more you will be like a lion and not like a lamb.'

Despite herself, just as when she had received the blessing from the old man in the temple of Krishna, Jenni felt moved.

Nadine, fondly holding her arm, told the guru that Jenni was world weary. 'She has seen too many sadnesses and worked too hard for too long. She needs to find some peace. This is why she has come.'

Maya turned her gaze (a true clichéd burning gaze) on to Jenni and held her eyes locked for a long pause, then she smiled.

'We welcome you to Kundi, sister. Nadine has told us of you for many years.'

Jenni noted that the guru used the royal 'we', and wondered if it meant Maya and her God unified as one.

'I, likewise, have heard of you and of Kundi,' she replied, aware of sounding positively Shakespearean, but Maya certainly emanated a regality of sorts.

'I know that you are not actually one of us,' said Maya, 'but Nadine tells me that you have learned how to meditate.'

Embarrassed, Jenni muttered 'Just a little – to help a racing brain when I get steamed up from work or something.' She refrained from adding that it hadn't helped a lot with a brain steaming from love.

'I hope that you will feel free to share in all the things we do here. Participate as little or as much as you want. You might find it helpful to Connect with the larger groups; there is great power to be gained from joining others in meditation and vocal unification.'

Jenni felt like a small girl. 'I did a little in Delhi,' she admitted. 'It was wonderful.'

'Good.'

She was positively warmed by the answering blaze in Maya's eyes. Though not tall, the leader of the ashram had a statuesque power and an expression which, though fierce, was full of love.

'Do all that you can. I am certain you will find that it was meant for you to be here now. Try to do intensive meditation for several hours a day,' Maya told her. 'That and the other disciplines we practise here. We rise before the dawn for the early morning Connection – as so many of the other eastern teachings also do. We call it the nectar time.'

She paused then spoke again with great intensity. Jenni was inadvertently reminded of the female Cabinet Minister she had recently interviewed.

'It is the time when, like a bee, you can fill yourself with spiritual power which will last all day. Try it. You will see for yourself, your burnout will heal.'

'Pre-dawn sounds a bit early for me.' Jenni tried not to giggle.

Maya looked at her with that same strangely tactful expression Jenni had observed certain Travellers use. The guru's eyes and attention appeared to be strongly on her, but without a really personal connection – it was somehow detached and non-emotional. In the end Maya smiled a little mysteriously.

'You may just find that you want to,' was all she said. 'Travellers do not take any form of artificial stimulant so that the mind can be kept pure. We also work on freeing ourselves from desires – the bondage of emotional or sexual attachment. These wants and needs, or what the undisciplined and un-unified mind designate as needs, are all a subtle form of bondage. You will realise that many of the things we think that we want or even need, though they may appear pleasant, will never bring us true happiness. We may think that they will do so, but that is illusion. With the disciplines of meditation we will become able to rise above them – free to unify with the power of the Life Force. Clear. Liberated. Unified. Our minds and bodies can then be used as tools of the Life Force, the Great Spirit, and we experience as the Gita tells us what it is to become like the lotus flower, a beautiful chalice which floats and is detached from the corruptions of earth and water.'

A silence, then Maya looked over towards Nadine and asked, 'Shall we Connect together now?'

Jenni settled down to meditate, making a strong effort to keep her eyes open, and concentrated on Maya's face. She sat staring open-eyed at the dot on Maya's forehead for almost twenty minutes, aware of the clever slanting eyes which became somehow bodiless, unseeing in the physical sense. She lost all sense of physicality and experienced a strange tranquil energy. Then suddenly she felt a great surge of power coupled with a sense of release which was akin to flying free like Superman. It was as though she was soaring up and up, high above the earth and beyond its boundaries to a place where there was a sensation of shimmering light and infinite space, and above all a feeling of peace which filled her like some magical fluid. She almost believed that she could see a glow like a halo round the guru's head. Rationally she told herself that it must be an optical illusion, but to be honest she really wasn't quite sure if Maya actually had a golden aura or not.

In the end she was still bemused by the whole business, puzzled by whether or not she had seen a halo. She was tired, she rationalised. Vulnerable. Michael would no doubt call it all a load of cobblers and talk authoritatively about the spiritual discipline of the Jesuits; but for the moment Jenni admitted to herself that she found the peaceful power of the Spiritual Travellers strangely seductive. Both Maya and Ram seemed to her impressive examples of what could be learned by a devout Traveller in the palace of Kundi.

I'll go for it, she decided. I'll give it a try. I need some of what they've got.

Seven

Meanwhile in Camberwell, London, Nella, a woman in her early-forties, fair-haired, pleasant-looking, could be seen standing in the ground floor window of a large house with a 'For Sale' notice in the front garden. Obviously waiting for somebody, her eyes ranged anxiously along the street without really noticing the children playing on the painted wooden structures in the small park opposite or the Alsatian which paused to sniff a lamp-post. She stood there for some minutes until suddenly she smiled and disappeared into the depths of the room. Moments later a second woman, short-haired, wearing jeans, red boots and padded jacket, walked through the garden gate past frosted rhododendrons and an uncollected milk bottle, up four steps to the front door which, before she had time to reach for the large brass knocker, opened to reveal Nella, who sighed happily as their eyes met.

'I thought you would never come.' The two embraced.

'I'm sorry, there was a bomb-scare on the tube. I've missed you so much. How are you?'

The first woman nodded, smiling. 'Happy now. Want a coffee?'

'Please.' The newcomer looked at her. 'Did the youngsters get off OK?'

'I dropped them off at the airport this morning – laden. Three sets of skis, boots, and Heaven knows what else. They're all so enormous. I don't know how we got ourselves and all the gear into the Fiat.'

'Lucky middle-class beggars. Who's paying, you or him?'

'Half and half, it's still being sorted out.'

'Have you seen Himself?'

'Not a word. I don't think he'll ever get over the shock.'

'That one's a survivor. Anyway, here we actually are. Have we really got a whole week?'

The blonde nodded. 'I can't believe it. All to ourselves. I told my neighbours you were my cousin. I still feel too confused by it all to tell them straight.'

'Straight seems hardly the best phrase!'

They hugged again. After some moments the woman in jeans pulled away. 'I'm not really desperate for coffee, Nell.'

'You're a devil. I can't help thinking what my old nuns at the convent would have said about all this.'

'Maybe they'd have said, "Greater love hath no man than to lay down his wife for his friend".'

'That is blasphemy, Fan.'

'Sorry, but I was actually his friend before I met you.'

Arm in arm they walked past hessian-covered walls and stripped wood.

'I can still remember him coming home telling me he'd interviewed this woman sociologist who was not only quite good-looking but could actually argue politics like a man.'

'Was that a compliment?'

'From Michael, yes.'

'Then I found you were my pupil.'

Nella turned to her. 'I am still learning.'

Jenni woke abruptly just before dawn and knew at once that she must get up and join the morning meditation. The luminous face of her watch showed half-past three, the nectar time when Maya had said it was possible to have the most powerful experience of meditation. Jenni washed and dressed as quietly as possible so as not to disturb the gently snoring Nadine. It was chilly as she pulled on thick socks and thermal underwear, but she had awoken as though summoned and wanted to experience the daily routine of the ashram as fully as possible. As she made her way in the darkness down the steps and up through the painted courtyard to the main meditation hall, she remembered the shock of last night's mealtime: they had climbed up a wide flight of stairs into the large pavilion which was the refectory and Jenni had been

66

delighted when Nadine greeted a young French sculptor whom Jenni recognised from Provence. He was a handsome man who looked even more impressive in the spotless white outfit which denoted that he was now a Liberated One. When Jenni had suggested that the three of them share a table for supper, she had been taken aback when the Frenchman's expression had suddenly changed to what she could only describe to herself as tactful. It was a look she had noticed several times on the faces of the Travellers – a mixture of earnestness and caution – but to her surprise Alain even withdrew a little physically. He didn't quite take a step back but it was almost that.

'I am very sorry, sister, but perhaps you don't know that brothers and sisters eat at separate tables on different sides of the refectory?'

Jenni, used to working all over the world in a profession with total ease of access between the sexes, was both disappointed and annoyed.

'Why on earth didn't you tell me?' she later hissed accusingly to Nadine as they stood in the food queue.

Nadine smiled blandly. 'You would never have come.'

Jenni had the grace to laugh, and in the end the meal which was eaten at a table with half a dozen other women had been exceptionally pleasant. The food was well-cooked, vegetarian with beguiling flavours, and the women all had interesting stories to tell. They varied from a hairdresser who had seen the light at a Spiritual Traveller's meet-up in Dublin, to a couple of young doctors, and an American practitioner of an obscure form of personal growth therapy who seemed to be a sort of Ashram groupie. The latter had experienced the Rajneesh one of which she told some hair-raisingly erotic tales, as well as the other more staid Maharishi Mahesh Yogi one to name but two.

'I like to experience wearing a uniform colour, and nobody has any make-up or jewellery,' declared Nadine at dinner.

'Except your bracelet.'

She shrugged. 'It's part of me.'

Jenni felt totally naked with her face scrubbed free of any make-up, short hair and nondescript collarless pyjama suit, but she confessed that she did have a strong sensation of relief at being let off her usual performance hook.

The decision the Travellers had made to live without sex was the one that puzzled her most.

'But what about the celibacy?' she asked as the life stories grew more intimate. The person she asked was the Irish hairdresser who drew back, her eyes suddenly sharp.

'I didn't enjoy all that sex-lust stuff,' she said so stiffly that Jenni forebore from investigating further. Then she asked an Australian actress who assured her with great conviction that she enjoyed the spiritual excitements she now experienced infinitely more than those of the body.

Margit, the rebirth therapist who had already caused them to disturb the ashram hush with giggles at her tales of earlier centres of learning, was still in full flow: 'I swear I arrived completely innocent at this Rajneesh place. I was led to this hut where I was to sleep, and there were three men there. I was supposed to pick at least one for the night if I didn't feel able to handle all three of them.'

Nadine was fascinated. 'What did you do?'

Margit, who looked as though she might well have handled the lot, laughed behind enormous yellow-rimmed glasses.

'I went straight to the office and demanded a hut by myself.'

'They gave you one?'

'Yes.' She smiled a little.

'And you stayed alone there?'

'For a day or two.' Margit coloured a little. 'It was an extremely liberating atmosphere. In the end I explored quite a few areas of myself.'

'And others too?' queried Nadine.

'Sshhh.' Margit put her finger to her lips. 'We're disturbing the peace.'

Nadine looked round and saw several people looking stonily towards their table.

'How about now?' Jenni persisted. 'Are you married?'

Margit sighed. 'That is quite a problem. I do have this life partner called Harry. We met in fact when we were with the Rajneesh outfit. Harry smokes and drinks alcohol,' she paused for these iniquities to sink in, 'whereas I have left that world well behind. I told Harry just before I came that things will have to be different from now on. I have made part of the bedroom into my early morning meditation place, and I've

68

warned him about the celibacy.' She frowned. 'But to be honest Harry has not yet completely accepted that I really have set out on the Journey. It is a bit of a problem.' She shrugged. 'He's a sweet guy, Harry, but completely un-unified.'

A cock crowed in the distance as Jenni walked sleepily to the Power House, and she met with more shrouded figures who murmured 'Peace – Connect' to her. She wondered if it were smug of her to wonder if any of the women she had eaten with the night before had ever had it as good as she and Michael had. The rebirther, Margit, still a highly attractive woman, certainly looked as if she knew about sensuality; she had also laughed so much at Nadine's jokes that Jenni had wondered if the silently devoted diners at adjoining tables might not ask them to leave the refectory. So why was the woman here? Why were any of them here? The unenlightened faraway Harry was probably quite a reasonable man, he sounded normal enough to Jenni, but obviously the drug of Spiritual Travel had proved stronger than sex for Margit. Perhaps it was her age, a menopausal aberration? Whatever it was it was all very puzzling, and all the young Travellers certainly weren't undergoing mid-life crises.

The large room was white, with glints of turquoise and gold. The pale stone floor had padded cotton coverings and there was a smell of incense and jasmine. Dimly lit, Maya's picture – the largest yet – stood near a table where incense glowed beside a bowl of fruit. When Jenni squatted down and took up the meditating position, carefully balancing eyes and body so that she felt centred, there were about twenty other meditators, one of them the fat American counter-tenor, sitting cross-legged, huddled in shawls, coats and woolly hats, staring hypnotically towards the central candle in front of the guru Maya's inescapable image.

In Camberwell, undressing, Fan looked round at the big bedroom with its jungle of giant green plants.

'It's very beautiful. Michael must miss it. How about you? It must hurt to sell up.

Nella sat on the bed a little wearily, her eyes thoughtful.

'D'you know, it all feels so odd and far away now, like another world. Since Sean left for university there's often nobody to cook for at all. It all began to seem like some play or opera that was over. I felt like a once-indispensable stage manager on a now-abandoned and forgotten set – to which, OK, I was most extraordinarily attached emotionally – but all that seemed to be left for me to do was pack up the worn-out costumes and used make-up and sweep clean the empty stage.'

Fan, naked, lay beside Nella softly stroking her arm. 'God, it sounds so sad.'

Nella, facing her, stared blindly out towards the large double windows. 'I don't really feel as though I will miss it, I just feel so empty now that all the energy and emotion has petered out.'

'Has it petered out with the children?'

Nella looked for a long time at a silver-framed picture of three smiling toddlers which sat by the bed. Sighing, she handed it to Fan.

'Lovely.' Fan searched the small grinning faces. 'They are such a mixture of the two of you. Sean's got Michael's jaw, hasn't he?'

'He is the image of his father.' She put the picture back in its place. 'I suspect that the business of mothering never really finishes. When I move I'll have to keep a space for them – at least one room. From what I've seen in my own mother and older friends I guess that the attachment is for ever: a huge invisible umbilical cord connects you to them and them to you for life. But what I find harder to understand is the marriage just fading away over the last few years like that, though that seems to be the way of it as often as not.'

'Don't cry, my love.' Tenderly, Fan knelt and kissed tears from blue eyes which suddenly overflowed. 'I'll take care of you.'

Nella's answering groan was deep-dredged. 'Can't you see that's exactly what I'm afraid of? Love, trust?'

Watching her, Fan listened intently as Nella gasped, 'It's because I've played this scene before. Years ago OK, but with Michael. He said those same things that you now say to me – and I in my innocence believed them. I wanted them to be true. And I did love him for a long time.'

'So what happened?'

Wet-eyed, sad and dignified, Nella shook her head. 'I don't know.'

Fan lay back to look at her, her expression soft. 'You are beautiful. And I know you don't like me to say it but I do love you.'

Nella sighed. 'I've been thinking about it all so much. I think the main problem was that we both got bored. At the end of it we both felt used up, sexually, mentally, all of it. We could always talk about the kids but he was away such a lot that I felt dumped. I was his hotelier, occasional bedmate, the mother of his children, and hostess when he deemed it necessary.'

'Maybe we all expect too much of love – especially heterosexual love. Men and women are expected to be such archetypal heroes and heroines to each other, to fulfil every need, emotional, financial, sexual . . . it's a helluva lot to ask of any one person.'

'So where does that leave us?'

Fan turned and pulled her closer. 'You really want me to tell you?'

'Yes.'

'Here, for starters. And here.' She watched Nella's eyes and softly moved her hand across and downwards.

'Oh,' Nella whispered. 'I begin to see . . .'

Nadine heard the same Rajasthani cockerel that had crowed earlier, but it came as a screech of terror in her dream. She was embroiled in a hideous nightmare which entailed a baby and tramping jack-boots. When she woke, she was sobbing and hardly knew for a few minutes if she was awake or asleep, she remained so overwhelmed by memories she had succeeded in neutralising and ignoring for years. As she slowly disengaged from them, she became aware of a headache: the small amount of whisky she'd taken as a nightcap the night before had been too much after the long journey. She sighed and would have liked to waft back to oblivion, but the evil images still disturbed her so she forced herself to get up and wash to avoid being sucked back into them. Using water which spluttered from an ancient heater into a plastic bucket, she dressed slowly, wrapping a yellow shawl around her head and shoulders and pulling on thick woolly socks. Tomorrow she would force herself to join the early meditators. She knew of old that only such discipline at the pre-dawn time when the human mind is at its most vulnerable and suggestive – for torture, prayer or self-hypnosis – could help to keep the blackness at bay. Nadine's ongoing flirtation with God at Kundi had become an essential and almost annual balancing act.

The dawn was bringing the world into pearly soft focus as she made her way carefully down towards the kitchen area of the ashram. One or two Travellers were already there, muffled and scarved, quietly sipping hot drinks, writing intently or gazing into space, blissed out. Nadine took a beaker and filled it from a large urn. Her hands grew warm from the heat of the drink and she went to sit on a balcony where she could see the lake turning to nacreous pink. As she sipped the spiced tea her headache lifted and the horrors of the night faded. She stood up as the rocky landscape dotted with palm trees became visible in the light of the new day, and leaned over the balcony to observe a large buffalo. A melancholy beast with great curved horns, it was licking its shiny black snout.

'*Bonjour, Madame,*' she called.

Black birds hopped on the creature's back and pecked for insects. Reaching into her embroidered bag for a small sketch book, Nadine set herself up on the wide balcony, her feet on a chair, the drink still warm beside her, and started to draw the buffalo's soft dark eyes with an equally soft black pencil.

'I have my way, Maya, and you have yours,' she murmured.

Her equilibrium was nearly always thus restored by attachment to, rather than detachment from, the physical world.

A young *Bhil* tribal girl of perhaps fifteen, wearing brilliant red, green and blue, carried a jug of milk over to the table. She laid down the jug shyly and crept over to look at what Nadine was doing. She watched fascinated as Nadine, frowning, continued to draw. 'Eh, what do you think?' Nadine held out the picture. The cow was clearly and decoratively depicted, a crow perched comically on its back. The girl drew

72

back, covering her face with her *odni*, but Nadine gestured for her to look properly and she did so.

'Photograph,' said the girl, pointing to the drawing. Then she burst out laughing. 'Hand-written photograph!'

'Hand-written photograph – yes, it is exactly that!' Nadine chortled in response and patted the girl's shoulder.

They were still gesticulating to each other when Jenni arrived at last with a group of self-absorbed fellow meditators from the early morning session in the Power House.

After the early Harmonic Unification the Travellers were expected to help in the kitchens, to experience the PPR (Present Physical Reality) of the School. A large man in a yellow apron showed Jenni and Nadine where to sit beside two young Australians who remained preoccupied as they devoutly prepared carrots from a huge heap in front of them, scraping and cutting with knives and boards given to them by the man who also carefully demonstrated to each newcomer exactly how the vegetables were to be sliced.

'It was beautiful this morning,' enthused Jenni, chopping briskly. 'If only I could get into a routine and get up at that time every morning, I could do a tremendous amount of work.'

Nadine eyed her ironically. 'Then you could be even more workoholic than before, you mean?'

Her remark caused the quiet followers of Maya to look up at the noisy white-haired woman as they worked. It was unusual to hear a raised voice at Kundi, but Nadine's high profile of noise and inescapable presence caused one or two of the less tediously pious Travellers to smile a little.

73

Eight

On the night of her seventh day at Kundi Jenni had a powerful dream. It was almost without images but with fierce physical sensation: a dream of power, love and expansion. As she dreamed she felt love as though for Michael and sex warmed its way through her body almost to orgasm, but then the sensations changed subtly and seemed to lift upwards from her body and heart and higher (this was the inadequate word she used when she tried later to expound the dream to Nadine) into her head – her mind in fact. There was a feeling of intense excitement and spreading out – but of intellect and understanding – not, as it had begun, of clitoris or vagina.

'It was marvellous.' She struggled to describe what was almost intangible. 'So full of future promise, and utterly indescribably pleasure. Honestly, I can only explain it as an orgasm of the mind.'

Nadine watched her. 'I understand exactly. I had a similar experience when I came here first and really followed the régime. Yes, it can be wonderful.'

'But what happened? You don't really seem to be hooked on the whole business now.'

Nadine shrugged and wiggled her head Indian-style, her eyes creased in a non-committal smile. 'It comes and goes, like everything else good in life.'

Feeling a great desire to hug her, Jenni put her hand on Nadine's for a moment. 'Thank you for bringing me here.'

'I knew what was needed. Been there, done it, like the ad' says.'

'It is an important time for me.'

74

'I know.' Nadine nodded for so long that Jenni was aware that she was very moved too.

The regime at Kundi was truly monastic if followed properly as Jenni tried to do. The most earnest Travellers rose early and went first thing to the Power Room to Connect with meditation and more of the bewitching wordless chanting with its eerily beautiful overtones. This was followed by the kitchen chores, or going back to sleep like some sleepyheads, then breakfast. After breakfast came physical Yoga, stretching and balancing the body in a serenely disciplined way, followed by talks on the meaning of the Journey and how to create a balance between the worlds of the mind, body, and spirit. Then lunch and more private study or rest. Some people went for walks, some wrote feverishly in their special Kundi notebooks with Maya's face and a gold dot on the cover whilst others made forays to the small local town where they could commission one of the numerous local tailors to create *kurta* pyjamas or sexless dresses in varying shades of yellow or white. After tea, more physical Yoga if you weren't too stretched from the last lot, study sessions, or long connections led by Maya or one of the Liberated Ones. There were workshops with protagonists from all over the world who would compare the problems of being a Spiritual Traveller in their various fields of medicine, teaching or theatre. ('It's a very middle-class religion,' Jenni commented dryly.) Jenni did attend one or two of the workshops, but found it a strain to keep her anonymity. A further hour of Connection was followed by supper. Early bed was advised, and Jenni was certainly glad of it after her early risings which had now gone on for over a week. Independently, Nadine spent much of her time wandering about with her camera, and Jenni was aware that she had several sessions alone with Maya.

'But what about the emotions?' asked Jenni as they rested in the sun on their balcony one afternoon. 'Surely they are as important as the spirit, mind or body?'
'You want them to have a world to themselves too, a fourth world?' Nadine threw a piece of banana to a chipmunk who daringly scuttled off to nibble the fruit in the safety of a tree.

'Yes. Surely our emotions are a separate entity just as much as mind and body are?'

'I think they permeate through all three worlds Maya speaks about and part of what the Journey is about is to separate out these different areas – worlds if you like – to get oneself into a state of control of them all, but in a strong way, so that you are not on automatic, tied helplessly and re-stimulatively to your past, your desires and fears.'

Jenni sighed. 'I don't really understand all that stuff. Much of what Maya says makes sense to me at the time she says it, but other parts I want to argue with, then when I do I am made to feel that I am not yet spiritually advanced enough on the bloody Journey to understand. They mutter: "Patience, sister" and tell me to keep on doing the physical and spiritual disciplines like I ought to be taking my daily dose of vitamins.'

Nadine chuckled. 'I had all that. I had it up to here.' She waved her hand over her head and rolled her eyes back.

'But even though you aren't really one of them, you keep coming. I still don't really understand the tie, or even why they allow you to keep coming back. Surely if you were going to be converted it would have happened by now?'

Nadine didn't answer for a long time. She busied herself with unloading and loading one of her cameras. 'I guess some people, mostly artists, have a sort of carte blanche spiritually speaking and Maya has a soft spot for them,' she said at last.

'A soft spot for you, you mean?'

Nadine shrugged.

'Anyway,' Jenni rolled over on her tummy, 'surely a guru should be so detached that she doesn't have any soft spots? It should be all equal, unemotional. If she has a soft spot for you or anyone else it means attachment and that's what this whole business is about, isn't it? Getting rid of attachment – or *bondage* as they so heavily describe it.'

There was a long silence.

'Well?' Jenni prodded Nadine who eyed her lazily.

'Well what?'

'Well I don't know, but I remain intrigued by your connection with this place. Something about it tickles the journalist in me.'

'Maybe Maya keeps me as a mascot.'

Jenni laughed. 'Some mascot. A liability more like. Mascots are usually quiet and cuddly. Docile.'

Nadine watched as Jenni adjusted her yellow shirt and trousers, newly-laundered and painstakingly ironed with an antique charcoal iron by the wrinkled *dhobi* man.

'You look different, what is it now?'

Jenni looked up enquiringly.

'Turn round.'

Obediently, she pirouetted, canary yellow shawl draped smoothly round her body.

'I know what it is.' Nadine pointed. 'It's your shoulders, that's what.' Satisfied, she nodded.

Jenni screwed her head round and peered down her back. 'I don't see anything.'

'I do.' Nadine's eyes gleamed.

'What are you talking about?'

'It's those two little bumps on your shoulder-blades. And – '

Nadine shielded her eyes. 'My God, the glare!'

'What glare? Are you feeling all right?'

Nadine smothered a chuckle. 'I guess they may grow quite fast. You'll have to be very careful with them.'

'What the hell are you talking about, Nadine?'

She smiled sweetly. 'Your wings, darling, your little budding angel wings. And that shining golden halo. Just don't fly too high, you can get lost up there. It's a long way to fall.'

Jenni gesticulated threateningly.

'Not now, liberated Travellers don't use violence, they're much too detached.' Nadine pulled her yellow beret hard down over her eyes and clutched her chest. 'And I mustn't get over-excited.'

'If you're not careful I'll report you to Maya for insubordination.'

Nadine responded by gazing heavenwards and chanting 'Aaaaaaah', open-mouthed, on a long extended note, a slightly wailing send-up of the Harmonic Unification. Then abruptly she sat up. 'It is a marvellous light. Let's go climb the hill behind the main buildings. I want to take some pictures. It's where the monkey tribe lives.'

Jenni stood up. 'OK. Let's go. I spoke to a woman yesterday

who said that this is the only known monkey tribe in the world with a female in charge.'

Nadine pulled herself to her feet with a hand from Jenni. 'Of course, with Maya in charge of the ashram, what would you expect? A man monkey wouldn't get a look in. She's quite a woman Maya. Always was.' She leant over the balcony and gazed contentedly at the magenta splendour of the bougainvillaea, the sweet-smelling orange blossoms and the blue pyramids of distant hills.

'How long have you known her actually?'

'Hmmm.' Nadine looked at Jenni enigmatically. 'You could describe me as her oldest friend. Come on.' She bent to pick up her striped bag. 'Let's go.' Then: 'Hey, look at him!' Excited, she pointed to a huge monkey who leapt up on to the balcony and stared at them. In an instant Nadine had the camera to her eye.

'Feed him some fruit,' she whispered.

Jenni reached slowly towards the fruit dish, picked up a small apple and threw it to him. He caught it elegantly and fled, bounding wildly away into the bushes where he met up with several small monkeys who immediately surrounded him and watched intently as he first minutely examined then ate the fruit.

They walked up behind the palace buildings, along a path bordered with dreamy blue-grey eucalyptus, tamarind and flaming poinsettia trees where green parakeets shrieked in the foliage.

'All this place needs is Adam and Eve and it would be complete.'

Nadine, somewhat breathless from climbing, stopped to admire the view. 'Yeah. They of course were celibate.'

'I suppose they were, until the snake came and Eve ate the fruit and offered it to Adam.'

That was his story!'

'But it's true enough. It was paradise when they were celibate, then it went, or rather they had to go.'

'It depends how you interpret it.'

They reached a large rounded boulder with a fine view of the lake and palace. Jenni put down her shawl bought in the village from a wicked-looking man in yellow pyjamas who swore he too was on the Journey. 'I am your brother, sister.

Spiritual Travel very good. Me and all my family Spiritual Travellers. I make you a good price . . .'

'Let's rest.' Still puffing, Nadine sat down heavily.

'Are you OK?' Jenni looked hard at her as she wiped her forehead.

She lay back. 'I'm OK.' Her eyes were closed.

Jenni gazed about her. 'God, it is lovely here. So lovely, everything about it. Do you know, I've started to imagine everybody I know and like back home being dressed in yellow or white with no make-up or jewellery. It would be amazing.'

Nadine's chuckle was her wickedest. 'Your mother?'

'I said know and *like*.'

'Ah, sorry.' More rasping laugh.

'I can imagine my brother and a couple of people I work with quite easily. I guess it's a sign of their being quite spiritual people anyway.'

Nadine mumbled agreement and seemed to doze.

'It's frightening,' Jenni was almost talking to herself, 'I even have these visions of my London flat made over to being a mini-Power House, the blue walls painted white, no pictures, pure and simple. It's crazy, but it's become a constant recurring image. By God, we could do with one in Fulham.'

'For poor tired businessmen and media people?'

'Sure. Anybody who needed it. That makes almost everybody.'

'Creeping in the door and taking off their business suits to reveal their yellow pyjamas like a new breed of spiritual Superman.' Nadine smiled. 'I like it.'

'But seriously, we should have meditation centres in cities.'

'Of course. Like churches once must have been. It's a basic human need.'

'It almost frightens me, but I can really imagine going home to do that with my place. The main room is big enough.'

'But what about the rest of it, the disciplines?'

Jenni was thoughtful. 'Even the celibacy I feel I could go for. The drink I wouldn't really find a problem except once in a while after a really tense bit of work, but I do begin to see the sense of the celibacy. After all, I hardly know anybody who thinks the world has much of a chance of survival so why create more children anyway?'

'But what about good old-fashioned sex? Sex, for fuck's sake? Our own dear good plain sex? Cuddling? You could really do without that?'

Jenni sighed loudly. 'As you well know I've been giving it much thought of late, both at here and at home. I haven't had a lot of it either, because of being attached you might say.'

'And?'

'Well, when I review my own history, the most painful things in my life have had to do with sexual relationships. Sex also creates families, and just think of all the mayhem they cause – and now there's AIDS as well.'

Nadine grunted then looked up, her eyes tight against the glare of the sun. 'What about Michael? Where would he fit into this new schema for living?'

'Where would he have, you mean? I told you, it's truly over between us, but oddly enough I can just imagine him in *kurta* pyjamas, and then . . .'

Nadine interrupted fast. 'Then you rip them off him double quick, heh?'

Jenni laughed. 'Not so. I just can't imagine him in them for more than a moment or two, then he goes sort of faint.'

'I don't think yellow is really Michael's colour.' Nadine sat up and choked a little. Jenni patted her.

'You shouldn't laugh so much at your own jokes.' Then she saw that Nadine was leaning forward, her eyes shut.

'Are you OK?'

Nadine managed to nod, but was obviously in pain. 'Pass me my bag.' She gestured vaguely, her eyes closed. Jenni picked up the bag.

'What do you want – whisky?'

'Small bottle – white pills.' It was a gasp.

Nervously, Jenni scrabbled through films, seed-pods, pencils, lens cleaning fluid – and at last found the right object. 'How many?' With some difficulty she managed to unscrew the child-proof lid. They must have brilliant children these days, she observed to herself hysterically.

'One.' Nadine looked awful. 'I put it under my tongue.'

Jenni handed her the pill and she lay back for some minutes, occasionally moaning a little. Her colour was very poor. At least, to Jenni's hypnotised relief, she seemed to

80

ease. 'It's OK. I'm feeling better. I guess you'll have to put up with me a big longer. Did I give you a fright?' Lopsided, her grin was vestigial.

'You certainly did.' Jenni held up the bottle. 'What is this anyway?'

'It's TNT. My bomb.'

Jenni read the typed label. 'Glyceryl Trinitrate. Take when required. Why on earth didn't you tell me you weren't well?'

'I wasn't too used to the idea myself.'

'What's wrong with you?'

Nadine sighed. 'Angina, but my bombs keep it OK. I stay quiet, put a pill under my tongue and it gets better.' Her eyes were still almost closed.

'When did it start?'

'Six months ago.'

'And you came here anyway? What did your doctor have to say to that?'

'He wasn't over-enthused by the idea, but I persuaded him it could be a good way to go.'

'Bloody hell.' Jenni felt close to tears.

'I'm sorry, Jenni. Most of the time I can ignore it.'

Jenni, looking at her dear friend lying there almost childlike in her apology, was suddenly overwhelmed with fondness for this funny, stubborn, brilliant woman.

'Sorry? I'm sorry, for heaven's sake. Shit!' She tried to compose herself. 'All I can say is you must damned well keep yourself attached to that body of yours for a long time. Don't you dare go and do anything silly like getting really sick. I need you, the world needs you, so you must take care and not do any more crazy trips up Indian mountains. OK?'

She was aware that what she was really trying to say was that if Nadine died, she would murder her.

'OK.' Nadine nodded contritely, then looked up at Jenni. 'You aren't really going to join up and become a nun, are you?'

Jenni eyed her. 'I might. Why?'

'Just asking. I like to keep in touch with who you are.'

Nadine was shivering. Jenni wrapped their two woollen shawls carefully round her shoulders.

'Are you able to walk?'

81

'Sure, a bit wobbly but I can. Don't worry, you won't have to carry me. I'm not dead yet.'

Slowly they made their way down towards the ramparts of the palace, Jenni poignantly aware of the orange sunset which was so beautiful as to be almost unreal. She held her as Nadine, half-stumbling, cursed exasperatedly in French. The photographer had always seemed the strong one to Jenni who had for years relied on Nadine's humour and wisdom to help see her through many a crisis of love or work. Years ago, soon after their very first meeting, Jenni had shocked her mother by describing the older woman as her best friend.

Ridiculous, her mother had snorted, and Jenni had realised with a pang that she was actually jealous. 'Best friend? She can't possibly be. For heaven's sake, she's old enough to be your grandmother!'

She eyed Nadine as she doggedly made her way down the Rajasthani hill, grumbling humorously at her own frailty, and realised that she still felt much the same way.

'We're nearly there,' she said encouragingly. 'You go and lie down and I'll bring you a cup of hot *chai*.'

Nine

Combing back to Kundi for Nathan was like returning to
base. He and Kalidas smiled at each other as the white
Land-Rover topped the hill which brought them to the view
of the palace across the lake. Kalidas was pleased because for
him too the place meant home. He had grown up running
round its deserted stables and grand galleries though his
actual home had been a brushwood hut under the big banyan
tree outside the ashram walls, where the tribal people had
their village encampment. Nathan had first befriended the lad
when he was twelve – before the whole exciting business of
helping Maya to acquire Kundi had begun.

Kalidas had been playing with a baby goat, and Nathan – on
his first field trip for NYAID – had stopped to chat to the
bright-eyed boy, squatting beside him in the dust and playing
with a small puppy which yelped with delight. Kalidas had
displayed a sharpness and humour which had immediately
appealed to Nathan, and each time he returned to Kundi,
where he had a couple of aid projects – a women's basketwork
and embroidery co-operative and a small factory for making
some mango pickles – he had got to know the boy better and
recognise his quality. Eventually he had even allowed Kalidas
to come with him in the vehicle and to sit in on the often long
and painful discussions with the villagers Nathan was trying to
help. The result of these episodes was that he was eventually
able to persuade NYAID to train and subsequently employ
Kalidas as a driver. It was an important appointment because
Kalidas was in fact the first ever Adivasi or tribal man to be
employed by the agency.

The boy Kalidas, like his entire family and all the people in the small settlement under the banyan tree, which was like a mini-village of its own separate from the larger stone-built village of Kundi itself, was illiterate when Nathan originally met him, but Nathan, impressed by the intelligence of the *Bhil* youngsters had managed to organise a small amount of schooling for them by doing a reciprocal deal with the local Jesuit mission. The mission, in return for funds to help set up a village shop up in the hills where the tribal farmers were being hideously exploited by a Muslim shopkeeper-cum-moneylender, sent a young brother (an Anglo–Indian from Calcutta who wore jeans and tee-shirts and looked like a rock star) to teach the youngsters for a couple of hours a day. This was later augmented by various willing young Westerners who came to Kundi as Spiritual Travellers.

The acquisition of Kundi had been extremely complicated and only possible because Maya had been married to an Indian national whose wealth she had inherited. Nathan, having been reunited with his friend Ram in Delhi where Maya had opened her first Indian centre, had succumbed at once to her personal charisma and had soon decided that the Journey she advocated was the one he too must take. It worked well for him with his work for NYAID: the main changes for him were that he now always wore white – which anyway was a perfectly normal thing to do in India – and that Kundi became his spiritual home. The celibacy and teetotalism had so far never seemed like problems or even major decisions. In the tribal village where he had spent three years he had always lived quietly like a *saddhu* or holy man.

There were *saris* and *odnis* of brilliant colour and pattern stretched out to dry beside the lake, and when the Land-Rover turned the corner to approach the palace proper the branches of the fig trees by the roadside were black with huge bats. Kalidas waved to the group of yelling kids in tattered rags who ran screaming after the vehicle and slowed down as the wheels bumped along the ancient cobbles. Nathan noticed a new painting of an elephant on the wall of one of the houses and saw that a white-haired woman was photographing it. It would be a beautiful picture if she caught the little black dog in the shot as well. The woman had a brightness to her expression which made him nod to her as she looked up. She waved back using the camera like a clenched fist and grinned.

'Well driven,' he told Kalidas who smiled gently back with almond eyes, and Nathan, longing to get out and stretch his body, was aware that his heart was beating faster when they drove slowly through the huge studded gates of what was now the ashram. He loved coming to Kundi.

The kids jumped up on the vehicle, still yelling, and a flock of white pigeons fluttered up behind them. They had arrived.

Jenni rationalised that Nadine's tetchiness was the aftermath of the angina attack and perhaps she was finding the unseasonably warm weather too much, but at heart she was uneasily aware that it probably had a lot to do with Jenni's own behaviour. She had unexpectedly become very deeply embroiled with the religious life of Kundi and Nadine was obviously dismayed by the amount of meditation she had been doing. Nadine liked best of all to wander by the lake or to explore the delights of the nearby village where you could buy embroidered slippers, incense or printed cottons, or take a canopied and cushioned boat out on to the lake. They had agreed to go their different ways in the afternoon and Jenni now found herself alone on the smooth stone hilltop above the palace. It was very hot and the lake stretched seductively below as she tried unsuccessfully to meditate. From where she sat she could see the whole of Kundi spread before her. The magnificent palace was built in tiers down the steep hillside, and at the bottom, nestling between the royal buildings and outbuildings, was the village. On the fringe at the bottom of the place ramparts, was the great banyan tree with the small encampment of brushwood and sacking huts where the Kundi servants lived in obvious poverty.

It was ironic, viewed from this height and distance. How many of the tribal people from those huts, she wondered grimly, had ever chosen to become Spiritual Travellers, even with the example of Maya and her followers right there in front of them? And how many had been invited? None, she supposed, except perhaps for an occasional favoured worker for whom it might appear politic.

Nadine adored those people with their circus colours and open smiles. She obviously related much more to them than to the more staid devotees of the actual ashram. Jenni was sad at the thought of being estranged from her. Perhaps she had as Nadine had teasingly suggested gone over the top with her devoutness. Jenni too found the tribal people enormously attractive and vital – especially the children. This morning when she had passed them on her way to the *dhobi* man she had felt aggravated with herself for being dressed in Kundi yellow, and had longed for her own bright clothes and largest earrings so that she could make the children laugh.

She stood up and started to walk down the hill which at this point was almost bare of trees or bushes. She had covered a couple of hundred yards when she realised with horror that she was in the middle of a sort of giant lavatory. For hundreds of square metres the ground was dotted with piles of human excrement which she had been too preoccupied to notice. Disgusted, she tried to flee, but wherever she walked or jumped there were more and more of the noxious mounds to bar her way.

Again she felt outrage on behalf of the tribal people. They were employed and kept alive by their slave labour for the ashram, but where the Travellers had all mod cons and plenty of them, the villagers had no choice but to take themselves to the bare mountain to fulfil their bodily functions. And here now was the supposedly level-headed Jenni Bartlett, that well-known television reporter, entirely dressed in primrose yellow, surreally tip-toeing her way through the turds. It was ridiculous. She suddenly laughed aloud and hopped even faster. She must go back to Nadine and make peace.

Michael, pleasantly dazed from the long flight to Bombay booked in last-minute frenzy from London, had twenty-four hours to kill before the eight-hour train journey to Ahmedabad. He had slept for a few hours in the Taj Hotel which overlooked the enormous triumphal arch built for the arrival of Emperor of India in 1911. The Gateway of India, and very impressive too: Edward VII must have felt quite the lad when he sailed in to be greeted by that giant edifice overlooking the great blue bay, though heaven knows what the Indians must have thought. Bombay was an amazingly attractive city: rococo Victorian Gothic buildings with Indian embellishments, domes, arches, and palm trees everywhere. Architecturally it was brilliant. The sea setting was fine too, and the glittering ocean which looked so inviting was actually warm. Michael had paddled in it after breakfast then had lain on the pale sand and drunk from a shiny green coconut, its top sliced off for him by a slender boy. Sweet rich juice, cool and satisfying. The lad had handed him a piece of coconut shell and showed him how to spoon the erotically creamy flesh from the dark interior of the nut.

It hadn't been very restful lying there however, there were too many people wanting him to give money or silkily offering a free massage. The beggars were unbelievable; there must have been hundreds of them, thousands even, though a man in the hotel had blandly informed him that begging was officially illegal in India. It was appalling to see such desperation. One woman he had passed had been bare-breasted. When he had raised his eyebrows she had laughed and her husband – also quite young, bearded, with a piratical headcloth and a towel tied round his middle like a kilt – had laughed too and they had run after him until he had given them a few rupees and asked them to go away. They had seemed oddly cheerful – hysterical almost – like cabaret performers. Then he had found himself almost engulfed by a crowd of scraggy kids and a couple of blind teenagers with miserable-looking keepers – their worn-out parents, he presumed. And lepers. He was sickened again at the memory of the fingerless injured flesh of the hand and half-face that had been thrust towards him.

He had shouted at them in the end. It had been impossible to move; he had felt as though he would be obliterated by an ever-growing crowd of outstretched empty hands and yearning dark eyes. It was hard to cope with emotionally. What could you do? Give away all you had and become one of them? Cut off entirely and pretend it wasn't happening?

He had wandered for a couple of miles past railings hung with European-style designer garments for sale for a few rupees each where he had bought a summer jacket and a couple of shirts, and had been tempted by dozens of cheap

87

amusing watches from Hong Kong. The city was like some crazy non-stop variety show.

He passed two large stone carvings of lion-bodied creatures with women's heads and breasts, and stopped to admire the latter dizzily. Near the statues was a bookstall where he lingered and bought a couple of paperbacks and an art book of erotic miniatures. Faint from heat and weariness, he went with relief into the pleasantly tatty air-conditioned interior of the Original Light of Asia Restaurant. Beneath a large black Victorian wall clock with Roman numerals and a brass pendulum he consumed a delicious meal of curried prawns and drank a lot of cold beer. As he ate, he had a sensuous jet-lagged daydream about the dark girls with long glossy hair who were eating at a table across the room from him. Dressed in brilliant saris, they in turn appraised the tall white stranger with the lantern jaw.

In the outbuildings of Kundi, in what had once been the dairy, gun rooms, and the offices for the estate in the time of the Raj, there still remained a few aged servants who had been allowed to continue living there when the Maharajah stopped being in permanent residence, and later when the Travellers took over the palace buildings. Nadine had explored these fascinating rooms on her first visit to the place and had taken pictures of the men, turbaned and peaceful, as they squatted smoking in the dusty rooms, watching the passers-by in the great cobbled courtyard. She had been amazed and delighted to discover several historic cobwebbed vehicles in the empty stables. A superb 1917 black Hispano-Suiza, elongated and powerful – truly a design for princes – was now home to a flock of domestic fowl who laid eggs on the mildewed seats and covered the torn leather upholstery with droppings. There were also several ancient carved carts with flaking paint lying abandoned beside a wheelless dog cart of elegant Victorian design. Some of her finest Indian pictures had come from these discoveries.

Frankly astonished that Jenni, after nearly ten days at Kundi, had unexpectedly become so indecently pious and bathed in sweetness and light, Nadine was feeling more than a little impatient.

'There's a picnic at the top of the hill above the lake

tomorrow, followed by a two-hour meditation,' Jenni had announced at breakfast. 'Are you coming?'

'I think I'd better not go hill walking again so soon.'

'Of course. I'm sorry.'

'You go. I don't feel in the mood, I'm feeling worldly.'

Jenni had looked at her. 'You sure?'

'I'm sure.' For once Nadine sounded almost grumpy. 'I have things to do here.'

Guiltily, Jenni had hugged her goodbye and left. Nadine, watching her thoughtfully from the balcony as she made her way down to the main meeting-hall murmured: 'Don't fly away, little one.' It was odd how in a matter of days Jenni was showing signs of becoming seriously hooked on the religious drug. Nadine almost wished she had never brought her here. She missed the girl already; she would never be the same if she really joined the Yellow Dots. Suddenly feeling very old and melancholy, she decided to entertain herself by looking up her old friend Piebald Pradip.

She found him gossiping under the shade of the awning which ran the length of the main courtyard which today was almost completely deserted.

Pradip's blue eyes had been one of their first talking points when Nadine, pointing to her own, had said: 'Our eyes are the same colour.'

Today he smiled in welcome, spat out his betel and offered her a fresh wad of spicy nuts and leaves to chew. He always wore the same tattered and grubby turban and a once-elegant brown Harris tweed jacket with a high collar. Even though the jacket was now completely threadbare, darned and held together with a safety-pin and odd buttons, the old man, who was about the same age as Nadine, wore the garment with dignity.

She opened her bag to give him a glimpse of the contents and suggested delicately that they should go inside the building to the former gun room where Pradip slept on a rope bed under the empty gun racks. He spoke mainly Hindi, but with the help of his friend Davinder who had picked up English from the Travellers, Nadine had learned his story.

He had originally come to work in the palace when he was seven and had seen service with four Maharajahs.

When Nadine had asked how much he had been paid in those days, the old man had held up two brown-and-white-patterned fingers. Two rupees a month. Pennies only.

Pradip's friend Davinder also had blue eyes. As she poured whisky for the three of them into little clay cups which the gleeful Pradip had produced for the purpose, Nadine wondered if the men had inherited their eyes from some blond young English officer who came to shoot tigers and play polo, or if they were a legacy from that earlier invasion of Aryan soldiers from the time of Alexander the Great. Nadine liked Davinder less than Pradip, though the latter did tend to become over-sentimental when he reminisced about the old days: 'Sir Michael Osbaldiston, General Farnham, Mr Hywell-Elliott . . . real gentlemen. They were all frequent visitors.' Perhaps Nadine had heard of them, or Sir Humphrey Mackintyre? 'He was a most important man – a fine person.' A fine person who, Nadine felt almost certain, had given Pradip his taste for alcohol.

Her mouth was scarlet from the betel wad she had dutifully crunched and chewed before she at last discreetly spat it out. She declined politely when Pradip urged her to take a second even larger wad, and offered him chewing-gum instead. Painstakingly, the three of them undid the little paper packs and ceremoniously set about chewing the spearmint as an accompaniment to the whisky.

They chatted, Davinder translating, and Nadine asked what it was Pradip had worked at when he first came to Kundi as a small boy.

He pointed to his legs which had the same strange skin as his hands – almost white with dark piebald markings. 'Because I was born with my skin like this I wasn't permitted to wait at table or to be a personal servant, so I became a messenger and helped to look after the pigeons.'

'Pigeons?'

He gestured through the door towards a carved stone screen on the far side of the courtyard where a few white doves still fluttered and cooed. 'We used the birds to send messages for many miles. There was no telex in those days. Even now, when the telex is broken, they still take messages. And Davinder, he sends messages to his village and even to

Ahmedabad . . .' At this information Nadine looked questioningly towards the unappealing Davinder who immediately wiggled his head in the enigmatic Indian way, so much so that Nadine feared for a moment that both his head and turban might fall off and tumble to the ground.

Pradip laughed. 'And me, I used to run for miles up and down with letters and parcels, round and round the palace and to the villages.'

Tiring of Pradip's reminiscences as they grew more bewhiskied and rambling, Nadine asked the men what they thought of the Spiritual Travellers' regime in the palace.

'Very good, very good . . . pleasant people,' Pradip immediately assured her, but from Davinder's body language and sidelong glances she had an uneasy feeling that neither of them actually cared too much for the newcomers. Pradip, however, grew vociferous in his praises.

'Maya Memsahib,' he said, miming with his blue eyes and camouflaged hands something that was admirable on a grandiose scale, 'very holy, very holy lady. Big, big *Shanti* – a mighty soul. Cheers.' He grinned toothlessly.

'Cheers,' said Nadine, and topped up the clay cups.

'And you are a widow?' enquired Davinder suddenly.

'Why do you ask?'

'You are travelling alone. Why does your husband or son not look after you?'

'It is different in my country,' said Nadine simply.

Pradip nodded wisely. He understood.

'And Memsahib Jenni?' asked Davinder.

'What about her?'

'She is your daughter?'

Nadine chuckled. 'No, no. She is my good friend.'

'She is not married?'

'To her work only.'

'Her work?'

'The television.'

Pradip was puzzled. 'Television?'

'She's a sort of story-teller. She tells the news.'

Davinder smouldered with interest. 'She is like an actress?'

'Kind of. You see her speaking on the television.'

Their eyes widened. Davinder leaned forward, fascinated. 'She is famous TV lady?' he asked huskily.

'In England she is, yes. Everybody knows her. She's a clever lady, Jenni.' She paused, uneasily remembering Jenni's wish for anonymity. 'But remember, shh. Now she is on holiday. Work is far away and best forgotten.'

'Shhh,' agreed Pradip obsequiously.

Amused by him, Nadine grinned back, her finger still on her lips. It wouldn't go down well if Maya heard that she was drinking with these two leftovers from the original Kundi, but she was in the mood to get pissed. She would be glad to get out and see some of the real India for a change, away from the Gold Dot Depot. Hopefully, too, Jenni would get back to normal once she was back in harness.

Ten

The setting for the picnic was a big plateau with vistas of lake and hillside intriguingly dotted with temples and ancient houses. As Jenni sat for a while with the blonde therapist whose partner hadn't yet been told that she had become a celibate, she eyed the woman's subtly put together outfit with quiet amusement. It must have taken a lot of decidedly unspiritual energy to fill in all the details: Margit wore exquisite yellow leather boots – Italian, surely? – which perfectly matched the rims of her huge designer spectacles. Even her head-combs matched exactly, as did her shoulder bag and superbly cut and obvious extremely expensive cashmere sweater and linen pants.

The picnic meal was beautifully organised and soon at least five hundred people were seated on the plateau eating spiced vegetables, rice, dhal, chapatis and sweetmeats. In a mood to be alone, Jenni took her food and climbed to the top of a large rock so that she could look down on the sea of faithful followers. She had noticed several times that Westerners looked unfinished here, like unbaked pastry. More than once, both in Delhi and the village, she had seen albinos – Indian albinos – and realised with a shock that that was how Westerners must look to Indian eyes. The women on the picnic were dressed as often as not in saris, regardless of their galumphing Western bodies, and the young men in pyjama suits and shawls. Jenni shuddered. Today they reminded her of some weird scene from a Fellini film.

She lay back on the parched ground and shut her eyes, filled with a sudden almost overwhelming distaste at finding herself part of this huge charade. Or was it a charade? Many of the people, if a little earnest, were intelligent, admirable even. She herself was feeling so much better already from all the yoga, and what about those marvellous meditations?

She was woken by a woman's voice, and looked up dazed to find a mousey girl, hair pulled uncompromisingly back, body ruthlessly encased in a sari, like a sausage in a yellow skin. Somebody should have a word with her.

'D'you mind if I join you?'

Reluctantly Jenni made a space, and the girl sat down and smiled faintly. 'I'm Madge. From the Liverpool Centre. I've seen you often.'

Jenni wanted to run. She knew exactly what was coming next.

Madge eyed her palely. 'It's Jenni, isn't it? Jenni Bartlett from the telly?'

Jenni had dark glasses on, the ones where you can't see the wearer's eyes, so she knew she looked inscrutable. But staring at Madge, for a terrible moment she didn't know how to act. Part furious, part afraid, she definitely didn't want the girl's attention and hassle. Deciding to be full-frontal, she removed the aggressively secretive sunglasses, and, with ponderous deliberation, laid them down. Then, very firmly, she gripped Madge's arm and stared into her now-alarmed face.

'Yes,' she hissed. 'I am Jenni Bartlett, but I'm here incognito and it is very important for the safety of the ashram that you tell nobody, I beg you – warn you – by all you hold dear in the movement, to say nothing whatsoever of this to anybody.' She gripped even harder. 'Do you understand?'

The pale eyes were glistening. Jenni stared into them. Madge gulped and nodded. 'I'll not tell anyone.'

'You promise?'

The girl nodded dumbly and Jenni stood up abruptly and put her specs back on. 'I have to go now,' she said. 'Important things to do.' Madge nodded again and Jenni fled, leaving the anxious girl abandoned on the top of the rock, disappointedly murmuring, 'Contain the light, sister.'

What is wrong with me? Jenni wondered frenziedly as she found herself running through the brush, past trees and rocks where assorted yellow groups compared their various levels of attachment, the vigour of their Journeys, and the subtleties of meditation. It had suddenly become too much for her. Too pure. Too claustrophobic.

'I need to get out of here,' she muttered grimly and looked back with distaste at the faithful five hundred. Madge was still sitting on her hill, a larger, acid-yellow version of the Little Mermaid.

Jenni kept on running. She didn't really belong here. She wasn't one of the Travellers, didn't want to submerge her ego in their embrace. True, she had been seduced by the peace and quiet, but now she wanted her own world again, the real world, the one that the *Bhil* people lived in, with their colours and clamour. The earthy world where people had passion, rage and laughter. Not this one where they appeared to want to feel nothing but sweetness and light, and certainly never a flicker of the clit.

'Out!' she gasped. 'I must get out!'

She stopped after a while beside a tree. She was sweating, but relieved that nobody was in sight.

She gestured to the sky: 'Infantilism, that's what it is!' She stayed by the tree for a while, panting angrily. 'Sheer bloody infantilism! The meditating is OK, but I have a body, I inhabit this world – my sexuality is a basic, beautiful part of me and my life. I need my passion. I love it. I need to find the balance with that and all the other parts of me – I do not want to cut off from it!'

She was still shouting, crying a little. She looked down and saw her yellow legs and yellow arms and yellow shawl and started to laugh. 'For God's sake, what am I doing here? I *hate* yellow! What am I, a fucking burnt-out clown?'

She laughed and walked on, giggling helplessly, until suddenly she found herself face-to-face with a grotesquely brilliant coloured effigy of a human. It was a scarecrow made of multi-coloured tattered rags which fluttered in the breeze. She stopped to examine him.

He was almost what you would call handsome – a fine sight, a live Rajasthani scarecrow. 'Hi there.' She gazed at the boldness of him, then carefully took her woollen shawl and placed it round the ragged shoulders which were made from two branches tied in a 'T'. Calmer, she walked back a few feet and admired her handiwork.

95

She must have stayed sitting near the scarecrow for over an hour, and at first didn't see the tall man in white. Intrigued by her, he had been standing there for some time. He had watched from a distance when she shouted and wept and had smiled when he saw her dress the scarecrow. When she sat down, he too had seated himself about fifty yards from her, watching. She looked so alive; he could see that she was disturbed but that very fact made her enormously attractive to him.

In the end he decided to approach her. He walked up quietly and stood looking down at her. 'Hi,' he said. 'Do you mind if I talk to you?'

Jenni looked up and saw him and knew in that moment for certain that she could never really join the Yellow Dots. They had it all wrong.

'My God, how long have you been here?'

He shrugged, smiling.

'You heard me yelling?'

'Uh huh.'

'I don't believe it! How embarrassing.' She shook her head.

'It happens,' said the man, who had a strange accent – American, with the sing-song of Hindi. 'Sometimes you have to yell.'

He was absolutely beautiful, dressed in dazzling white and with dark curly hair.

'What's your name?' he asked.

'Jenni. And yours?' she replied, praying that he wouldn't preface his answer with the word 'Brother'.

She watched his face as he answered; it was fine-featured, intelligent and sensitive. Pow!

'I'm Nathan,' he said quietly, now sitting down beside her. 'Would you like some?' He offered her a piece of chocolate.

They chewed in silence for a little. 'It's my greatest weakness,' he said mildly.

'What is?'

'Chocolate. I always get the European and American Travellers to bring me Mars Bars.'

Kalidas loved polishing the white Land-Rover. He could spend hours painstakingly washing, wiping, and making every millimetre of the glass and paintwork shine. He was a good-looking young man, sturdily built, with glossy blue-black hair and a sleepy smile which only partly hid his extreme modesty. He was proud that he had responsibility for the vehicle and enjoyed coming back to his village. He had a young wife in Ahmedabad, but his parents were here and growing old. He stood back to examine his work and, satisfied, opened the door to put away the polishing cloth. Pradip, in his tattered tweed jacket and scarlet turban, squatted near him puffing contemplatively at a smelly *beedie*. Kalidas, neat and clean in a new white shirt, leaned back against the Land-Rover and chatted amicably with the old piebald man.

Kalidas was proud of Nattan *Bhai* too. Nathan was a good boss who treated Kalidas as his friend; they often laughed together. Nathan was apart from the other Westerners here – the girls and tall men who pranced about in yellow, the women looking like comic dancers in saris, whispering together and writing in their holy books and wearing those silly gold *tikkas*. Sometimes Kalidas imagined squirting them with paint as though it were Holi. He would like to make them react, to be more alive and not so serious, though to do them justice they were friendly enough, honest and kind, and they appeared happy.

He was glad that Nathan never wore a *tikka*. When Kalidas was little, he had jumped up and pointed to the tall American's bare forehead asking shrilly why didn't he wear the same gold dot as all the others. Nathan had responded by swinging him up high and setting him on his shoulders, Kalidas shrieking with joy.

'If I have a clear spirit it will show by itself,' he told the boy. 'And when I go to the villages I don't want to seem even more strange and foreign than I am to the people I have to meet and work with.'

Jenni came back from the picnic in a strange mood. Nadine, still jolly from her session with Pradip and Davinder, was in fine fettle and was surprised and delighted to find that Jenni seemed to have undergone an almost complete de-conversion, and to have retraced her steps down her personal road to Damascus. In fact, she seemed to have returned

97

almost too abruptly to the world that was familiar to them both.

'I will continue to do yoga and meditate, that's for sure . . .' flinging herself on the bed Jenni kicked off her sandals '. . . because it makes me feel good. But when I saw all those people gathered together there – honestly, they reminded me of Wordsworth's bloody daffodils!' She recited falsetto:

'"Ten thousand saw I at a glance,
Tossing their heads in sprightly dance,
Beside the lake, beneath the trees
Fluttering and dancing in the breeze".'

She laughed helplessly. 'Only the Travellers don't even want to recollect emotion in tranquillity as Wordsworth did – they want the tranquillity but without emotion. Anyway, I just suddenly felt I'd had enough. It was so oppressive, so well behaved, so *boring*! All those young people and no sex. It's beyond me.' Energetically, she threw one of her sandals at the framed picture of Maya, hitting it so that it hung sideways.

'Oops, sorry!'

Nadine watched, open-mouthed with delight.

'I can't deny that Maya is a very powerful teacher, but I know now it's not for me. I reckon I was in a vulnerable state . . .'

'You certainly were.'

'But I do feel alive again. I'm grateful to them for that. It has helped me. It's a very healing place, but by God I'll be glad to get out!'

'We're due to leave the day after tomorrow anyway. We just have to telex NYAID in Ahmedabad to fix our lift to the dam.'

'We're going with NYAID?' Jenni stared at her.

Nadine was leaning back, beret askew, smile benign. 'I told you I'd fixed it through my American agency friend.'

'You just said it was an aid agency. I was too miserable for it to register.'

'Jenni, you keep smiling to yourself. What's going on?'

'I just feel positive, but I must tell you . . . I have met the most lovely man.'

'That's what's cheered you up! Don't tell me he's a Traveller?'

'He is, but he's different. He's real.'

Nadine watched her intently. 'Good-looking?'

'Incredibly attractive, and he doesn't have that strange cut-off thing that the others have – you know how usually they seem to have utterly subjugated any frisson of sexuality?'

Nadine nodded.

'I hated that part of it today.'

'Two days ago you were talking of becoming celibate.'

Jenni shrugged. 'I know, but today's massed rally of Babes in the Wood was too much. I just wanted out. Anyway, to get back to this chap I met – he seems to have been connected with Maya and Co. for ever, but he works outside. He actually works for NYAID.'

Nadine clapped. 'It must be Nathan!'

'You know him?'

'Tall? Dark-skinned?'

'Yes.'

'I know of him. He's an old friend of Maya's. A wonderful man, I believe.'

Jenni nodded. 'It shows.'

'He comes here for retreats from his agency work in Ahmedabad which I gather is very hard – they're terribly pushed coping with the drought at present. I've never actually met him.'

'He told me he was leaving tomorrow to go up towards the Chittokundi dam.'

They looked at each other.

'Where is he now?'

'With Maya.'

'He's the one who can give us a lift.'

'I'm getting twitchy to get back into the real world.'

'You wouldn't mind leaving so soon?'

'The sooner the better.'

'Me too. Bravo!' Nadine threw her beret in the air.

Jenni stood up. 'I'm cold.' She rummaged in her bag and pulled out a black jersey.

'Where's your shawl?'

'I don't have it any more.'

'You lost it?'

Jenni put on the jersey and pulled out her make-up bag,

unused for two weeks. 'I gave it to somebody whose need was greater than mine.' She produced her mirror, peered into it, and set about firmly lining her eyes with a navy blue pencil.

On their last evening at Kundi, Nadine and Jenni had agreed to attend a special two-hour meditation in the main marble hall of the palace where the Maharajas of Kundi used to hold court. They gathered with three or four hundred Travellers and sat side by side enjoying the shared silence.

There was a vast marble throne with polished carvings set in the centre of the wide pavilion with painted and mirrored walls, marble floors and pillars, hung with large pictures of Maya. As they meditated, the assembled disciples were able to see the mountains change colour in the sunset glow. After some minutes, dignified in her perpetual white, Maya entered through a fretted gateway and made her way to the throne, capacious enough for even the fattest Maharaja to sit cross-legged. She placed herself carefully on the smooth stone before wrapping her body in a cocoon of shawl.

There was a heady aroma of incense in the air. Peter watched attentively to see that his guru was settled before he came forward and ceremoniously lit a large white candle which he set on a table in front of her. She nodded to him, then, when he had retreated and sat himself on the ground beside the other Travellers, looked out at the waiting audience with a strange sweet smile.

'Peace, my Golden Ones,' she whispered. Connect. Contain the light.'

Confused by her own ambivalence, Jenni once more felt herself helplessly seduced by the intensity of the experience. Nadine was well away: she was swaying slightly and looked almost ready to levitate. Bemused, Jenni recalled her own, earlier outrage but shrugged it off. She was determined to enjoy the here and now. To Connect. To allow herself to feel the power of the shared silence.

After an hour there was a gentle rustle of movement, triggered by a barely noticeable flicker in Maya's masklike face which seemed to have become uninhabited during the meditation. Out of the body, they called it. Simultaneously, as darkness fell, all over the royal pavilion people started to

100

sing quietly. Jenni and Nadine, stirred by the sound, joined in with the others and both felt unaccountably moved as they hummed and chanted. The long sustained notes swelled to an ocean of noise which thrummed and surged with subtle interlocking rhythms which were sustained for some minutes until the sound crescendoed magnificently. It stopped quite abruptly, just as a flock of birds will suddenly cease singing for no obvious reason but the mystery of their shared consciousness.

The congregation watched as Maya rose regally, slipped on a pair of sandals and glided away from the dais and out of sight through an archway. Half-hypnotised Jenni watched the tall figure who was now taking up Maya's position. Immediately she was alert. It was him. The lovely NYAID guy. He looked so intelligent, so sensitive; he immediately put everything back into focus.

Nathan's warm gaze enveloped the sea of Travellers who stared raptly back at him, gold dots glinting. His look seemed to embrace every individual in the audience but Jenni was certain that when he and she looked straight at each other something very powerful happened. For her part it certainly didn't encourage thoughts of celibacy. It had been a long time since she had felt such a strong pull towards a man. She slid into the second hour of meditation filled with a warm anticipation of tomorrow's journey.

After the Harmonic Connection had finished, Peter came to Nadine and Jenni and said with great earnestness that Maya had asked for them to come to her room.

'Head mistress's study,' whispered Jenni. 'She's found the empty whisky bottle.'

'*Non.*' Nadine was emphatic. 'She knows we're leaving. She simply wants to say goodbye.'

'Oh God, I hope nobody's told her about my shawl on the scarecrow? She might find it insulting.'

'Don't worry,' Nadine patted her arm. 'Maya has a good sense of humour under all that guru polish. She would laugh.'

They slid off their shoes in the doorway and entered the dimly lit room where they found Maya seated in contemplation. She looked up to smile at them both and motioned to them to sit.

They remained in silence for a long minute. The guru's yogic gaze seemed to be even more intense than usual tonight.

'So.' She addressed Jenni at last. 'How was the time here been for you?'

'It has been wonderful. I have never experienced anything like it.'

'How did you cope with the disciplines – the food, the early risings, the studying?'

'I loved it all.' This was true. It had just all become a bit much after two weeks solid.

'I am glad for you.' Maya smiled. 'Perhaps when you are back in London you will join us on the *Jivan Yatra* and help to bring others on the Journey with you?'

Suddenly defensive, Jenni wondered if Maya had somehow been able to see her persistent if unexpected vision of running a meditation centre in Fulham?

She paused before answering. It reminded her of being before a BBC board, you had to think before you spoke. 'I will certainly tell others what I have seen and heard and what I have experienced. Much of it was impressive, and for me extraordinary.' Once more she was uncomfortably aware of sounding theatrical.

Maya looked at her intensely. 'Sometimes new-born Travellers find that they need to retract for a while before making a full commitment.'

Jenni didn't reply but nodded uneasily. She was sure the guru knew what was going on.

Maya nodded to Peter who rose and went behind a white curtain. He returned almost immediately with several woollen shawls which he laid carefully on a stool beside Maya who picked up the top one and held it in front of her.

'Sister Jenni?' She smiled full-beam at the suddenly nervous Jenni who was convinced that Maya must know about the abandoned shawl, now blowing in the wind along with the multi-coloured Rajasthani tatters.

'We thought you might find a use for this.' Smiling, Maya held up the shawl which was of fine wool, dyed a deep apricot-yellow, towards Jenni. She stared for a moment, aghast.

Nadine, watching, knew exactly the conflicting emotions

102

Jenni was undergoing. She must feel that she couldn't possibly be so hypocritical as to accept this gift after so dramatically rejecting her own shawl only the day before.

She prodded her softly.

'Jenni, take it.'

It was a present. She must accept it. Jenni breathed deeply and moved forward awkwardly until she found herself kneeling in front of Maya, feeling unaccountably emotional. 'Thank you very much. I will wear it when I meditate back home in London,' she managed to stutter.

Maya handed her the shawl and Jenni tried to say thank you again but was unable to speak for tears.

Peter, next in line, was also rendered almost speechless by his gift. At last he was given a white shawl which denoted that he had evolved to being an Advanced Traveller.

'Oh gosh, Maya,' he murmured breathlessly. 'Hey . . . I just don't know what to say. Thanks. And I shall . . . Contain the Light. Connect.' He was so overcome that he got mixed up with the peaceful power and the ashram salute and couldn't quite remember whether it was finger or palm first. Still half-kneeling, he stumbled back to his place, blinking like a little boy who has just been awarded four gold stars.

'And now we come to our dear Nadine.' As Maya turned her gaze Jenni was struck by how alike their rather strongly defined profiles were, each with its slightly jutting jaw, fierce brow and emphatic nose.

'This one is for you.' The guru held up a dazzling white shawl of softest, finest cashmere.

Nadine eyed the shawl ironically. 'For me? you must be joking.' She was obviously both embarrassed and surprised. 'No,' she looked at Maya, 'I can't take this. That's for saints and angels, not for Nadines.' The yellow beret quivered.

Maya countered her tense refusal with what Jenni could only later describe as a glow. 'Some souls make their own special journey, and you, dear Nadine – our beloved sister, friend and Traveller – you are one of those. You shine for the lost souls among us, you lead, you inspire, by being the soul you are. White is the only colour to give you.'

'C'est fou,' muttered Nadine. She looked as though she was about to jump up and run. This time Jenni touched her arm.

103

'I think she's right,' she said. 'Please take it. It is a gift, freely given.'

Nadine shook her head.

Watching, Jenni saw an expression cross Maya's face which was uncannily similar to Nadine's. She thought for an instant that the guru was going to take the white shawl and use it to throttle the stubborn Frenchwoman, but the tension passed and to everyone's relief Nadine capitulated. In the end she even meekly allowed the shawl to be placed round her shoulders. Jenni had never seen her friend look quite so vulnerable.

Dawn the next morning found Kalidas leaning against the Land-Rover chatting to piebald Pradip. 'You leave now?' the old man asked, carefully extracting one of his thin *beedies* – wrapped in a leaf and tied with string – from its paper pack. Kalidas nodded and they talked desultorily. Davinder, heavily shawled in the early morning chill, slithered himself between them.

'Where to today?' he asked.

'Sapatdongri today and tomorrow, then straight up the Chitto Valley.'

The men grunted in commiseration and Davinder's head turned from side to side.

Kalidas looked up and smiled shyly in greeting as Nathan appeared carrying a travelling bag.

'I'll open the back.' He motioned for the keys. 'We have two extra coming with us.'

Kalidas didn't question who the extra passengers would be; he would discover soon enough. They didn't often take people out of the ashram, only Guru Maya sometimes. Nathan was amazing: once he had persuaded her to come out for a picnic in the Land-Rover – just the three of them. She had laughed and talked with Nattan *Bhai* for ages and had actually even drunk Coca-cola, eaten chocolate bars and played badminton. Kalidas had been astonished at all this. The guru had legs! Later, when Nathan had seen him smiling at the Coca-cola bottle, he had said, 'Even a guru needs a break sometimes.'

He turned and caught Pradip's blue eye. Pradip nodded, scrambled to his feet and shuffled off across the courtyard

104

through an archway at the far end. He returned a minute or two later bearing two red roses which he handed carefully to Kalidas who took the flowers and went to open the driver's door. He was climbing into the vehicle just as Nadine and Jenni, accompanied by Peter, arrived. Kalidas was pleased that it was those two: he had noticed them both several times. They looked good fun. No gold dots either.

'You are taking the Memsahib Nadine and her friend?' enquired Davinder. Kalidas nodded and helped the women to stow their luggage. As they climbed into the vehicle, joined by Nathan, Davinder stared at the women and nodded in recognition to Nadine. Then, to Jenni's surprise, he suddenly approached very close and, leering, performed his own circuitous version of the ashram salute to her, his palm ending up stretched entreatingly towards her instead of remaining vertical in the normal way.

'Is he crazy or something?' she whispered as Nadine frowned and gestured for him to go away. 'Why pick on me?'

Nadine shrugged. 'You're young and beautiful even at this time of day.'

'That doesn't mean I'm going to give him any handouts – the ashram people forbid it anyway. It creates subtle *bondage*, remember?'

Nadine chuckled croakily, and returned Pradip's farewell *namaste* with elegance.

Nathan introduced them. 'Kalidas, this is Nadine and Jenni.'

Blushing a little, Kalidas nodded an almost imperceptible acknowledgement and Jenni and Nadine watched entranced as with no apparent self-consciousness the handsome young man prepared for the journey by placing the freshly plucked roses on the dashboard. He followed this by producing a stick of incense which he lit and attached to a metal holder beside the glowing blossoms. He contemplated this for a few moments before at last turning shyly to Nathan and asking something in dialect.

Nathan nodded and told the women: 'We will spend a couple of nights at the Jesuit mission at Sapatdongri. It's a four- or five-hour drive, but I have several projects to look at on the way which might interest you.'

105

Kalidas waved to Pradip. Davinder had already disappeared. A sleepy cow moved aside and a flock of pigeons whirred into the clear morning as the gleaming Land-Rover, heady with perfumes of incense and roses, swung slowly out through the palace gates.

Eleven

On the flat roof of a house in Ahmedabad, a tall grey-suited man with yellow eyes was busy. He held a pigeon in his hands and carefully removed a roll of paper from its leg before putting the bird into a hamper. Frowning a little, he sat on the parapet of the roof to read the contents of the message, before gazing out over the hazy flat-topped houses. He scarcely noticed the exotically coloured corpses of fallen paper kites. It was the kite-flying season in Ahmedabad and they hung everywhere from the trees bushes and telephone lines of the polluted city like forgotten Christmas decorations.

He climbed down a rickety ladder into the tiled interior of the house and went to a desk in the small room which led into the kitchen. A plump woman in a sari was occupied in rolling out *chapatis* on a circular wooden tray painted green and red. She eyed the man non-committally as he searched through the desk drawer and continued to roll out her balls of dough, flattening them into circles before laying them neatly one on top of the other in a round tin decorated with a jazzy picture of blue Krishna playing his flute to a milkmaid.

The man sat down at the desk to read the roll of paper again, his eyes narrowing to a saffron slit as he concentrated on the message. He sat in thought for a while, his expression serious as he stared at the blue and pink curves and black plait of the woman in the kitchen.

He put down the paper, eyed his shiny chrome wristwatch and nodded to the woman who had stopped in mid-roll to look at him. He stood up, adjusted his tie and spoke quietly to her in Gujarati. She listened, shaking her head unhappily, then he muttered something emphatically and went out of the room. He returned quickly with a small briefcase which he opened and examined before closing and locking it firmly. This done, he checked his breast pocket, nodded at the woman and walked purposefully out of the house.

She watched him go and turned dolefully to roll out two more discs of *chapati* which she added to the others before snapping on the lid of the tin. Then she washed and dried her hands and went into the sitting-room where she knelt in front of a garish poster of a goddess standing in an idealised land-scape – wooded, with a waterfall and many flowers. In front of her knelt a prince with a brilliantly caparisoned white horse set before a triple-domed temple with a fluttering pennant. The goddess, who was smiling and haloed, finely dressed and garlanded with jasmine and roses, held a long-pronged trident in her left hand. Her right hand, intricately patterned and dotted with henna, was held up in blessing, and her feet, bejewelled with gold rings and chains, rested on the scaly body of a huge grimacing crocodile.

The woman stared at this image of radiant power, a goddess who had subjugated a fierce creature – symbol of ignorance – with jewels on tail and claws. Then, with care, she lit a stick of incense and started to pray in a wailing voice for the goddess to protect the yellow-eyed man in the turban who was obviously up to no good.

'Eh, what a river!' Nadine gazed in wonder out of the Land-Rover at the wide stretch of water.

'That's the Chittokundi; the dam is only about forty kilometres from here.'

Jenni sat up. 'Will we actually see it today?'

'No, we're heading east to spend the night at the mission where we have a couple of projects with the Jesuits, but the day after tomorrow you will.'

'It is so beautiful, so wild.' Nadine was almost falling out of the passenger window.

'It is one of the loveliest bits of country I know. There are crocodiles down there. You have to be careful in certain parts of the river.'

'You're kidding?'

Nathan shook his head. 'The Chittokundi is famous for two things: crocodiles and dacoits.'

'Dacoits?' Nadine smiled doubtfully. Yesterday Nathan had told her that camels pee backwards and she had giggled in disbelief all morning until they had actually seen one in action and discovered it to be true.

'No kidding. Tomorrow we go up along the river through the Chitto Valley and that, I have to warn you, is really scary. I had hoped we could by-pass it but the flash floods have washed away the other road.'

They had already driven through villages today where many cattle lay dead, drowned in the sudden massive rainstorms, the flash floods that ironically flooded the drought-dry land, too dusty to absorb the water quickly. There had been vultures everywhere, perched on the corpses, savaging the rotting flesh.

'What do the dacoits do?' Jenni asked.

'They stop vehicles – take anything they can. They're like old-fashioned highwaymen.'

'Do they injure people?'

Nathan shrugged. 'I don't want to scare you ladies. As I said, I'd hoped not to have to go that way, but once in a while you can be unlucky.'

'You say there are lots of dacoits?'

'Yeah. Since the dam construction started and the tribals are being displaced – lots of them.'

'Like how many?'

'I dunno. Don't worry, we'll be OK. They're unlikely to attack an official-looking vehicle like ours.'

'How many Adivasis have been displaced?'

'Three hundred villages. More maybe.'

Jenni had her notebook out. 'How many people on average to a village?'

'Seven hundred and fifty souls; the villages are spread out over two states.'

'My God, that's hundreds of thousands.'

Nathan nodded sadly.

'What compensation do they get?'

'I spoke to the elders of a couple of villages last month who had been offered a hundred and fifty rupees per acre. It would cost them ten thousand rupees an acre to buy land in a new area.'

Nadine hissed in disgust.

'It's even worse when you realise that the actual land value now is two thousand rupees an acre.'

'Is there nobody to help these people?'

'It's tricky. NYAID has to keep a low profile; we do what we can but because we aren't Indian nationals we have to be extremely careful. I could lose my work permit overnight. The Jesuits where we're heading – they're involved. We're all doing what we can but in a quiet way.'

Jenni, happily daydreaming of Jesuit priests looking like film stars in long white robes, asked what the brothers did to help.

'Brother Francis who you'll meet tonight at the mission is an amazing guy. He has learned to be a lawyer so that he can represent the tribals in the courts here; he's a real fighter. You'll enjoy meeting him.'

'What nationality is he?'

'Indian, Jesuit educated from Bombay. Now he's had some real tough experiences.'

'Like what?'

'He's been badly beaten up several times.'

'No?' Nadine was appalled.

'Oh, yeah. The field workers from agencies like ours – NYAID, OXFAM and the various missionaries – are natural targets for violence.'

'Why?'

'Violence is a common occurrence here because by necessity the grass roots work of raising the consciousness of the poor, which is a basic part of our task – perhaps even the most important part – creates anger among the exploiters when they lose out because their workers become unionised and politically aware.'

'Have you ever been beaten up?' asked Jenni.

Nathan was frowning. Nadine caught Jenni's eye and shook her head warningly, finger almost imperceptibly to lips, and Jenni saw that Nathan's knuckles, though he still appeared not to have heard, were white. Then both women, watching his face in the mirror, saw his eyes slide unhappily to the side and stare out of the window.

'Perhaps you don't want to talk about it,' said Nadine softly, and Jenni watched transfixed as Nathan's hands gradually relaxed and he exhaled at last. It was some time before he spoke:

'A couple of times, yeah.' He smiled grimly. 'Once in India. It put a great strain on my passive resistance. That time was in a tribal village. I actually got mad and banged a stick on the Land-Rover and scared them off.' He grunted and turned to them. 'It was a lucky escape. I know three or four people out of not very many field workers who have escaped from beatings and are lucky to be alive.'

They were quiet for several minutes then Nadine asked to know more about Brother Francis.

Nathan chuckled. 'Poor guy. Last year he had to go into hiding for a couple of weeks.'

Jenni, fascinated, was scribbling fast. 'Why?'

'He had forty-five accusations of rape levelled against him.'

'Rape? A Jesuit priest?' Nadine crowed in amazement. 'Forty-five?'

'Yeah, really. The accusations were all signed with marks made by illiterate women who believed they were giving their signatures to the ongoing government-sponsored buffalo scheme which is intended to give a buffalo to every family.' He smiled.

'What happened to him?' Jenni imagined the charismatic Father Francis hidden away in a dark hole.

'Fortunately for him the case was laughed out of court, but he really has experienced a lot of violence.'

'I'm looking forward to meeting him.'

'He's a great soul.'

They were coming into a small town with a few shops and shoddy low-roofed buildings. Nathan murmured something to Kalidas then turned to the passengers. 'We're coming up to the border post – it's usually just a formality. They check the papers and have a look at who's coming and going.'

Ahead of them were two armed policemen who did not look at all friendly. They gestured to Kalidas to stop the vehicle and he pulled slowly to a halt. Nathan handed some papers across to one of them. The man frowningly examined them and abruptly motioned to Nathan to get out. The three of them stood talking for some minutes. The tension was obvious. Nathan came back and leaned in the driver's window.

'They're being quite awkward. I'm afraid I'll have to go with Kalidas to sort it out. You two just stay here. Don't leave the vehicle.'

'Do you think it will take long?'

'I don't expect so.' As usual, Nathan sounded incredibly calm. 'We're not doing anything we shouldn't, the papers are all in order. Just sometimes things can get a bit sticky.' He shrugged and smiled. 'Boredom, I guess – and avarice.'

Kalidas nodded to Nathan, climbed out of the Land-Rover, slammed and locked the door.

Jenni and Nadine watched the two men go off up a narrow lane between the houses, escorted by the policemen.

'My God, Kalidas looked scared,' said Nadine.

'So did Nathan. He looked positively grim.'

The moment the Land-Rover halted anywhere on the journey it was almost immediately surrounded by a bunch of curious little boys who grinned, giggled, jumped up and down and touched the bodywork of the vehicle. Normally Kalidas would yell at them to scare them off. Today the usual crowd of youngsters had gathered round them, but now they were alone the children melted away and the women found themselves completely surrounded by a circle of men. Many of these were very handsome, fierce-looking with large moustaches. They all wore the local blood red turban. Jenni smiled feebly, but there was no response. Then Nadine smiled and said, 'Good morning,' loudly, but the men only answered by staring at them with an even more frightening intensity.

'I'm scared,' whispered Jenni, trying not to move her lips.

'Me too.'

'What if they keep them at the police station?'

'Don't.' Nadine patted her arm.

'These guys are absolutely terrifying.'

Nadine nodded. 'If you do make eye contact, it's still just that terrible dead stare.'

'Maybe they're afraid of us?'

112

'They don't look it. They've probably simply never seen European women before.'

'Is it possible?'

'Sure.'

They waited for ages, feeling more and more threatened and exposed, their minds, they both confessed later, filled with baroque imaginings of imprisonment and multiple rape. Then at last they saw Nathan and Kalildas come back. They both looked as stern as the policemen accompanying them and Nadine and Jenni expected the worst, so were very relieved when Nathan motioned to them to unlock the doors and he and Kalidas climbed in.

Kalidas started up and drove off without looking back at the checkpoint. They ran a gauntlet of gloomy stares as the intimidating circle of red-turbaned moustaches parted into two lines to let them pass like a macabre guard-of-honour.

'What happened?' asked Jenni at last when the last buildings of the town were behind them.

'They wanted a bribe.'

Nadine gasped in disbelief. He nodded grimly. 'It's illegal, but they sometimes try. Most people pay up.'

'Did you?'

Nathan shook his head.

'How did you avoid it?'

'I shouted at them.'

Nadine laughed at the unexpectedness of his reply.

'I did,' he insisted. 'I used it as a tool.'

'I didn't think you could get angry,' said Jenni quietly.

'If I think it's necessary, I can summon it up.'

Jenni shivered. 'It really was frightening.'

'I hate such people,' murmured Nadine.

'It's never only the fault of the individual. There is a lot of corruption here. They grow up absorbing it as part of life. They need education and good leadership. It is slowly improving.'

Nadine told him about the staring men and he cheered up. 'They didn't mean any harm, they were probably just fascinated.' He smiled round at Jenni. 'It's because you're so beautiful.'

She didn't really believe him but part of her was ridiculously pleased that he had said it.

Brother Peter, former lifeguard, blond and twenty, who hailed originally from the Los Angeles School for Spiritual Travel, had not gone on the day trip to the Temple of Krishna. He had stayed behind to host a new contingent of arrivals from Bombay, due in a couple of hours, and if he had not been eager to merit his newly awarded White Shawl, he might almost have admitted to himself that he was a little bored. But Maya had taught him that truly Enlightened Travellers – the spiritually clear and pure – were never bored. Tireless, perennially cheerful, hard-working and helpful, their faces should forever shine with enlightenment and display spiritual joy. Eyeing his reflection in a mirrored pillar he carefully combed his hair. There were few mirrors in the palace: it was agreed that they made for bodily awareness of the most harmful sort which Maya was always warning them so strongly against.

He went up to the main terrace where there was a fine view over the lake and settled himself down to meditate on a white embroidered cushion. His large blue eyes remained open and his wide-cheekboned, somewhat innocent face wore a slightly vacant expression that he believed to denote supersensuous joy. He sat like that for a long time, but found that it was not easy to meditate today. The body obtruded into his thoughts, and to his dismay was even beginning to obtrude into his *kurta* pyjamas. He closed his eyes and meditated harder, bringing in some rather chilling images of graveyards which he had in his pre-celibate days found a helpful device to prolong erection when needed, but which in these celibate times had precisely the opposite effect. When he opened his eyes and saw a tall figure standing silhouetted against the glare of the afternoon sun, he had detumesced and was breathing deeply, his face perhaps a little flushed, his sense of spirituality triumphant.

Peter blinked guiltily and smoothed the new white shawl over his crossed legs where a vestigial warmth still stirred. Dazed, he touched finger to forehead, as did the tall stranger in the sweat-stained yellow shirt, and both simultaneously held up their palms in greeting as Peter scrambled to his feet.

'Peace – Connect,' murmured Michael politely, 'I'm sorry to disturb you but the place is virtually empty. A couple of old guys down in the courtyard sent me up here. Are you Brother Peter?'

114

He nodded, somewhat hurriedly adjusting his shawl.

'I am. Has the bus arrived from Bombay already?'

'I'm alone. I came by motorbike from Ahmedabad.'

'Ah, which centre?'

'The ah . . . I actually just touched down there from Bombay and came straight up.'

Peter was a little surprised. It was unusual for Travellers to undertake solo journeys. Once on the Journey, never alone. The Life Force was always with you, and to help you keep connected, so always were your fellow Travellers. The knots and attachments of the Present Physical World always reared their ugly heads when a Traveller was alone for too long and not properly Connected.

'Would you like some lime juice? You look kinda hot?'

'Please.' Michael nodded gratefully and followed Peter down to the main courtyard. Here they passed an elderly man, turbaned, with blue eyes. He was preoccupied with a white dove to whose leg he seemed to be fixing something.

'What's he doing?' asked Michael.

Peter glanced to where the man now stood up to let the bird fly from his hand. 'Davinder lives here. Sometimes he sends messages by pigeon – to his village maybe. They can fly for hundreds of miles.'

In the kitchens they found refreshment. Michael gulped the lime juice with relief.

'I've never travelled a road as bad as that. There were boulders all over the place – the rule seems to be if you see an obstacle, overtake it, no matter what. I saw one burned-out tanker and two overturned lorries. I must have had more near-misses in a day than I've had in five years at home.'

'I don't drive here. The ashram has Indian drivers.'

'It really was bloody hair-raising.' Seeing Peter's slightly puzzled expression, Michael realised that he wasn't being low key enough and stopped in mid outburst.

'If it is your Karma, it is your Karma,' murmured Peter. 'I guess you can't do a lot to prevent it, but you can be spiritually prepared if it is time for you to leave the body. Then it is less frightening to ride a rough road.'

Michael responded with an expression that he hoped was

115

suitably spiritual. 'When are they due back from the day trip?' he asked after a while. 'I have come to meet up with a couple of friends here.'

'Friends from the London Centre?'

'One of them, yes. The other is French – she's quite an old lady.'

'Ah. Sister Nadine?'

'The very one.' Michael's heart lifted. 'They travelled together from London. Nadine was with a younger friend – er – sister. Jenni.'

'Very lively people.' Peter nodded. 'Sister Jenni got right into the routine, even though she was a newborn Traveller.' He sounded enthusiastic.

Michael tried not to double-take, but chose to nod wisely instead. 'She's been busy here, has she?' he asked carefully.

'You bet. She was so keen, so thirsty for knowledge. A truly refined and gifted Traveller. A natural Liberate, almost.'

'Really?' Michael managed not to reveal surprise as he nibbled the rather cloying square of orange sweetmeat Peter had offered him.

'It's a pity you missed them though.'

'Missed them?'

'They left this morning.'

Michael gawped. 'When will they be back?'

'They're not coming back. The two ladies had some sort of PPR assignment to do – I think they were interested in the work of the agency.'

Michael groaned. He remembered that PPR meant Present Physical Reality, as opposed to past or spiritual. Easy enough once you understood the jargon. Ever since he had boarded the plane for Bombay Michael had felt certain that he would meet up with Jenni at this place. He had even researched Kundi of which Rudyard Kipling had written that 'The royal palace of Koondi must surely be one of the most beautiful places on earth', but its beauty was lost on him at this particular moment. 'Damn,' he groaned.

Peter, eyeing his slumped body sympathetically, was shocked by the intensity of Michael's response. The man suddenly appeared almost alarmingly un-tranquil and obviously highly disturbed by his ongoing attachments. They must be strongly knotted ones. Judging by the way he behaved so reactively Peter reckoned he couldn't possibly have been a Traveller for very long, and certainly hadn't responded as well as Jenni to his spiritual journeying.

'Why don't you come down to the Power House with me?' he suggested gently. 'Looks like you need to Connect. It might help to centre you if we harmonise together.'

Michael tried not to show his panic. Frantically, he wondered if he ought to announce that he was heterosexual, then he understood what Peter actually meant. 'Ah . . . yes,' he murmured, 'that would be – er – excellent.'

On a dusty hill, a small boy in ragged shorts stood barefoot, staring out across the barren country to where the river showed silver in the distance. Round his neck was a short necklace of blue and white beads from which hung a square copper amulet of Hanuman the Monkey God, especially beloved of tribal people. His near shoulder-length curly hair was circled with a red headband. Before he died, the boy's grandfather had told him that soon the river would be a lake and the hill he now stood on an island. It was difficult to imagine: he didn't like to think about it too much. The huts and familiar fields where his grandfather's goats and the cows now wandered, where would they all be? he wondered.

He had picked up a handful of carefully chosen stones and was amusing himself by throwing them at the trunk of a palm tree when he heard the distant noise of a car's engine. It was unusual for a vehicle to come so far up the track which was really just bare hillside except where the village men had cleared a token road for the well, built a couple of years ago. Ravi grinned at the sight of the jeep and dropped his stones. The fastest runner of all the children in his district, he could run for miles on his hard bare feet. He laughed aloud as he approached the jeep and ran after it, trying to jump up on the tow bar at the back where he managed to hang on for a minute until the big man in the passenger seat – a fellow with a curly black moustache and scarlet turban of the district – thrust his head out of the window and roared at him to get off. The vehicle was going very slowly because of the rocks on the path, so the boy laughed to show he wasn't scared and quickly ran on ahead, grinning as he passed the thin unfriendly man with yellow eyes who was behind the wheel.

The mud hut was set alone halfway up a small hill, almost a mile from its nearest neighbours. It was a widespread community because the land was so arid.

'Wanita! Wanita!' shouted the boy running full tilt into the hut where a fierce-eyed young woman wearing bracelets on ankle and wrists and a heavy silver collar sat polishing a rifle. She looked up, her expression harsh.

'What is it today? An escaped elephant?'

'A jeep, it's coming now!'

Wanita leapt up and grabbed a couple of cartridges from a rough wooden shelf above the sagging *charpoy* bed, slipped them into the open rifle and decisively snapped it shut.

'Stay.' She pushed the boy back and peered out of the hut. 'Where is Ramdas?' she asked, tensing as she saw the jeep appear over the brow of the hill.

Ravi giggled. 'He is in the jeep.' He screamed with laughter and lay on the bed giggling helplessly, leathery feet kicking the air.

Wanita shouted at him, 'Why did you not say? Idiot child! I was afraid!'

'You didn't ask.'

She slapped his legs so hard that he almost started to cry. Then he laughed again, very loudly this time, to show that he was a brave tribal man.

Wanita, bright trousers pulled well above her knees in the local fashion, midriff bare, ankles, wrists and neck gleaming silver, stood outside the hut, rifle at the ready. She eyed the jeep warily as it drew to a halt near a couple of buffalo and watched intently as the two men jumped out. The larger man, seeing Ravi peering out from behind the hut door, motioned impatiently to him to disappear. He ran off as Wanita dubiously viewed the tall stranger in the grey suit and turban, pulling her orange and green *odni* across her face so that only her angry eyes showed. Her grip on the rifle tightened as the men approached and she shouted to the tribal man in dialect.

He answered quietly, pointing to the yellow-eyed fellow

118

who stopped some feet behind him, watching the two of them uneasily.

Wanita slowly unwound her headcloth, revealing long black hair which curled in tendrils round her forehead. Ravi, watching from behind a tree, thought she looked just like the painted clay goddess they had in the shrine in the hut – fierce and strong, but wonderful.

'How do you know you can trust him?' hissed Wanita.

Ramdas frowned then winked. 'I can trust him.' He tapped his moustache. Slyly, he slipped his hand under his embroidered waistcoat into a shirt pocket and pulled out a filthy wad of notes.

'It's a simple job for us, just the usual, but it's big money.' He grinned and winked again.

Wanita snatched the money from him and expertly counted the notes, her eyes gleaming. It really must be an important catch for them to pay so much. She thrust Ramdas towards the hut.

'Get the other gun. You keep guard. I'll speak to him.'

Ramdas sullenly did as ordered and tried to look as though he didn't mind handing over to her. Wanita peremptorily motioned the stranger to go into the hut, then stood for a moment in the doorway looking up the hill.

'Ravi!' she yelled, her voice piercing. The boy's head appeared round a tree trunk. She motioned to him to come.

'*Chai*,' she commanded. 'For our guest.'

The boy nodded, and eagerly scrabbled on the floor to make fire with a bundle of twigs from the pile in the corner.

Twelve

At a tea house near a bridge, on the outskirts of a small town where Nathan had almost imperceptibly motioned to Kalidas to draw in, the four travellers were drinking hot sweet tea made with spiced buffalo milk, watched by more silent men who stared at the women. Nathan had pretended to find a worm in his tea – but it had proved to only be a leaf – and had just told Nadine and Jenni that at the NYAID sponsored hospital they were about to visit, one of the patients with a wasting disease had a party trick for visitors which consisted of poking her tongue out through her empty eye-socket.

'Ugh! Stop it!' Nadine grimaced.

'I'm sorry.' Nathan looked contrite. 'It's been a long time since I spent time with – '

Jenni suddenly felt sure that he meant normal, ordinary people who weren't Travellers.

'Well?' Nadine and Jenni waited for him to finish his sentence.

He shrugged, a little embarrassed. 'People who make me laugh.'

'I think you need to laugh. You have a serious job. It must be very hard.' Nadine stood and picked up her striped camera bag. 'Is there time for us to walk by the river for five minutes, to take some pictures? I find it very beautiful.'

'Sure. Fifteen minutes. See you back here. I'll sit and write my report for the office.'

'Coming?' Nadine motioned to Jenni.

The two of them made their way down a sandy path flanked with thorny bushes on either side to the bank of the wide river.

'Watch out for crocodiles!' called Nathan over the parapet of the bridge.

'He's a fine person,' said Nadine as she set up her tripod. They were already surrounded, even in this remote country place, by a crowd of children and several heroic but ferocious-looking men, handsome in those brilliant turbans.

'He's wonderful.'

'I still don't understand.' Nadine shook her head.

'Understand what?'

'How can a young attractive man like him be celibate?'

'Maybe he isn't.'

'Wishful thinking, girl. I see how you like to look at him.'

'Oh, come on.'

'It's true. But maybe he's gay.'

'I'm sure he's not.' Jenni watched an old woman, naked but for a pair of ragged shorts, carefully bathing her wrinkled body in the river. There were many people washing clothes and themselves. Saris, shirts and trousers were draped to dry on bushes, and dogs wandered around sniffing.

'You sound like you've had feedback.' Nadine peered through her camera lens.

'I almost think I have. It's confusing. He kind of sticks his head out then retracts like a shy animal.'

'But to be celibate is his calling.'

Jenni nodded. 'I just sometimes get the feeling that he might be getting restive.'

Nadine clicked the camera and grunted with satisfaction. 'It's is so fantastic this country, I love it. Come.' She snapped the tripod shut. 'Let's walk a little.'

They wandered along the bank watched by people who smiled and waved and giggled at them, and were followed at a distance by half a dozen children. Nadine suddenly grasped Jenni's arm.

'Oh my God, look at that.'

Ahead of them was a breathtaking sight. Two young boys of ten or twelve were holding out a long pale length of cotton sari to dry. The nearest boy – who was wearing only a pair of shorts – held his arms outstretched in a wide vee above his head and clasped the two end corners of the cloth. His friend, perhaps fifteen feet away from him, was naked, hands held downwards at his sides, wide enough apart to tightly stretch the fabric. He gripped the opposite corners firmly, making the material billow magically and undulate like waves so that you could see half of his gleaming golden body through the flimsy material.

'Aaah . . . what choreography.' Nadine knelt slowly and aimed the camera. She watched the ballet the oblivious boys were performing and clicked several times, until at last she muttered, 'I got it.'

Then she stood up. 'Wonderful,' she said simply and took Jenni's arm. They walked further along the river, past a bank of pink flowers. There were herons, hoopoe birds and even a couple of kingfishers flashing past, bright green and blue like jewels. Entranced, Jenni pointed to a group of more than thirty egrets grouped by the water's edge like an enchanted gathering of Enlightened Ones.

'I have regained my happiness in India,' said Jenni.

'I can see. You keep it, Jenni. Happiness is the equilibrium between our desires and needs.'

They looked back and saw Nathan's tall figure standing on the bridge. He waved to them.

Nadine waved back. 'He is lovely. Did you know he had been married?'

'When?'

'Back in the States, but I think something bad happened; he seems to retreat somehow when he remembers.'

'He was very strange when we asked if he'd ever been beaten up,' said Jenni thoughtfully.

Nadine grunted. 'It must have been something very bad.'

Ahead of them were the remains of what seemed to be a bonfire on the sand. They walked without thinking towards the ashes, dreamily aware of the startling bright blue of the water and the long skeins of grass-green weed. Occasional figures, tall bearded men or young girls, were bathing apart from the crowd, self-absorbed, innately elegant.

'Oh.' Nadine stopped. 'Look.' She pointed in awe to the bonfire and Jenni turned from gazing at the river and stared at the ground.

There was part of what could only be a human pelvis in the still-smoking ashes. The river water lapped peacefully nearby.

They stared wordlessly at the remains of what had been part of a live human being, only yesterday perhaps.

'We must have come to the ghats,' said Jenni at last, pointing inland to where she could see small domes and what must be memorial stones.

Nadine nodded. 'I would like to have my body burned like that, to be given back to nature. No box, no brass handles. Just simple, fire and water, dust to dust.' She smiled. 'India is a wise country. She understands life. I feel I am swimming along in the River of Life when I am here,' Beaming, she turned to Jenni. 'What joy, *hein*?'

Jenni put an arm round her shoulders. There were not, she mused affectionately as they retraced their steps back to the waiting Land-Rover, many people with whom one could have a spontaneous celebration of life inspired directly by the unexpected sighting of a half-incinerated human pelvis.

Ravi hated it when his sister and Ramdas shouted at each other. They had been fighting for ages now at the far end of the hut, yelling, followed by a long silence, then more angry noise. The man with the jeep had gone away after talking alone with Wanita also for ages. Ravi, watching and listening to the preoccupied adults had gathered that the man would return in two days' time after whatever task he had asked Wanita and the men to do for him had actually been performed. He would bring more money – lots from the look in Ramdas's greedy eyes. But Wanita, as usual, was less trusting. She wanted more money now as surety because it was a big job: they would need four more men and even Ravi to be used, as well as the whole flock of his dead grandfather's goats.

He sighed as he lay in the dark on the mud *otla* under the projecting tiled roof of the hut and wished that they would make up their minds as to what they wanted to do so that he could go to sleep. The voices died down until he could hear only an occasional grunt. Ravi sighed and shut his eyes. It was always like that: shouting, yelling, thumps, followed by a bit of quiet, then laughter, then those funny little puppy yelps from Wanita, culminating in a deep groan or two from Ramdas. It was at this point that Ravi always knew that he would get some peace. He giggled and snuggled his head

123

firmly into the crook of his arm so that the bright light from the upsidedown crescent moon did not also keep him awake with its silver smile.

At the Jesuit mission at Sapatdongri the travellers washed and rested before supper. The mission had a small farm attached where the brothers bred rabbits and goats, and there was a boys' school on the far side of the main building where the three brothers lived and worked together.

Jenni, lying on her single bed, which she had been relieved to find had a mosquito net tented above it on an iron frame, smoothed the patchwork bedcover idly as she watched Nadine unpack and potter with her photographic gear.

'I feel quite let down that the brothers aren't wearing robes.' She confessed.

Nadine chuckled. 'Yeah, but he's a pleasant young man, that Basque one, Antony, who welcomed us with tea. Sincere, hard-working and committed to helping the poor, he's more like my idea of a communist than a christian. I like him even if he does only wear jeans.'

'I went to do an interview at a boys' school in Wales a few years ago and the priests there wore cassocks. Very sexy. There was one man I really fancied. He had very hairy wrists sticking out of his robes. Such a turn-on . . .'

Nadine, amused, eyed her over half-spectacles.

'I think that you are developing a penchant for *célibataires*. What is it that draws you to them? The challenge of forbidden fruit?'

'Maybe. But I do actually think Nathan is pretty admirable, don't you?'

'Oh, yes. Seeing him at work with those poor farmers and the hospital staff in that place near the bridge, he's superb.'

Jenni sighed.

Nadine took out a tiny telescopic brush and delicately tickled a lens. Jenni watched her practical hands with their almost spatulate thumbs as she busied herself, packing away the clean lens into a small cotton bag and counting out several films ready for the next day. This done, Nadine rose to find her striped bag and eyed Jenni tenderly, patting her lightly on the shoulder as she passed her by.

'You OK?' she asked.

Jenni's face puckered. 'I guess so,' she said quietly. 'Love. It's hard to eradicate completely for some reason.'

'Ah.' Nadine took off the half-specs which made her look a little gnomelike. 'It is the barbs.'

'The barbs?'

'Do you think it's merely a dart Cupid has? It's a barb – and barbs remain embedded in the flesh.'

Jenni rolled on to her stomach. 'I never thought of that. True, I suppose.' She gazed at the ceiling. 'Michael used to sing me a Scottish song.' She crooned, a little wistfully:

'"And my false lover stole the rose.

But, ah, he left the thorn with me."'

Nadine listened, and nodded.

Jenni sighed. 'How long do the barbs remain?'

'Too long, usually. How long were you and Michael lovers?'

Jenni shrugged. 'Six or seven years.'

'How long since you saw him?'

'Four months.'

'It's not really so long.'

Jenni grunted.

'But at least you're aware of other men again.'

'Yes. And it's not that I would want Michael back really. I think there are times when you yearn for the past or for some imagined togetherness. Anyway, in a way this one is married too.'

'Of course. Perhaps you are simply attracted by the unattainable?'

Jenni thumped her pillow. 'Maybe. I don't understand these things. There are moments when I really can sympathise with the celibate Nathans and Mayas of the world. It can seem like a crop-out, but on the other hand it is a very strong statement to choose to avoid the turmoil that intimate relationships cause.'

She looked at Nadine lying on her bed. 'I just get lonely sometimes. That's why it's so good to be here with you.'

Nadine nodded. 'It is hard to live alone, but you get used to it and even grow to like it.'

'Why did you never live with anybody?'

125

Nadine sighed and gazed up at the crucifix hanging on the wall near the wardrobe. Jesus's nose was chipped.

'I was married once.'

Jenni was open-mouthed. 'I never knew that.'

Nadine's eyes crinkled. 'There are still one or two things you don't know.' Her jaw jutted forward.

'But when? How long? Who was he?' Over the years Jenni had learned the various loving liaisons – some with women – but a husband was something new.

'He was a Polish painter. We met in Paris.' She sighed.

'What was he called?' Jenni dared to ask.

'Mordecai.' Nadine's voice sounded far away. 'Now that one, he was truly beautiful, soul and body.'

'How long were you together?'

'Five years.'

'Did you ever want children?'

There was a long silence as Nadine watched a bluebottle circle the bed. Its giant buzz reverberated through the whitewashed room like an aeroplane. As Jenni looked at Nadine she thought how striking she was, the simple navy blue shirt and trousers offsetting the silver of her earrings and wide bracelet she always wore.

'I did want children then.' Nadine's voice was quiet. 'I was only twenty.'

Jenni tried to digest this new chunk of her friend's past. 'What happened?' she asked at last.

Nadine grunted and sat for a while with closed eyes. At last she turned and looked full at Jenni, her eyes very blue and bright. 'How does your Shakespeare say? "It was a long time ago, and in another country".'

Nadine sat up and felt for her shoes, busying herself with the laces, then she looked up at Jenni again just for a moment. 'It was the war. That was why it ended.'

Jenni longed to ask dozens of questions. Was he Jewish? She enquired at last.

Nadine nodded and looked away. 'I don't want to talk about it,' she said simply. Abruptly, she stood up and looked at her watch. 'Shall we meditate together? There's time before supper.'

'OK.'

Nadine sounded cheerful 'Then hopefully we will meet the marvellous brother Francis, *hein?*'

'Ah, yes, the rapist.' Jenni had sat up and was in the important process of making herself symmetrically comfortable, legs crossed, hands lying palms upwards, when there was a knock.

'I'll go.' Nadine went to open the door and found herself face-to-face with Nathan.

'Hi,' he said. 'I wondered if you two would like to Connect with me?'

Jenni, Buddhalike on the bed, smiled up at him. 'Come and join us.'

Next to the refectory, in the kitchen of the mission, a small plump bespectacled man was busy with colanders and pots of bubbling vegetables. The three entered and found Kalidas talking shyly with the bearded and be-jeaned Basque brother, Antony, whom they had already met. He showed them where to sit and introduced them to a third brother who spoke little English but smilingly offered them iced water from a plastic jug.

The little cook was muttering and clattering temperamentally in the kitchen.

'Do you think he needs any help?' asked Nadine nervously.

'He prefers to do the cooking alone,' Brother Antony assured her.

They chatted quietly until the cook, glasses somewhat askew, at last arrived bearing a steaming dish which he laid on the wooden table.

'Will you bring the rice, please?' he asked. Antony rose obediently to fetch a second pot while Nathan brought *chapatis*. Endearingly, the Jesuit had a flowery apron round his tight little belly. He stood at the end of the table to serve the guests.

'The dhal too, Antony, please.' He motioned to the kitchen and wiped his brow with a corner of his apron. 'And then,' he beamed round his guests, 'we can eat.'

Antony handed round plain white plates heaped high with the delicious food.

Nathan, seeing the bespectacled man suddenly go back to

the kitchen, called after him: 'Are you not eating with us?'

'I'm coming, I'm coming,' he called. 'Please begin.'

'It smells so good my mouth is watering,' said Nadine.

'It's is his favourite recipe, cauliflower and coconut,' Antony told them.

There were murmurs of appreciation from everybody at the table.

'Marvellous food,' said Jenni when the cook returned clutching a large plastic bottle. He was scarlet and shiny from his efforts, but beaming.

'I thought you might perhaps enjoy a little of our communion wine,' he said, flourishing the container. 'We have more than we need, and as it's a dry state, it's the only wine you will find in Gujarat. I know Nathan is teetotal, but perhaps you ladies will join me?'

He sat down and removed his apron, knocking his spectacles into the rice as he did so. He giggled. 'It is the excitement of having female company,' he told them, joyfully pouring Jenni and Nadine each a glass of the dark red wine.

'Now,' he said, 'tell me why you are here?'

Jenni told him a little about the sort of work she did at home and explained that Nathan had offered them an extended lift. 'He's a marvellous guide – seems to speak about five dialects and can explain exactly what's happening. It's fascinating . . . such an opportunity to see what's really going on.'

'It is a complex country.' The little man, eating with his fingers as they all did, pushed dhal into *chapatis* as fast as it was possible. 'There are so many layers to any part of the society here.'

Jenni nodded. 'I could see myself becoming sucked in.'

He nodded. He had spilt vegetable curry on his shirt and looked even more untidy. 'There are worse ways to spend a life.'

The Jesuit looked at Nathan. 'I understand you are going through the Chitto Valley on Tuesday?'

'We have no choice.' Nathan had been almost silent up till now.

'I know that the other road is still impassable, but the valley is not very safe. Is it wise with ladies?'

'It's the only way. It's a small chance.'

'How far is the valley from here?' asked Nadine.

'About sixty kilometres as the crow flies, a little further by road.'

'But is it really dangerous?' asked Jenni, who still thought Nathan had been exaggerating. 'I'm sorry.' She touched the cook's arm. 'I don't actually know your name.'

He beamed at her. 'I am Father Francis.'

'Oh!' Both women were astonished.

'You are the legal expert?'

Father Francis wriggled modestly. 'Hardly that.' He had a high-pitched laugh. 'I had to study to be a lawyer so that I could represent the poorest people in this corrupt place.'

'Do you know people who have met dacoits?' asked Nadine.

'One or two. I know some of the actual dacoits quite well too; they are desperate people because they have been terribly exploited, but don't worry too much. Many vehicles pass through the Chitto Valley unchallenged. You will almost certainly be OK.' He chuckled. 'Don't be afraid, ladies. If there is any problem we will come and rescue you, I promise.'

He was so small and plump that he would look a lot more like Sancho Panza than Don Quixote, Jenni thought, but she smiled at the priest. 'That makes me feel much safer.'

'We will pray for you too,' said Father Francis. 'Will we not Antony?'

He inclined his head. 'Of course.' He sounded as if he really meant it.

'I believe you have spent time in Nathan's ashram?' Francis leaned across to Nadine and refilled her glass to the brim.

She nodded, and they talked a little of Kundi which now seemed strangely far away, with its singing circles of yellow people.

'It's quite near here really,' said Nathan. 'We are as far from Kundi as from the dam – it's like an isosceles triangle on the map.

'Anyway,' Francis raised his glass, 'here's to our guests. May you find out many things.'

'And may you travel safely,' said the young brother Antony in his careful English. Nathan translated this to the bashful Kalidas and to the third brother, and they all smiled hopefully as they drank together.

129

Thirteen

'Please,' said Michael, 'I have come all the way from England to find her. I have been to Kundi and just missed them. It is a personal matter. I am a friend and colleague of the lady. I must find her, and I believe that you can tell me where they might be staying.'

The thin young man in the brown shawl looked at him deadpan as he answered. 'I am very sorry,' he said, 'but I do not know who you are, I do not know the particular lady, and it is not part of my job to give out information as to where our field workers are. We have had a lot of violence, you know.'

'Please,' said Michael again. 'Do I look like a violent man? I have my passport, my ticket.' He pulled out these things from his shoulder bag and waved them at the man who took the green Irish passport and stared at it before handing it back.

'I am very sorry, Mr O'Brien, it is not for me to give this information.'

'Who could authorise it?'

'Only Mr Robson.'

Michael was suddenly hopeful. 'Where is this Mr Robson?'

'I'm afraid I cannot tell you.'

'When would it be possible for me to see him?'

'I'm afraid he is not available.'

'He's away?'

The man wiggled his head almost imperceptibly and didn't answer.

'When will he be back?'

'In four or five days perhaps.'

'I can't wait that long. Can you tell me who's in charge here?'

'Mr Robson is the chief executive for NYAID in Ahmedabad. I am in charge when he is not here.'

Michael shut his eyes. 'Is this Mr Robson the person who has accompanied the two ladies on their trip?'

The man stared at him blankly. 'I am afraid I cannot say.'

Michael wanted to explode but knew that he must keep his temper. It had taken him almost two hours to find the office; Ahmedabad was not a city where you could find a street map in any tobacconist's shop. There weren't really any tobacconists in the London sense: there were tiny kiosks and market dealers and perhaps an occasional monkey, but no actual street maps, at least not that he could find, and the street signs if there were any were in Gujarati. There was little written up in English except for an occasional sign for Kodak or a bank, and after two hours in the city Michael felt sure that he must be the only European within miles. In the end he had found a helpful rickshaw driver whose vehicle he had followed on the motorbike he'd hired, until he had arrived here at last, tired and very sweaty.

Once more he looked at the man in the shawl, but he didn't seem very bribeable.

'Excuse me, would you like some tea, sir?'

Michael turned to see a girl in jeans, pretty, with the dark eyes and luscious glossy plait you saw everywhere in India. She handed Michael's protagonist a cup and saucer and waited for Michael to reply.

'Thank you, Shirin.' The man looked at his watch and muttered: 'You will please excuse me? I have to go to a meeting; I am already late.'

He nodded impersonally to Michael who in turn nodded a grateful acceptance to the girl who disappeared out of the room; then to Michael's enormous relief, the man drank his tea quickly, picked up a couple of files from the table and after calling down the office corridor that he was going, slammed the front door behind him.

Michael's smile was at its widest when the girl came back. She motioned to him to a bench which was under a large wall-map of Gujarat and he sat down with relief.

131

'Lovely. Thank you.' He looked across at the girl who was now seated at the desk by the window. He gulped down the tea and laid down the empty cup. 'I didn't have a lot of success this morning with your Mr . . .' he said conversationally.

'Mr Sen,' she helped him. 'No?' From the way she said it he got the impression that she wasn't too keen on old Brown Shawl either.

Michael sighed. 'I want to get a hold of Mr Robson. It's rather urgent. I believe he's travelling with a couple of friends of mine – ' He was relieved to see that she was definitely listening '– an elderly lady, Nadine, and a younger one, Jenni. I just feel so frustrated because I've come all the way from London to meet up with them and only just missed them at Kundi.'

'Ah, Mr Robson is often there.'

'So I understand, but where is he now? I do know roughly where my friends are aiming for but I want to be sure to find them.' He smiled helplessly.

The girl eyed him levelly. 'Where to you think they are going?' she asked.

'Towards Chittokundi, I guess.'

She nodded. 'Yes.'

They looked at each other and at last, to Michael's relief, she relented. 'They are staying with the Jesuits at Sapatdongri. We have several ongoing projects there.'

Michael eyed the map on the wall. 'Could you possibly show me?'

'Of course.' Shirin got up and went over to the map, studied it for a moment, then pointed. 'That's the mission. The dam is there – a bit further up the valley – about two hours' drive.'

He realised that he would have to retrace his steps, but even so he wanted to hug her and sing. Instead he asked if it would be possible to phone the mission, and offered to pay.

'I can try.' She looked through an office address book until she found the number and dialled the operator. Michael heard her ask for a 'lightning call', which she told him had three times as much priority as an ordinary call. She listened for a while, spoke to the operator a couple of times, then sighed and put down the receiver. 'No luck, I'm afraid.' She looked up at him with melancholy eyes. 'It is out of order.

There have been flash floods on the way. But I will write down the address for you and draw you a simple diagram of how to find it.'

Ravi lay on his belly under the thorny *bawal* trees which covered the scrubby ground between the road and the river and sighed; it was very hot and he found it hard not to fall asleep. He had long ago eaten the snacks Wanita had thrust at him when he set off with the ten black goats, and was now really hungry. He had found a few wild berries to nibble, but they were pithy and bitter so he had spat them out. His water bottle was empty, but he was afraid to leave the goats to go to the river bank for a drink, and, to be honest, he was scared of the crocodiles. A woman from a village a few miles away had been eaten by one only last spring. He watched a gecko and pounced at it, but it flashed away into the undergrowth. The goats were fairly quiet at the moment; they had found grazing, though the smallest one had wandered off again almost to the edge of the road. Ravi groaned and stood p to run after it. It took him a couple of minutes to catch the animal, but when he did it nestled up to him and tried to chew his vest as he murmured to the little creature, nuzzling it, enjoying the soft warmth of its tight dark curls and floppy ears.

Ravi squinted up through the trees to where Ramdas sat on the small hilltop which gave a good view up the valley. He was still sitting in exactly the same position he had taken up early in the morning. Ravi stood looking at him for a minute and tried to catch his eye, but Ramdas didn't respond to the boy's wave. Ravi lay down again and lifted a stone to watch a line of marching ants. A half-chewed *chico* fruit was now almost completely obscured by the busy insects, and a couple of them were determinedly carting a huge crumb of *chapati* along the ant road. Ravi rolled over and groaned. He wished that whatever was supposed to happen would hurry up and do so: he wanted to go and fly his kite.

Michael stopped the motorbike by a dusty thorn tree and climbed down the dry bank to have a pee. He stood for a little to admire the hot landscape, which was dry and red, rocky, with prickly bushes, an occasional lonely palm tree, fields of young sugar cane and dramatic pyramidal blue hills in the distance. He wiped his face and hands with lukewarm water from his bottle and swallowed some thirstily. As he scrambled back up to the bike he stopped to admire a large bush with flat leaves of a dullish grey-green which had star-shaped blossoms, pink, five-petalled and slightly waxy, growing in clusters. It had an almost cloying smell. Exotic, a desert flower.

He looked at his watch and eyed the sun. With luck he would reach the mission before sundown, if only the machine would hold out; for the last few miles it had been making nasty splutterings. It was worrying. Michael was no mechanic, and he certainly hadn't passed a lot of local garages on the way.

He smiled as he imagined Jenni's face when she saw him. He had envisaged the scene so often, the images becoming more and more operatic as he grew hotter and tireder. Jenni, her face radiant with recognition; himself climbing off the bike, looking at her and standing there open-armed. He chuckled at his own romanticism. Knowing Jen, she would probably yell at him.

'What the fuck are you doing here? I thought I was free of you at last!'

He warmed at the thought and tried not to remember how adamant she had been in reality. Just stay away, she had said. It's over. I'm tired of feeling dragged down by a no-hope situation. He remembered too his angry wife, Nella, wholesome mother of three, his friend and ally since they were younger than their youngest now was, poised to leave him after almost a quarter of a century. He shivered as he recalled his bewilderment at the ironic volte-face, the rage which she had hurled at him when he had dared to confess that he wanted out.

'Go, for God sake!' she had yelled. 'I'm sick of the lies and secrecy. You're not the only one with a double life. Let's get it over with, for God's sake!'

Ridiculously, he had felt appalled by the reality of her wanting out. To be cuckolded by another woman, that was the real joke – and a woman he knew and liked at that. The ironic part of it was that he simply hadn't realised what was going on. He smiled grimly as he remembered telling Nella that he had interviewed this highly intelligent woman after the Brixton riots.

'Ask her over,' she had said. 'It's time we had a bit of decent social life.'

In the end both of them had laughed rather bitterly and they had cried together, but the fact that it was a woman Nella loved was still hard to take. Michael had felt catatonic for weeks: hadn't wanted to tell anybody. The kids had been very upset, except for Maggie. She, astonishingly, seemed to think Nella was making a wise move. It was a funny bloody world.

He must get going. Trying to subdue a new image of a Jenni who shouted at him to piss off and stay away for ever, he climbed purposefully back on to the saddle of the old Enfield which was radiating heat, wiped the orange dust off his sunglasses and kicked the starter pedal.

To his horror there was no answering roar. Cold with dismay, he tried again several times, but the engine only uttered a dry cough and remained mute.

Michael cursed, then climbed off and stood looking at his impotent white charger.

'I don't believe this,' he groaned. 'The bugger actually isn't going to start.'

There was no dwelling in sight, no live creature but for a vulture soaring high above a distant clump of trees, and a scraggy couple of cows across the road, and he hadn't seen another vehicle for a while.

There was only one thing to do. Wearily, he wiped the sweat from his eyes and squatted down in the roadside dust to search in the cracked saddle-bag for the tool kit that he had been assured was complete.

'How long is the Chittokundi Valley?' asked Jenni as they prepared to set off from the mission after their second night there.

'Fifty miles. We'll get there early this afternoon after I've looked at a women's project on the way. I think you'll find it interesting. Most of the workers in that particular village are employed on constructing the dam and haven't been paid for nearly a year. We're doing what we can to help.'

Nathan climbed into the front of the vehicle beside Nadine and turned to look for Kalidas who was still busy outside.

'He's giving it an extra good polish for luck,' whispered Nathan. They watched as Kalidas carefully burnished the driver's mirror and windscreen before climbing into the cab.

Today it was Nadine who handed him a fresh blossom for the journey – jasmine this time, with its heady perfume. The three brothers came to say goodbye.

'We will expect you the day after tomorrow,' called Father Francis. 'If you're not here by nightfall we'll send out a search party.' He giggled like a kid. Antony waved impassively as Kalidas, his dark eyes unusually serious, started up the Land-Rover.

Hours later, as they squatted to relieve themselves in a field watched by a bright-eyed mongoose, Nadine whispered to Jenni: 'I think our two men are really nervous.'

She nodded. 'Nathan hasn't said a word for the last hour.'

'He bites his nails a lot.'

'So does Kalidas today. He's even quieter than usual.'

'We must be nearly at the dangerous bit.'

'We are. Nathan said when you were asleep.' She pointed across the fields, beyond a grove of bamboo, to a forested cleft in the landscape. 'That's the entry to the valley over there, where you can just see the river. Exciting, huh?'

'Only with you, Jenni, would there be a chance of dacoits. You are like a magnet for drama.'

They returned to the men and climbed back into the Land-Rover. Kalidas, eyes watchful, drove off once more and Nathan, obviously tense, pointed out the occasional landmark. The landscape was almost Antipodean, with occasional patches of eucalyptus and stony barren hillsides.

'There has been terrible deforestation all over this area,' Nathan told them. 'It's all been used for buildings and fuel. As you see people already walk for many kilometres with their bundles of firewood, and they are having to walk further and further.'

'Is the eucalyptus indigenous?' Jenni pulled out her notebook.

'It's imported. It grows fast but it's a poor crop, not good for constructing, only good to burn. This used to be all good rich jungle and woodland, full of panthers, tigers and peacocks.'

'Snakes?'

'Sure, there are always snakes.'

'Are they dangerous?'

'Yeah, they can kill you.' He looked at her, amused. 'I saw one last week when I was staying in one of the villages; he came and slithered up to have a look at me when I was lying in bed.'

'Ugh. What did you do?'

'I said hello, talked to him a little. Connected.' Nathan smiled. 'It was good. I think he liked it. In the end he just went away. They won't hurt you unless they're threatened.'

Jenni shivered. 'I couldn't commune with a snake.'

'I like snakes,' murmured Nadine. 'They are so mysterious.'

After some time Nathan showed them an eerie stretch of river. Out of the almost unreal vibrant blue of the water, many dead trees, naked of bark, branches stark white, thrust up like skeletons. Nathan explained that the river had changed its course at this point, adding that when the dam was built a lot of the landscape would look like that.

'It's weird, a moonscape.' Nadine's hand crept to her Leica.

Nathan turned to her. 'I think you had better miss this one, Nadine, it's wiser not to stop here.'

She nodded and stared wide-eyed as they passed the ghostly trees, trying to engrave the image in her head. Taking out her sketch book she scribbled a few hurried notes.

Kalidas mumbled something and she looked up. They all tensed as he slowed down to pass a large parked lorry facing the way they had just come. A man was kneeling in front of it, busy with matches. He looked very strained.

Nadine gripped Jenni's arm.

'Trouble?' asked Jenni levelly, professionalism to the fore.

Nathan relaxed. 'It's OK. It's just a driver doing *puja*. He's putting up a prayer because he's come through the dangerous bit.'

'I begin to believe you,' said Nadine. 'Like I didn't believe camels pee backwards.'

Nathan laughed, and translated for Kalidas who smiled his sweet fugitive smile.

137

They continued for three or four miles almost in silence, except occasionally to remark on a bird or tree. The wide river was visible from time to time through the greenery and the four in the cab were united in tension.

Jenni's mind had strayed from the road ahead when she heard Nathan murmur, 'Uh uh. This looks funny.'

Ahead of them, a small boy wearing a necklace and a red headband was standing with a flock of goats spread out across the road. The women smiled at the idyllic sight – then suddenly there was uproar.

There were loud bangs – gunfire, Jenni knew at once – shouts and horses rearing in front of the vehicle, which abruptly lurched to a halt, crunching on to a huge boulder. A great thump on the windscreen and myriad shining squares of glass sprayed over the three in the front seat.

'No!' Jenni heard herself yell, and clutched Nadine.

Nathan blinked and put up his arm. Take it easy,' he ordered calmly. 'This is it.'

The driver's door was pulled open and Kalidas violently dragged out by a heavy man with a moustache. The man shouted at Kalidas and forced him to the ground until the young driver was curled up almost foetally, hands behind his neck, his face on the tarmac. Kalidas winced and made to start up, but the man whirled round and swiped him on the head with the rifle butt. The others watched appalled as he gave a terrible groan, fell over on to his side and lay bleeding profusely, eyes closed.

The small boy had scuttled away, leaving a couple of goats still wandering on the road. There were several other men and a wild-looking girl on horseback, who dismounted and came up to them yelling. Nathan, Jenni and Nadine winced as she reached them and watched breathlessly as she pointed to the recumbent Kalidas and roared at the big man.

She's telling him that he's an idiot,' Nathan whispered. 'She's obviously the boss. Just don't move.'

Jenni eyed the car keys which were still in the starter. 'We could drive through them . . .'

'We can't leave Kalidas.'

In moments, they were tumbled out of the cab and on to the ground. The dacoit girl demanded the keys and forced

138

Nathan to get out to unlock the back. The luggage was quickly emptied out by the big dacoit man; two other turbaned men stood by with rifles at the ready.

Ramdas demanded that Nathan show him how to undo the handbrake and the horsemen dismounted and heaved the Land-Rover off the road and through the bushes until it was hidden from sight. The woman, fierce and tense, stood guard. None of the three on the ground were in any doubt that she would shoot to kill if they moved at all.

'Are you OK?' hissed Jenni. Her head was pressed into the road near Nadine's.

'Yeah. I'm OK, but my pills . . .'

The female dacoit kicked Jenni when she saw her speak, shouting incomprehensibly.

Nathan tried to talk to her but was ordered to shut up. Their bags were unzipped crudely, the contents spilled out, and all four were roughly tied up with randomly assorted clothes. Jenni wanted to laugh hysterically when her wrists were tightly knotted in the despised yellow pyjamas and winced when she saw Nadine's impeccable white shawl bloodstained from Kalidas's head wound.

'Nathan,' she whispered. 'Nadine needs her pills.'

He put his head up gingerly and called to the woman who was supervising the tying-up. She frowned and listened without sympathy.

'She wants to know where they are,' he told Nadine.

She was breathless. 'A small bottle in my camera bag.'

Nathan spoke again and the striped bag was produced. Ramdas grabbed it and Nadine groaned despairingly as he upended it clumsily and the cameras smashed down. The woman reached regally across, snatched the bag and searched it thoroughly before producing the little bottle which she flourished at her prisoners. Nadine nodded and Nathan told her that it was the right medicine.

In an instant Ramdas had seized the bottle from Wanita and tried to open it, but he couldn't manage the child-proof lid and glared. Cursing, he took the bottle and, watched by the horrified prisoners on the ground, hurled it away as hard as he could into the undergrowth under the eucalyptus trees.

They barely knew what happened next. They were kicked,

punched, bundled and heaved up on to the backs of horses, heads hanging down. Kalidas, unconscious, groaned deeply when he was lifted.

Jenni called Nadine's name and heard her answer: 'OK.' She noticed Nathan's strained face upside down near hers for a moment.

'They want us out of sight . . .' he muttered, 'before more cars come. Hang on in there.'

'I don't think they want to kill us or they would have by now,' whispered Jenni, but he didn't seem to hear.

The next thing they knew was that they were blindfolded, and the last thing Jenni glimpsed before her vision went black was the little boy's huge dark eyes peering out at them from behind a tree.

Fourteen

It was dark at the mission. The brothers had finished supper and were washing up when they heard knocking on the front door. Brother Antony went cautiously to open it and found himself confronted by a tall dark man who looked scorched from too much sun, and obviously ready to drop.

'Is this the Jesuit Mission?'

'Yes, it is. Can I help you?'

'Please. My name is Michael O'Brien and I'm trying to find two women friends – an English woman and a French one. The French one is called Nadine, and the English one . . .'

'Miss Jenni?' the young brother asked.

Michael lit up with relief. 'They're here?' He wanted to shout for joy.

'No, but they have been here.'

Michael slumped visibly at this news.

'They went out on tour yesterday morning but we expect them back the day after tomorrow.'

Michael's sigh of relief was heartfelt. Brother Antony, looking at the man's unshaven, haggard face thought for a moment that he was going to swoon. 'I have been chasing them for days.'

'Er – may I enquire why?'

Michael blinked a little then laughed, a small tired sound. 'It's a long story. Jenni is an old friend and I have a great personal need to see her.' He looked at the young man and wondered how a celibate Jesuit brother would feel about it all. Michael was a lapsed Catholic but the roots went deep – ineradicably deep he had thought until recently.

Antony was joined by a small plump Indian with spectacles who looked enquiringly at the stranger. Antony turned and spoke quickly to him, obviously reiterating what had already been said. Michael, alternately hopeful and exhausted, stood feebly by.

Francis came out to take a better look at the stranger. How had he travelled, and how far had he come? Michael sighed and shook his head ruefully.

'I am sorry to arrive so late. I tried to phone from the NYAID office in Ahmedabad, then my motorbike broke down and it took several hours to mend – somebody stopped to give me a hand in the end. And after that I passed a bad accident about three hours away, near Rajkooti.'

'What sort of accident?'

'A jeep got crushed by a lorry carrying wood. The lorry was overloaded and toppled over.'

The brothers nodded sadly. It was always happening. Lorries and buses were filled twenty feet high, higher than the lorries were long, with people if not wood; they had seen it all too often.

'Was anybody hurt?'

'The driver of the jeep. I helped him as best I could but he only lasted for an hour. An ambulance came after a couple of hours but it was too late. The jeep was a write-off.'

'Poor man.'

'It was strange, he had a gun with him. He begged me to take it before the police came.'

'What did you do?'

Michael shrugged. 'I left it. I didn't want problems with the police.'

The brothers nodded sympathetically.

'Your friends have been here,' Father Francis told him. 'But we don't expect them back for two more days.'

'Could I find them where they are going?'

The brothers eyed each other. 'I think it would be better that you wait for them to come back. You wouldn't find them easily; it is politically sensitive territory.'

'So I understand.'

'Do you have somewhere to stay?' asked Francis after a pause.

'I – er – had hoped to find a hotel somewhere in the town.'

'Have you eaten?'

Michael shook his head. The brothers looked at each other.

Perhaps, Francis asked tentatively, Michael might like to accept their hospitality for the night and wait for his friends here? As he stuttered his thanks the Jesuit added that he was lucky because there was still some most excellent curry left over.

'What's happening out there?' Jenni, kneeling by Nadine on a *charpoy* bed in the ten by fifteen foot hut where they had been unceremoniously dumped, looked up at Nathan, peering out through the square window opening which had straight wooden bars socketed firmly into mud-finished walls.

'Not a lot. They're raking through the bags trying on our clothes. Still arguing.' He came over and knelt beside Jenni.

'How is she?'

Nadine's eyes opened. 'Better.' She smiled a little. 'How is poor Kalidas?'

There was an answering moan from the other side of the dark room where Kalidas, his head cradled in the bloody shawl, lay on his side.

'I'll go.' Nathan touched Jenni's arm and rose to look at the driver. Kneeling by Kalidas's rope bed with its threadbare cotton covers, he leaned across to touch his shoulder and murmur his name.

Kalidas moaned and turned round painfully, his hands shaking. Nathan smiled at him and spoke quietly and Jenni came over to watch as Nathan unwound the shawl and examined the wound.

It's actually not as bad as it looks, quite a small cut really, but it's a massive bump.'

'Hello,' said Jenni softly, and the young man managed to smile a little, then asked Nathan several questions which he answered before standing up decisively.

'We must ask them for some water. Kalidas's head needs to be cleaned and we need to drink. I'll ask them.'

He went to the window, held on to the bars and stood watching for a little before calling out. Standing behind him, Jenni was able to see the girl dacoit coming towards them

143

frowning, gun at the ready. She was wearing Jenni's black zipped jacket over her brightly coloured tribal trousers.

Nathan spoke to her for a minute or so and she listened without replying, then turned and shouted to one of the men who had been on horseback and pointed to a canvas bag which lay with the others beside a heap of books, clothing and papers.

Nathan came back and squatted between the two beds. 'She's ordered somebody to get us something to drink.'

They waited for a little until Wanita appeared at the window. She had a blue box with her which she gave to Nathan. He took it and thanked her. Moments later, a plastic bottle was handed through the bars. Nathan spoke with her for several minutes. The girl's voice was shrill at first, then calmer.

'She's given us the first aid box,' Nathan handed Jenni the water bottle and went back to Kalidas. 'Give Nadine some to cool her down, but don't drink it yet, just bathe her. We'll have to drink it if there is really no alternative, but I doubt if it will be good news for European stomachs. She's agreed to bring us tea. At least that will have been boiled.'

'Can you find out what they intend to do with us?' Kneeling, Jenni bathed Nadine's face with a torn-off piece of cotton.

'I tried, but I gather that they don't have a plan. They're arguing because some guy they were expecting hasn't turned up.'

Jenni stood up and went to Kalidas. Nathan unwrapped the shawl completely and used the water to clean the young man's wound. He worked carefully and efficiently, wiping with water then applying antiseptic from a bottle which made Kalidas wince, but he looked better after Nathan had fixed him a neat bandage with sticking-plaster. Nathan sat back to admire his work and said something which made the injured man grin a little.

'I've told him he looks like a warrior-hero.' He came to Nadine and squatted beside her. 'How about you? Are you still in pain?'

She tried to sit up, but Jenni gently pushed her back.

'Stay resting. That was a bad go you had.'

144

'Bloody bodies,' murmured Nadine. 'Ach.' She sighed and closed her eyes.

'If only that great oaf who looks like Atilla the Hun hadn't chucked away the TNT pills. They help immediately when her chest feels constricted.'

'Maybe they could find them for us.' Nathan looked thoughtful. 'I think we've got to be as amenable as possible – try to build up some sort of relationship with them. That is a very tense bunch of people we've got out there . . . trigger-happy, quarrelling amongst themselves. It doesn't make for a good scenario.'

'What do you think they meant about a man?' asked Jenni. 'A sort of bandit's pimp or something? Might they be part of a bigger gang?'

'I don't know. She seems very much the boss lady, but the big guy obviously doesn't like it that way and as we've seen he's impulsive, so we mustn't make them any angrier.'

'I feel absolutely murderous! To hell with passive resistance. I'd like to blast the lot of them.'

Nathan looked at her calmly. 'It wouldn't make it any better.'

Jenni glared. 'I hate to feel so impotent.'

'You may learn from it.'

His softness riled her. 'Surely there's something positive we can do other than wait?'

He shook his head. 'I truly don't believe so.'

Impatiently, she got up and went to peer out. It was beginning to grow dark and two men in turbans were sitting about twenty yards away idly watching the hut. One man was fat, the other very thin. They made her think of Laurel and Hardy. Three horses were tethered nearby and a few yards from the hut by a small tree she could see the little boy busy beside a fire on the ground. He appeared to be cooking something and was still wearing Nadine's yellow beret set comically sideways above his blue and white bead necklace with the copper amulet of Hanuman. The woman, obviously waiting for someone, was standing near him looking out across the hillside. Ramdas was not to be seen. He'd been away for several hours.

Eventually it grew too dark and Jenni gave up looking. She

145

came back into the body of the hut and sat against the wall near Nathan who was meditating. Nadine seemed to be asleep. Kalidas was awake but very quiet. For a while Jenni tried to meditate too, but she felt too disturbed for it to help. She was incredibly tired, and ached all over. She had never been so thirsty. She tried to lick her lips which were already cracking, but her mouth was almost too parched. In fact she herself felt like cracking. She was glad when Nathan moved a little. Thank goodness he was coming back, she didn't like him to be absent in this situation. She eyed him sideways as he stretched and took a long deep breath in and out. Then he stood up and smiled at her, a really intense look like Maya did after being Connected, and she felt his gentle power flow through her like a current.

'You OK?' he asked softly.

She nodded, her annoyance evaporating. 'Just impatient.'

'Sure.' He held her arm for a moment and she wanted to shout at him to hold her some more but he withdrew his hand and stood up. 'We've got to have something to drink or we'll be dehydrated.'

Jenni watched his silhouetted figure and heard him call. The woman shouted something in answer.

'She says they're bringing something to eat,' he said.

Kalidas was sitting up. Dimly, Jenni saw that he had put his feet on the floor and was looking around.

'OK? she asked and saw his eyes and teeth show white.

'OK,' he said. 'All OK now.'

Nadine was shifting around too. 'I'm starving,' she said from the bed, 'and where on earth do we pee in this awful place?'

In the sitting-room of the house in Ahmedabad the woman in the pink and blue sari sat waiting. She had tidied the house, swept it out, dusted and wiped. She had washed clothes and hung them up to dry in the sun on the flat roof, prepared a batch of fresh *chapatis* and made almond sweetmeats with honey and cardamom. She had been so the market to buy vegetables and had attended to the plants which grew round the house, watering them and pulling off dead leaves and blossoms, and she had swept the dust from the step and yard outside the house, but still the man with yellow eyes had not returned.

She jumped with fright when the phone rang. It always made her anxious to answer it and she became more nervous when she heard a male voice speaking in a language unknown to her. She listened, fearful, and thought that she heard her yellow-eyed man's name spoken.

'He is not here,' she told the man in Gujarati. The voice repeated the name and she repeated louder that he was not here. More foreign words came crackling through to her. She spoke louder so that perhaps the man might understand, but she neither understood his babble nor did he understand her shouts. At last, distressed, she put down the phone and sat unhappily alone.

'Ramdas,' she murmured slowly, then said it again, puzzled. 'Ramdas . . .'

She shook her head uneasily and stood up. For a moment she stared at the little shrine where the bright picture of the beautiful goddess with the crocodile stood, the goddess forever triumphant. But the woman did not draw comfort from the image today. Instead, sighing, she went into the kitchen and slowly cut herself a square of cooling *halwa*.

Ravi was running. Ramdas had hit him again this morning when the boy had asked if he could take food to the white people and the tribal man in the hut. Last night Ravi had cooked for them and had been allowed to give them *chai*; he liked the funny old woman who had laughed at the yellow hat he was wearing and had been kind when he gave her the hot drink though she didn't look very well. The young woman – who looked as though she might cry – had held her in her arms and helped her to eat and drink. The tall man with curly hair was a good man, you could tell by the look in his eyes; he also spoke Ravi's language well. The tribal man with the sore head hadn't said a lot. He had simply thanked the boy and quietly sipped water and eaten a little of the plain dhal. The young woman was very watchful but quite nice. She had thanked him too. Ravi liked her smile. He was glad Ramdas had gone off early on the horse. He felt angry with the big man and was still bruised where Ramdas had hit him on the arm.

Wanita and Ramdas were always arguing, but this time it seemed worse than usual. Ravi didn't fully understand why but knew that it was something to do with the man with the jeep not coming back. It probably had to do with money as usual. Ramdas had been almost cheerful the night after the man had come to the hut; he had even joked with Ravi and given him some sweets when he came back from the village where he had gone to round up the men who were now guarding the prisoners.

He ran along the stony track, up and down, until he came near the place where he had helped in the attack by spilling the goats out on to the road. He felt curious to see it again because he wondered what had happened to the big white vehicle. He half hoped it would still be there so that he could sit in it and see what such a thing felt like. It would be very exciting. He would pretend that he was a rich Maharaja or a Bombay businessman and play with the steering-wheel and all the little knobs and dials.

Still wearing the yellow beret and carrying the tall wooden stick he used for herding the goats, he came to the place at last and stood breathlessly trying to recognise the exact spot. He was puzzled at first because the vehicle was no longer where he had last seen it – pushed out of sight into the bushes. He wandered about for a while until he found tracks – footprints and tyre marks – and bushes trampled and hanging loose. He frowned and followed the broken branches, jumping horribly when suddenly a monkey screeched behind him; then he found himself near the river bank which at this point stood steeply several feet above the water. He peered over the edge cautiously, ready to jump for his life if a crocodile was any-where in sight, but through the greenery he saw only the blandly flowing water. A bird squawked, then there was silence. Puzzled, the boy stood up and was about to go back, but some instinct made him pull aside more foliage and look once more.

He stared and felt a thrill of excitement: about three yards from the edge, his disbelieving gaze fell on a white pyramid of metal sticking innocently out of the water.

Mystified, he crawled further along the bank and hung over to look more closely. There, dimly in the muddy water, he

148

could make out the shape of the Land-Rover. He sat back on his haunches to stare at it and frowned. It was very strange. He knew that a big machine like that must be worth millions of rupees, millions and millions. It must mean that the yellow-eyed man was extremely rich and that the prisoners were very important to him.

'I wish I could understand what's actually going on,' said Nathan. It was noon the next day. They had all slept intermittently the night before, but they had been cold and much disturbed by scuffling rats. They were still locked in the hut though they had been allowed out a couple of times to water the hillside, presided over by the formidable armed guard with a tattered vermilion turban whom they had christened Rambo.

'I don't understand either. It's all very mysterious. Who do they expect to pay the ransom? Who do they think we are? Is it because we're Westerners and they automatically think we're very rich?'

'We are by their standards.' Nadine had seemed asleep but obviously wasn't. She had had an alarmingly bad night and had been almost silent all morning, except occasionally to swear and feebly swat at some of the hundreds of flies which tormented them.

Nathan looked at Jenni. 'I think it's more complicated than that. I have a strange feeling it has something to do with you.'

'You're kidding. Why me?'

He shrugged. 'Just what I heard them arguing about.'

'What did they say?'

'Well, first of all the woman, Wanita, is furious that it's a NYAID vehicle that was stopped.'

'How does she know? It wasn't labelled.'

'She's illiterate anyway – most of the tribals of her age and older here are – but she knows who I am. I've worked in the district for six years. We're pretty well known and generally welcome in the villages, so she's not happy to have taken me. But she keeps talking about this other man they expected. She was mad at Ramdas about the whole business.'

'Is kidnapping unusual?'

'Yeah. Some villages are known criminal villages: it's

149

accepted that it's their livelihood. These people are like that. They have no alternative way of living because the land is so poor and they have been so exploited. Generally the dacoits round here simply stop a vehicle and strip it and the people in it of everything – sometimes they literally strip them naked – then they either force them to drive on, or shoot the car tyres and leave them stranded. Occasionally they kill people, but actual kidnapping is rare.'

'What on earth makes you think I might have been the target?'

'A couple of things she said.'

Jenni suddenly felt cold. 'Like what?'

'She said TV Memsahib very big.' Nathan looked searchingly at her. 'Are you? I understood you were a journalist.'

'I am a journalist, but on TV. I do my own reporting.'

'So you perform as well as write?'

'Yes.'

'Ah.' He was silent. 'You famous?'

Jenni shrugged.

Nadine's eyes fluttered. 'She's famous.'

Nathan nodded. 'I didn't know. That brings its own pressures.' He smiled a little, then turned to her again. 'Do you have any enemies, Jenni?'

Jenni's insides did not feel good. Whether it was the water she'd drunk in desperation this morning when nothing else had been forthcoming or her suddenly recalled unease about the programme, she could not tell. She frowned.

'Well?' Nathan's gaze was intense.

'Not enemies. Rivals perhaps.'

'Surely nobody who would organise a crazy business like this.' It was Nadine speaking; she had rolled over on her side and was very pale.

Jenni was still puzzling. 'I can't imagine it, and yet – ' she frowned ' – there is something niggling.' She shook her head. 'It's mad.'

'This whole situation is mad, but something odd is definitely going on.'

'It's just that I did a programme about illegal arms sales from Britain. It's a complicated story: a British ship was bombed in the Gulf of Iran by British-made weapons, and I

found out a few things about the business and made a programme about it.'

'Recently?'

'It was due to come out just before I came to India.'

Nadine muttered something.

'Come again?' asked Nathan.

'They censored it. Idiots.'

'They stopped it?'

Jenni nodded. She felt awful, dizzy. 'I came away to escape
it all. I was incredibly angry but helpless to do anything. They
were having a meeting in London about it when I was at
Kundi.'

'I'm confused.' Nathan squatted down, his back against the
wall. 'Who actually cancelled it? The TV channel?'

Nadine grunted. 'Good question.'

Jenni sighed. 'Officially it was them, but you see the television company has what's called a Board of Governors, and
they – well – ' She shrugged unhappily.

Nadine heaved herself up. 'Government approved,' she
said harshly. 'Censorship I call it.' She glared and swiped
fretfully at a fly before shutting her eyes again.

'Ah. I begin to see – or think I do. But surely they
wouldn't . . .'

Jenni shook her head. 'No. I'm sure we haven't been kid-
napped because MI5 is after me – that would be too high camp.
Anyway,' she laughed unhappily, 'they would have done the
job properly, not delegated it to these people. But I just – '

'What?'

She shook her head. 'Forget it. I'm imagining things.'

Nadine leaned towards her. 'Say what the thought was,
however stupid it seems.'

They watched Jenni, who frowned and closed her eyes.
Kalidas, who was standing looking out of the window, turned
to watch her too.

'It's too far-fetched.' She shook her head again.

Nathan gestured round the hut. 'Too far-fetched? This is
almost beyond belief.'

'No, forget it. I have no answers. I think our dacoits simply
want to go up-market but don't quite know how to do it. What
else did you gather from Wanita?'

'No more than I've told you. She's in a mess because this other guy hasn't turned up.'

'But it can't really be because of me. OK, I'm well known on the box in Britain, but here nobody has ever heard of me, and anyway I'm not rich.'

'Maybe somebody recognised you?'

'No. I even look different. I had all my hair cut off before I came, and changed the colour.'

Nathan nodded. 'Must have been bad, huh?' His handsome face was sympathetic, designer-stubbled now.

'It was.'

Their eyes met.

'But say somebody had recognised you somehow, maybe they thought you had money?'

'It's crazy.'

'Sure it's crazy, but it is within the realms of possibility. A little money to us is a fortune to them.'

'What if . . .' Nadine tried to sit up but obviously found it an effort.

'Lie down,' said Jenni gently and went over to sit beside her.

'What if this man or somebody else actually *did* know who you were, and thought the BBC would pay for you?'

'You must be joking!'

Nathan looked up. 'I don't see why. In the States television companies have a lot of money. Is Britain not the same?'

'No way.' Jenni was adamant.

Nadine stirred. 'It still seems a possibility to me. What about that girl on the picnic or . . .' She paused. 'Oh my God! Davinder.'

'Who's he?' asked Nathan.

'One of the two men who live in the old rooms off the courtyard at Kundi.'

'That creepy one who wanted money from me?' Jenni remembered.

'Yes.'

'How would he know anything?'

'His friend, the old piebald man. I like him . . .'

'And?'

'He asked me about Jenni – or one of them did.'

152

'What did you say?'

'Not a lot.' Nadine frowned. 'We were chatting – drinking a little whisky – but I did say she was on the TV.'

Nathan turned to Jenni. 'And the girl on the picnic?'

'Just a Traveller from England who recognised me.'

'She might have told somebody who told somebody else.'

'No.' Jenni was adamant. 'I really can't see it. It's all too far-fetched.' She was almost amused at the thought. 'Though the BBC's not what it was.'

'Financially?'

Jenni sighed. 'That too. They're always moaning about cutbacks. But I mean the ethical side – like my programme being held back.'

'Is that a new syndrome?'

Jenni nodded. 'Fairly, but very worrying. I'm afraid it's happening more often. A Member of Parliament put it rather well a while ago when he remarked that the BBC is tired, battered and dishonoured, but the best thing we've got in a third-rate country – though all that doesn't help solve our mystery.'

Nathan suddenly looked keenly across at Nadine. 'Are you OK?'

She looked anything but. Her eyelids fluttered and she nodded faintly. 'So thirsty . . .'

Nathan got up. 'I'll try again.'

He joined Kalidas at the window and stared out for a moment. 'Wanita and the kid seem to be bringing some food.'

'Thank goodness for that.' Jenni started to get up but felt Nadine grip her arm.

'Jenni darling, I need to go outside.'

'Sure.' She looked at Nadine, then knelt down again quickly. 'What is it? You look awful.' Nadine, she realised, was also very hot.

'I feel bad. I need to – very quickly – '

'Tummy?'

'Yeah.' It was almost a gasp.

Panicking, Jenni called Nathan who yelled out through the window space. A moment or two later the door was opened and Wanita stood there with Stan and Ollie, rifles at the ready.

The women, Nadine painfully doubled up, were escorted to the thorn bushes. Meanwhile, Ravi carried in a clay dish of rice, water and some *chapatis*. Carefully, he laid the food on the floor, watched by Wanita.

Nathan looked up at the bandit woman. She was glowering, had a savage look about her. He spoke to her, telling her that the old woman was ill and needed a particular medicine. She shrugged. Had she not given him the medicine box yesterday?

It had been thrown away, Nathan reminded her. Her special medicine. At which Wanita looked even angrier and muttered invective against Ramdas.

How long, Nathan asked, did she intend to keep them prisoner?

As long as it pleases me, she answered.

But our friend needs help, she is an elderly lady, not in strong health, he told her. It would make big trouble with the authorities if she becomes worse or even dies.

Wanita's eyes flickered.

There was a silence, then he tried again gently. He had friends who helped the tribal people, he said, people who would allow her case to be heard fairly in the courts. Nathan understood that life was hard here and that Wanita and the men must have had good reason to do what they did, but their prisoners were innocent tourists who meant them no harm and who brought income to the country.

Wanita muttered that she didn't know about that. The authorities he spoke of, she added bitterly, were evil and totally corrupt men whom she would trust no further than a rat or a snake.

Nathan bowed his head as she spoke and nodded sympathetically. Then he looked up. It seemed a pity, he dared to say, that they had stopped a NYAID vehicle with field workers like himself and Kalidas inside it.

Kalidas, who had been listening nervously, now joined it.

Surely she knew, he asked, how much help Nathan and NYAID had brought not only to this district, but also to the whole of Gujarat and Rajasthan?

Wanita had had enough. She pounded the rifle butt on to the mud floor and roared at them to shut up. She wanted no more moaning. She was in charge, she knew what she was doing, and it was justified if they only knew what toll had been taken on her family. Her father and mother were dead; her

154

brother and his wife were dead. She was an orphan with her brother's orphan to care for, and sometimes they almost starved. She then shouted even louder that nearly all the people here believed that the poverty and misery of their lives was Karma and that they must atone for sins committed in past lives.

Nathan watched her keenly. Yes, he said, he knew many people thought that thing, but what did Wanita believe?

The girl blazed, with anger, legs planted wide, strong toes gripping the ground, and yelled that she believed that she and her people were held down, exploited by evil greedy men. She also knew that many of her fellow tribal people were stupid and ignorant, but she intended to change this and to be a leader for them. The dacoits took from the rich travellers who passed through their valley in cars and lorries so that they and their families could survive. Not to be comfortable or have a good time, simply to survive. She stopped, breathless.

Nathan and Kalidas watched her intently. Nathan felt incredibly moved; Kalidas thought she was a very wild woman and was glad that his eighteen-year-old wife was not like that at all. She had a great power this Wanita, though it was frightening when you thought about it. She had the gun and was obviously all set to use it on any of them. Ravi, who had crept back in during his sister's diatribe, was kneeling on the floor near the food, gazing up at her, big-eyed. Kalidas, glancing at him for a moment, noticed that the boy was carrying Nadine's striped bag.

There was a silence, then Nathan spoke. 'I understand what you are telling us, Wanita, and much of it is justified. Your people do need help and good leaders, but I believe that they need education most of all, and for my part I cannot believe that violence will ever be the answer to their problems.'

Wanita was breathing heavily. She knew only that she must not cry. Warriors did not cry, and certainly not in front of prisoners. She was glad to see the two women were coming back at last, but not so glad to see that the young one was half-carrying the white-haired one. She stood aside to let them back into the hut, and Nathan, seeing how ill Nadine looked, leapt up to help Jenni lift her ashen-faced friend on to the *charpoy* bed.

155

Fifteen

At the ancient palace of Kundi young Peter was perturbed. In his two years of service with the Spiritual Travellers he had never known his leader appear ruffled in any way or to display moodiness, but today was different. At lunchtime, Maya had seemed distant, her mind definitely not on the matters in hand, and at the end of the meal – which she had barely touched – she had almost abruptly asked him to take over from her in the afternoon. There was a new contingent of people from Adelaide expected shortly and she had close friends among them whom it had been arranged she would be there to welcome. When she asked that she be left in her room and not disturbed, Peter wondered uneasily if she might be unwell.

In fact Maya was intensely disturbed. She tried to Connect with her spiritual centre, but strange images welled up, and her whole body felt uneasy. Her normally subjugated, reactive mind swirled about, clouding her vision of what in her lectures she termed PPR – Present Physical Reality – and pulling painfully at the hidden knots and ties of memory. At first she didn't know herself what was causing the disturbance, only that she was uneasy in an area to which she had some deep atavistic attachment and which had not yet been made to disperse by the refined tool of meditation. There was still a knot and it was refusing to unravel however hard she employed her gentle power on it. She remained immobile for hours, eyes open, her expression tense. In the end she rose and went to the door and opened it. She found Peter waiting nearby, leaning on the balcony looking out towards the darkening lake.

156

He turned anxiously towards her, automatically touching his forehead and raising his palm.

Atypically, today May only nodded wearily in response and asked, 'Have the Australians arrived?'

He nodded. 'They've gone to rest and freshen up so it's all quiet. Would you like anything?'

'I'd love some hot milk.' She looked pale.

'Sure, I'll fetch it.' He nodded and went away.

Maya returned to her room, went across to the bed and sat down cross-legged, her back against the white wall. Her eyes roamed unseeing round the room, out to the balcony and beyond to the evening sky. Shivering, she pulled her shawl round her, smoothing as she did so her long cotton sleeves. Nobody ever saw Maya's arms uncovered; even in the full heat of summer she always wore a muslin blouse with tight sleeves which ended at the wrist, but tonight, almost idly, she pushed back one white cuff and for a moment her dark eyes rested thoughtfully on her inner wrist which she fingered briefly before pulling the sleeve back down so that the arm was covered as usual. Sighing, she lay down on her side and closed her eyes. She was still in this position when some time later, there was a knock at the door. She called for him to come in, and Peter, slipping off his shoes, entered softly and laid a metal beaker of warm cinnamon milk on a table by her side. Unsure whether to go or stay, he stood for a moment.

'Are you feeling OK Maya?' he asked. 'You seem a little quiet.'

'I'm all right.' She took the milk and sipped it ruminatively.

'Is there something worrying you, D'you want to talk?'

She sighed. 'I can't explain. I just have this very strong feeling about Nadine, that something bad has happened to her.'

'Nadine? but when she set off she was in great shape.'

'There's something wrong, I know it. Something very wrong.' She looked up. 'Do you know where they were heading?'

'She was going to travel with Nathan, wasn't she?'

Maya nodded. 'For several days.'

'Well.' The boy was relieved. 'No harm can come to her with him.'

157

Maya frowned. 'That's the thing. I think there's something up with him too. I'm sure of it.'

Peter didn't question the statement. He knew that when a Liberated One had a gut feeling it was always with good reason.

'Do you want me to try and find out about them, I could try to telex Ahmedabad? The lines may be OK by now.'

Maya thought for a moment. 'What time is it?'

'Almost six.'

'The NYAID office will be closed.' Her grim look was not at all guru-like. It struck Peter how old she suddenly looked. Really old – like thousands of years old. He thought for a little, then brightened. 'Tell you what we could do . . .'

Maya looked up heavy-eyed.

'The Catholics. They were heading for the mission at Sapatdongri.'

Maya brightened minimally. 'Yeah, I guess we could contact them.'

'Shall I go down to the office and try? It takes hours sometimes.'

'Soon. Shall we Connect together first? I have a need to clarify.'

'Sure.' He nodded respectfully and looked away discreetly as Maya shifted herself on the bed, carefully adjusting her long white garments, prepared once more to meditate. Peter glanced round the room and chose to sit on a floor cushion over near the balcony. It was almost dark and growing cold when he obliterated the contours of his strong young body, using the white shawl like a woollen bandage, his wide blue eyes fixed on the still uneasy centre of her forehead.

At the mission Michael had slept and eaten well. He found that he enjoyed the conversation of the brothers and had stayed up late with them to discuss and compare the life and politics of their two countries. In the morning he went with Father Francis and watched him at work in the local town where Francis held a weekly surgery to help and advise people on legal problems. It was a fascinating day for a journalist; Michael eagerly took notes, listening avidly to Francis's running commentary of translation. There were poor farmers who had mortgaged their land for more than they could ever earn in a year, who had got so deeply into debt that they were almost starving; and there were family rows – a murder even – and many people who were oppressed by years of too little money and the drought conditions which had made their crops fail for five years running.

'I feel humbled,' Michael told Francis at the end of the day as they drove back to the mission. Francis, giggling on the back of the motorbike, on which he had begged to be allowed to ride, waved the comment aside.

'No doubt I would feel humbled and intimidated if I were to come to England and see your grand offices and fine machinery at work. It is a matter of different environments, different tasks to be done. Here we do what we can to help, but I am afraid it is very little and it is slow work. You see the results in generations rather than months or days. Consciousness-raising is the main problem. That and education. They are always the two things that must go hand in hand. The empowerment of information.'

Relieved that there was seldom talk of God or higher things, Michael nodded. It sounded to him more like socialism that the brothers were dispensing than religion. A good thing too, in his opinion; he warmed towards his tubby little passenger. Francis, clutching Michael's waist as hard as he could, shouted as they travelled past camels and bullocks pulling carts overburdened beyond belief: 'Your friends should be there when we get back, or soon after!'

Michael, slowing the bike down to allow a superb line of six girls in dazzling saris, carrying wide and obviously heavy basins of cow dung on their heads, grinned and shouted back to his passenger that he couldn't wait and reckoned that now he had travelled far enough.

He felt incredibly light and happy, like a lad in love. Jen would surely be pleased to see him, even after his unforgivable silence. He was certain that he would be able to explain it all to her. Just thinking of her made his blood surge. He wanted to take her to Udaipur, to the Lake Palace Hotel. They had once watched a film about it: the great white palace set romantically in the middle of a cerulean blue lake, encircled by mountains, now a place for the rich to relax. You

159

could hire the Maharaja's bedroom suite if you were lucky. He had promised her that they would go there together one day. There, like a Mogul warrior, he would re-possess her at last.

Ravi had brought Nadine's striped bag because Wanita, not interested in what looked to her like children's toys, had given the boy the artist's drawing things and tiny black enamel paintbox. He liked the paintbox best. The latter, surprisingly heavy for its size, was about seven inches long, cylindrical in shape, but flat down one side which hinged open to reveal bright squares of colour and a white enamel mixing tray. Ravi had tried to use the little brush which came with the box, but when he wetted it with the strange-smelling liquid he found when he unscrewed the brass cap on the end of the box, it didn't work very well. Spit was better. He looked at Nadine's drawings in wonder and chuckled at some of them. There were cows, birds, people sitting and standing. He guessed they must have been made by her because there were even some clever pictures that he recognised as the memsahib Jenni and the two men.

After her outburst, Wanita had left the prisoners to eat their food, and to his delight had allowed Ravi to stay in the hut. He watched the four of them shyly, as, except for the old woman who was lying very still, they ate plain boiled rice. He was shocked to see that the Jenni lady used her left hand to eat with as well as her right. Nathan and Kalidas did not, of course, they knew it was bad to do that. You were only supposed to use your right hand for eating; the left one was for wiping your bottom.

Seeing the boy's amazed and slightly horrified look, Nathan said something to Jenni who looked at Ravi apologetically, smiled, put her left hand firmly out of the way, and continued to eat only with her right. Kalidas, his rice finished, drank from the water bottle and pointed to the bag Ravi was still clutching tightly. What had he there? he asked amiably.

Shyly, the boy took out the pencils, paints and drawing books, and showed them. The precious cameras – one of them badly smashed – Ramdas had already sold in the nearest town.

160

'Ask him if he likes to draw,' said Jenni, and Nathan spoke to the boy who grinned shyly.

Nadine was sleeping deeply as Jenni played with Ravi. They drew little pictures of each other which made the boy chortle, then she taught him to count in English.

'One, two, three . . .' he said slowly, then in a burst he got it right and chanted with her '. . . four, five, six.' When they reached ten he doubled up with laughter.

'He's so clever,' she said to Nathan. 'He should be at school. He's so quick and bright, it's a terrible waste.'

Nathan nodded. 'It's slow, but it's changing. We're working on it in this district, but there's still only thirty-five percent literacy in many of the country areas, often much less.'

He joined in and taught the small boy – who didn't know how old he was but guessed he was about nine – to play Boxes by marking a series of dotted squares on Nadine's best watercolour paper and showing him how to join up the sides of the dots to create squares. The more squares you made the better you did. Ravi, happier than he ever remembered feeling, picked up the game incredibly fast, counted his wins and proudly initialled them with his newly-learned capital 'R'.

Nadine woke up. She was very hot, but the griping pains had stopped for the moment. After watching Ravi for a little, she called him over to her, pointing to him to bring the paper and pencils. Ravi stood by her bed and with a flourish she drew him a crocodile with zigzag teeth and a portrait of the mangy dog that hung hopefully about the door of the hut. He gazed in wonder as the images appeared and looked as often at the artist's concentrated expression as she worked as he did at the emerging drawings. When the pictures were ready he was awestruck, his mouth and eyes open wide.

Nadine, obviously uncomfortable, pulled herself on to her elbow.

'Are you hungry at all?' Jenni asked. 'We kept yours for you.'

Nadine grimaced and shook her head. 'But,' she pointed to the little black paint-box which was abandoned on the floor, 'I might try some of that.'

161

Jenni wondered for a moment if she were delirious.

'Bring it to me.' Nadine pointed again and Ravi, understanding, jumped up and brought the black enamel paintbox to her. She took it and carefully unscrewed the small brass cap on the end. She sniffed, then, smiling, inhaled.

The three adults and the boy watched puzzled as she put the top of the cylindrical black metal paintbox to her lips.

Nathan suddenly got up and waved the plastic water bottle at her. 'Hey, Nadine, drink this. The stuff in there will be old.'

Nadine smacked her lips and smiled what Jenni called her monkey smile. 'This isn't water.' She sipped some more with obvious enjoyment. 'It's whisky.'

She sighed with contentment and lay back. The three adults watched her and looked at each other.

'You're a terrible woman,' said Jenni fondly, then instantly jumped up. Nadine's benign expression had suddenly become horribly distorted.

'Oh, my God. Ah!' She clutched her stomach and gasped.

'What is it?' Jenni rushed to her.

'Pain . . . ach!' Nadine groaned dreadfully. I'm sorry. I have to go out again – quickly.'

Nathan shouted to the guards outside. Stan Laurel, half-asleep, leapt up and came and unbolted the door quite quickly as Jenni helped the agonised Nadine to her feet.

'*Merde!*' she muttered, still grimacing. Then she managed a small grim smile. 'If whisky has this effect on me, I must really be bad.'

Jenni supported her and Ravi ran to help on the other side. When they reached the thorn bushes, he walked away and kicked stones, trying not to look over to where the marvellous crocodile lady was obviously in much pain. Jenni, trying to shield Nadine's dignity, glared at the moustachioed guard who had no such discretion. Smoking a *beedie*, he stared insolently at the women. After several minutes of spasm, Nadine lay back on the ground.

'There's nothing more to come,' she said faintly.

Jenni and Nathan helped her back to bed where she lay looking suddenly very small, her face a horrible bluish-white, her eyes closed.

Jenni felt her forehead. 'She's freezing now.'

'Diarrhoea still?' Nathan asked.

Jenni shook her head. 'She's retching bile.'

'She needs help.' He paused and shook his head. 'That and angina – it's too much.'

Jenni bent over Nadine. 'Here, try a sip.' She poured some water from the bottle into a clay saucer and held it to her friend's lips. Nadine sipped obediently, then clenched her teeth in obvious pain, her hand clutching her chest. She lay back breathless.

Jenni felt panic rising. 'Is your chest bad too?'

Nadine managed to nod. Jenni's terrified eyes caught Nathan's. 'We must get help. Where's Wanita?'

Kalidas had been standing at the window. He turned and murmured something.

Nathan frowned. 'She's not here, just the three guys.'

He went to the window and called out and one of the men shouted back that Wanita would be back soon.

Ravi had followed Jenni and Nadine into the hut and stood worriedly watching all that happened. He came forward now quietly and looked up at Nathan, but Nathan was too preoccupied to notice. The boy put out his hand and tugged at Nathan's filthy white shirt which bore little resemblance to the saintly garment it had once been. Looking down at the boy, his face sweet with affection, Nathan touched his head tenderly and asked him what he wanted.

Jenni and Kalidas watched curiously as the child put his hand into the front of his holey vest and, very shyly, pulled out the familiar small glass bottle filled with little white pills.

Jenni gasped in amazement. 'It's her heart pills. He must have found them after Ramdas threw them away.'

Nathan bent down and hugged the boy who was overcome by shyness, but smiled nevertheless. Then, looking up at Nathan and round at the others, he very deliberately took his right index finger, put it slowly to his lips and shook his head, his eyes enormous.

Still hugging him, Nathan promised him that they would say nothing. From the bed Jenni beamed her gratitude towards the little boy and mimed that she too would be silent.

The pills in fact had disappointingly little effect. Nadine took one immediately but reacted by retching violently. Then she lay back quietly, looking very strained. As it grew dark she slept intermittently. Kalidas still stood staring out of the window opening – he hadn't spoken for ages – and Nathan sat and played cat's cradle with the sleepy Ravi who at last fell asleep, his head across Nathan's chest. Jenni, watching them, felt almost envious, and recognised that in this situation Nathan might have to miss out on his evening meditation.

At one point Nathan looked up towards Kalidas and asked something. The driver, half-smiling, answered and pointed outside. After gently laying down the sleeping boy on the bunch of rags which was his bed, Nathan rose to look out too. He stared for a while then came over to Jenni and sat beside her.

'What's happening out there?' she asked. 'Any sign of Wanita or food?'

He shook his head. 'She hasn't come back, but the guards have found a whisky bottle.'

'It was full – a litre bottle. We bought a couple in Duty Free.'

'I think they're pretty drunk.'

Jenni shivered. 'Let's hope it doesn't make them trigger-happy.'

When it was almost completely dark but for a faint silvering of moonlight, the other two saw Kalidas go over to his bed and sit down. He didn't speak but they heard him reach for his shoes which were lying on the floor and heard him slowly put them on.

Nathan looked at him. 'Going for a walk?' he asked.

Kalidas nodded bashfully. He picked up his cotton jacket and, walking to the window, looked out towards the men who were drinking noisily by the fire. Then he bent down quickly and picked up something which he tucked in to his shirt. Jenni realised with surprise that it was the black enamel paintbox. Puzzled, she watched Kalidas's silhouette as he returned to the window and called quietly to the men outside.

There was raucous laughter, a shout, and an almost interminable pause before the wooden bolts were pulled aside again. One of the men, heavy-eyed and grinning inanely, but still clutching his rifle, peered in, swaying slightly. Kalidas told him he needed to go to the bushes and the man grunted, motioning with the gun for him to go out.

Nathan and Jenni sat quietly together.

'What did you do back in the States?' she asked, surprised as she did so that they had not had this particular conversation before.

'I was a musician.' He put his head back against the hut wall and looked at her sideways.

They had been talking for perhaps fifteen minutes when they realised that Kalidas had not come back. Then they heard two shots followed quickly by a third.

'My God!' Jenni leapt up. 'What's going on?'

Nathan rushed to the window and they both peered out but it was too dark to see anything except the fire where the men had been sitting. They heard shouting, only much louder and angrier even than the usual. At first there were only men's voices, then there was the sound of a horse arriving and they heard Wanita's voice too. She was obviously enraged and making a lot of noise.

'I can't bear this!' Jenni was crying with tension. 'I can't bear it if they've hurt him again or killed him. It's too bloody much.'

She wept, then to her amazement she felt Nathan's arms round her. He hugged her and she sank down and wept against his lean hard chest with marvellous relief.

Ravi woke at this point, asking what was wrong.

There was a terrible thud as the hut door was flung open and Wanita appeared, yelling like a madwoman. Behind her, Ollie Hardy, also carrying a gun and a dangerously flaming torch, swung about unco-ordinatedly. Nathan and Jenni leapt apart and stared at Wanita's flailing shape. Obviously something bad had happened and she blamed them. Her virago yelling continued for some time, then stopped abruptly. Nadine, oblivious, moaned from the bed, Ravi started crying and Jenni, desperate, turned to Nathan and shouted: 'What on earth is happening?'

'It's Kalidas,' he said. 'He knocked one of the guards unconscious. He's escaped.'

Sixteen

At the mission house Father Francis, in celebratory mood, appeared from the garden carrying a basket of vegetables and smiled at Michael.

'Antony is the cook for tonight but I will help him a little as we will have so many pleasant guests.' He pulled out a large marrow and examined it minutely before setting about slicing it with a murderous-looking knife, humming to himself as he did so.

'Beautiful, beautiful,' he murmured appreciatively, nibbling a small piece of the crunchy vegetable.

Michael, sitting at the table relaxing with a mug of tea, watched him. 'Can I be of any assistance?'

When Francis smiled, the thick lenses of his spectacles made his eyes look as large and benign as a labrador's. 'Not at all. You may rest until they come. Perhaps you would like to bathe before they arrive? They will all be eager to use the water so it is better if you use the bathroom now.'

'When do you think they'll get here?'

The little priest chopped dexterously. 'I am frankly surprised they're not yet here, but perhaps they have been held up at one of the projects.'

Michael fetched a towel and clean clothes and went to wash and shave. There was hot water which you carried yourself in a bucket, then poured over yourself with a jug. He examined his face in the mirror and carefully removed the navy blue stubble, shampooed and washed, and splashed on a modest bit of after-shave. Straddled before the mirror, much too low for his gaunt frame, he parted and combed his hair which was wild from his vigorous towelling. Clean and wearing a favourite blue shirt Jenni had given him, he felt good when he rejoined the brothers in the kitchen.

Francis and Antony were busily cooking. Michael inhaled the rich smells of ginger and freshly chopped coriander.

'It smells very good.'

'I hope you'll like it. We don't make very highly spiced food, but we have fine vegetables this year. We enjoy the garden.'

Antony, busy with flour and water, smiled. 'Some of us enjoy it more than the others,' he observed mildly.

'I like it,' said Francis simply. 'Have you seen our garden, Michael?'

'Not really.'

'You should go and look what we grow there.'

Michael wandered out into the pink evening and enjoyed the sunset. There were banana palms, *chico* and orange trees, a magnificent flower garden with riotous blooms, and an impeccable vegetable plot where beans, peas, sweet corn, onions and potatoes grew in abundance. He lit a cigarette and sat quietly, enjoying the noise of birds and the richness of colour which was everywhere. A large lizard stared at him as he watched a young family in the field across the way. The pretty young mother, her skirts pulled up above her knees, was giggling as she and her husband ran after a lost kite which had got caught up in a tree. They gazed up into the branches, their two small children shouting and pointing upwards, and tried to ease the trapped kite down by pulling at the pink string.

Francis had explained that the pink kite strings were dipped in powdered glass so that they could cut down their opponent's kites in mid-flight. The first task this morning had been to present each boy in the mission primary school with one. The kites – all hand made, of tissue paper stretched on bamboo – were a cottage industry in Gujarat. Square in shape and all different, hand-painted in brilliant designs with chequers, circles, dots and fishes, every single one had a small streamer of tissue tied on with gold or silver paper. They cost only one rupee – about a halfpenny each in English money – so the mission could afford to be generous. Michael smiled as he remembered how the beaming Francis had looked as he dispensed the magic toys from his rainbow armful of paper squares.

Michael wandered over the darkening field to see if he could help get a hold of the trapped pink and orange kite but it remained firmly stuck in the branches. He admired the fat baby of the family who was sitting playing with a necklace of marigolds, blissfully chewing the orange petals. He tickled the baby under the chin, and chatted in sign language with the young parents – the father half-toothless, grinning amiably beneath his checked headcloth. Michael was sad to see that the woman, though apparently friendly, kept discreetly wiping at the baby's face where Michael had caressed it. He looked at his watch. It was almost seven-thirty and would be dark in a minute. Where the hell are they?

'Did Kalidas tell you he was going to run away?' asked Jenni. She could see Nathan's tall shape standing in the window, black against the night sky. Wanita's shouting had been very fierce; she blamed them for his escape and they had all feared for their lives for some minutes before the dacoits had locked them up again.

'Not a word. He's always been quiet.'

'What do you think he'll do?'

'I'm not sure. He does know the territory well, so he'll probably try to get to the main road and maybe walk or try to get a lift.'

'But where to? The police? I wouldn't trust that lot an inch.'

'I doubt it. He might try to get back to Kundi and ask for help there.'

'How could they help?'

'I guess they'd contact the embassies.'

'All three – English, French and American?'

'It could make a big stink. I just hope he gets somewhere quickly before these people get too impulsive.'

'Atilla hasn't come back yet.' Jenni stood up and peered out into the darkness. The fire was still glowing and she could dimly see two figures beside it. 'And where's the guy Kalidas clunked with the paintbox?'

Nathan chuckled. 'It hadn't struck me that that was why he

168

was taking it. The victim is lying over there under the brushwood shelter where they sometimes sleep.'

'D'you think he was badly hurt?'

'I guess it was the whisky as much as the rather unusual weapon,' said Nathan drily.

'It's almost nine. D'you think we'll get any food tonight?'

'No. It's punishment time for us from what she said. Wanita is so hopping mad and scared, I don't think she knows what to do at all.'

'She must be wondering whether to move us. After all, if Kalidas did go to the police they could be here in a few hours. That's surely what she would be afraid of.'

'I guess so. She might even want to . . .' He paused.

'Get rid of us?' Jenni tried to see his face, but there was a cloud over the moon so it was too dark.

'She's frightened enough to do anything.'

'What do you think has happened to Ramdas? He's been away all day.'

'My guess is that they were both trying to locate the mysterious missing gentleman.'

Jenni laughed hollowly. 'The MI5 one who was after my body?'

'That's the one.'

On her bed Nadine stirred. Jenni went to her at once, felt her hot brow, gave her some water and wiped her face.

'How are you doing?' she asked softly.

'Weak, no strength, but I'm not sore at the moment. It's just if I move.'

'Hungry?'

'No.'

'There doesn't seem to be anything, so that's lucky.'

Nadine moved around on the bed and groaned angrily. 'Damn it, I hate to feel like this.' She lay back, obviously uncomfortable. 'And Kalidas – he really ran away?'

'He really did.'

'Maybe he will get help?'

'We just hope they won't move us before he does.'

'Yeah, that could be bad. She's a crazy one, that Wanita. Like a kid really, but dangerous.'

'Mmmm.' Jenni stroked her arm and encountered the

169

heavy silver bracelet – the four-inch-long cylinder, intricately clasped and beautifully engraved with images of fish and sun. She looked at it. 'Wouldn't you be more comfortable with that off?' she asked.

'No. I like to keep it, it's almost part of my body.' Nadine chuckled weakly. 'Like the Tin Man, eh?' She touched Jenni's cheek softly. 'You are a good girl. I love you, you know, as though you were my own.'

Jenni blinked. 'I love you too.'

'One day,' Nadine's voice was quiet, 'I would like you to have the bracelet. I know you've always liked it.'

'No.' Jenni drew back. 'It's yours. I can't imagine you without it.'

'I mean when I'm gone.'

'Shut up.' Jenni, gripped Nadine's hot hand tightly.

'It's OK, I'm not dead yet.'

Jenni wanted to howl.

'I'm cold though.' Nadine shivered.

'Here.' Jenni fetched a ragged cover from Kalidas's bed and tucked it round her. 'Better?'

'Thanks. I'm just so tired – ' She sighed a thin juddering sigh.

'More water?' asked Jenni.

'No.' It was almost a whisper.

'What about another of your bombs?'

'Maybe one.'

Jenni took one of the tiny pills out of the bottle and gave it to her to dissolve under her tongue. She watched the outline of Nadine's head on the bed and stayed by her until her breathing was regular and she appeared to be asleep. Nathan, sitting near the window, called quietly to her.

'Come and sit beside me.'

She did so and shivered.

'You chilly?' he asked.

'Freezing.'

He took off his tattered cotton blanket and wrapped it round them both so they were cocooned together. Then he put his arm round her.

'Better?'

'Mmmm.' She leaned against him. They sat together

170

quietly until he heard her sniff. He turned to look at her, and she tried to hide her face but he put his hand out to her cheek and wiped her tears. She saw his face silvered by the small moon which was now in full view from where they sat.

'I'm sorry.'

'You're very fond of her, aren't you?'

Jenni gulped. Then, without realising it, she found herself folded in his arms, weeping on his chest.

Nathan, holding her, experienced a strange unfurling of memories and emotions. He remembered the dead girl, Laura, and how good it had once been to hold her and make love with her; and he remembered the awful pain that had overwhelmed him when she killed herself – his guilt, rage and sorrow. He had almost forgotten those feelings. Dazed, he felt his body stir in animal response to the warm presence of the sobbing woman in his arms and held her closer to him. There were other memories too, vile ones. He hardly realised what he was doing when he bent his face towards her wet cheeks. Almost without thinking he found her lips, searching like his own, yearning for contact and affection, as they met in a long kiss.

At nine o'clock Francis declared that they must eat the supper which had been prepared to welcome the expected guests or it would be wasted.

'Maybe they had a mechanical problem,' he said hopefully, offering Michael water from the jug.

'Surely they would have got a telephone message to us?'

Brother Antony, who was obviously worried, smiled. 'It's not so simple to telephone here. You have to do it through the operator and our local one is probably already asleep with her chickens and goats.'

'They might simply have broken down far from a telephone,' reasoned Father Francis. 'We mustn't worry.' He turned to Michael. 'We teased them so much about dacoits.'

'There are dacoits though, aren't there?'

Francis sighed as he served out the aromatic vegetables and rice. 'A few.'

'When do we start getting really worried?' Michael, looking at the food, realised that he didn't feel at all hungry.

Francis polished his spectacles on his apron. 'We can't do

171

anything until it's light. Then I suppose if they haven't turned up we should go and look for them. I know their itinerary and which projects NYAID have in that particular area. But I have faith that they will come soon.'

He was disappointed to see that Michael ate very little.

'There's so much of it, but perhaps you don't feel well?'

'I'm OK. Just anxious, I suppose.'

'She is an old friend of yours, Miss Jenni?'

Michael nodded. 'For several years. Nadine too.'

'They are both strong women. Is Miss Jenni married?'

Michael shook his head.

There was silence as they ate.

'Are you a married man, Michael?' asked Francis.

He paused. 'I – er –'

'You are divorced?' The question was quite straightforward.

'In the process of.'

'Ah.' Francis nodded. 'A pity, but it happens more and more these days, especially in the West, I understand.' He smiled. 'Here they sometimes assassinate the old wife when they get fed up with her by setting fire to the house when she's locked in it.' He shook his head cheerfully. 'I don't mean to suggest . . . but I really have had several of these cases in the last year.'

'It wasn't quite like that with me,' said Michael wryly. 'Painful, yes, but not overtly murderous.'

Francis was embarrassed. 'I really didn't mean to suggest – or to pry.'

'Don't worry,' Michael said amiably, 'I didn't take anything you said amiss.'

'Our lives here are so different.'

'I know.'

The young brother had made tea and was handing it round when the telephone rang. Brother Antony went to see who it was and the others waited expectantly. He came back after a couple of minutes looking bewildered.

'Any news?' asked Francis.

Antony shook his head. 'No, it was strange. It was that young American man – the blond fellow who helps run the School of Spiritual Travel at Kundi. He said he'd been trying for almost three hours.'

Michael sat up.

'He was asking if there was any news of the others. Apparently Maya is worried.'

'Why should she be worried?' asked Francis.

Antony shrugged. 'He didn't really say, but he made me promise that the moment we knew anything about where they were we should try to phone them back, even if it was the middle of the night.'

'Odd.' Michael looked at Francis for enlightenment.

'It is odd, but I understand that the guru there and Miss Nadine have a strong connection which goes back for many years.'

'But why should they suddenly phone?'

Francis shrugged. 'I don't know. Maybe they know something.'

'I'm sure they don't.' Antony sat down. 'They were simply worried. He said she had a bad feeling about it.'

'Mmmm.' Francis now looked really anxious.

Michael felt terribly dispirited. He wished that he had gone towards the dam today as he had suggested. He felt sure some lover's instinct would have brought him to Jenni: she had so often convinced him that lovers shared some magical extra-sensory perception. Suddenly weary, he stood up.

'I hope you'll excuse me,' he said, 'but if there's nothing we can actually do, I think I'll go to bed. Will you wake me if anything happens?'

Michael looked out of his bedroom window at the pale moonlight, listening uneasily to the unfamiliar noises of the Indian landscape. There was a man's wailing voice singing somewhere, and he was viscerally disturbed by a strange throbbing drum beat which became more and more frenzied. It sounded alien and almost frightening and he wondered what on earth it meant, until he realised to his chagrin that it was only the slow rotating of the roof fan which he had inadvertently turned on when he came into the room.

Once in bed he found he couldn't sleep at all. He kept remembering the bloody accident with the dying man with amber eyes who had begged him to take his gun. When at last he put out the light, the moonlight shone into the room and he was disturbed by the dive-bombing of mosquitoes. He got up and found a spray gun and sprayed the room all over, then he leapt about for a while with an old newspaper, swatting the insects who seemed impervious to the chemical though to Michael it was almost asphyxiating. When he looked at his watch it was half-past twelve and he was still wide awake. It was well after one when finally he thought he might manage to fall asleep.

Kalidas was running. He had given the thin man a hard thump on the temple with Nadine's paintbox, which he was still carrying, tucked into his shirt like a talisman. He had managed to hit him by telling him he had something to show him. The guard, woozy from booze, had wandered over to look at the little black box, then Kalidas had struck. The fellow, grunting horribly as the blow landed, had dropped his gun before falling to the ground. For an awful moment Kalidas though he might have killed him. Trembling, he bent down to listen but the man was still breathing heavily, arms sprawled out, mouth open and reeking of whisky.

Kalidas had hurriedly washed his hands and drunk from the water crock the guard had brought to refill. Then, without thinking, he had bent to pick up the gun and set off, running as fast as he could towards where he knew he would find the main road. He kept the gun with him until he reached the road then dumped it, hiding it under some brushwood beside a dry stone wall. There was just enough light from the young moon to see by, so he decided to cut across the hillside, knowing that he would save almost twenty miles that way. He was a strong young man, good on his feet, and when he was younger he had run and walked for miles in the countryside round Kundi. Two hours later, exhausted, he met up with the road again and reckoned that he was far enough away from the encampment to chance travelling along it for a while. He still had his bandage, but decided to take it off and wipe himself down as best he could. He was unshaven and knew the head wound must make him look pretty wild. He kept up a steady jog for ages. Only two lorries passed by, neither of which even slowed down when he signalled to them.

He had been running for a couple of hours when he heard a car. He turned and tried to see what it was, praying to his

174

tribal god that it was not going to be a police car. It turned out to be a local official who had been attending a meeting. He was not going as far as Kalidas had hoped and was obviously uneasy and curious as to what had happened to him, but he agreed to drop him off about five miles from Sapatdongri. Kalidas told him that he had been attacked and robbed in the Chittokundi Valley, and though the man appeared to believe him he was still not willing to go out of his way to help him.

He was exhausted and had no idea what time it was when at last he reached the mission. He reckoned that he must have escaped from the encampment after seven, and guessed from the state of the moon, to say nothing of his aching chest and shaking legs, that he had been on the move for at least seven hours. He arrived at the gates panting, and hung on the bars almost fainting. Then he saw that there was a light on in the kitchen.

He bent down to pick up a handful of gravel from the road and reached through the iron bars to throw it at the illuminated window, but missed. He waited for a moment, still breathless, then tried again. This time the gravel hit the glass, and a moment later the door opened and he saw a tall European man peering out; the man looked rumpled, and was wearing pyjamas under a woollen sweater. Kalidas called and the man came to him, a cup and saucer in his hand.

Kalidas spoke in Gujarati. Then, seeing the man didn't understand said, 'I Kalidas – driver – NYAID, Nathan, Jenni, Nadine . . .'

'Oh my God you'd better come in.' Michael put down his cup and tried to open the gates but they were bolted. Then he stood up, but seeing Kalidas slumped exhaustedly against the barrier, picked up his cup and handed it through the bars to him. '*Chai*,' he said. 'You drink.' He disappeared, but came back after a couple of minutes with a sleepy Father Francis, also in pyjamas, a brown stole wrapped round his shoulders against the chill of the night. Francis peered at the battered Kalidas for a moment before recognising him through the filth, then at once unlocked the gates to allow him in. He took the young man gently by the shoulder and, followed by Michael, whose heart was beating furiously, led them to the kitchen.

Seventeen

Wanita and Ramdas were arguing again. She was for moving the prisoners at once, but he was adamant.

'Kill them. Dump the bodies. Then if the man who ran away fetches help there will be no sign here that they ever existed.'

'Not possible,' said Wanita. 'Somebody, somewhere would find out. Anyway, what about these four?' She indicated the four men. The wounded Stan was lying nursing his head, Ollie and Rambo were in a drunken stupor, the fourth man, Manoj, was huddled blearily by the door of the hut. Sleep had become a problem for all of them. They were afraid to lose consciousness in case something happened, except for Ravi who was asleep beside them now, his face lit by the flicker of the fire, a pencil still clutched tightly in his hand.

Ramdas, his voice getting louder, was still for calling it a day and finishing the prisoners off. Wanita reminded him of what Nathan had said: he could get legal help so they would not be too severely punished.

That made Ramdas laugh horribly. Wanita watched him severely as he stood up and went over to the whisky bottle which still had an inch left in it. He unscrewed the top and gulped it down, smacking his lips.

Anyway, what about the man with yellow eyes? He had given them all those rupees. She patted the bag at her side meaningfully. He had promised more, much more. Perhaps he would still return.

Ramdas was quite certain. He knew the man would not come back. Forget it.

176

But why? Why would he waste his money if he didn't really want the Jenni woman? He had promised to pay more when she was delivered to him.

Ramdas looked as wise as he was able. He just knew, he told her. The man would definitely not come now.

'The old woman.' Wanita gesticulated towards the hut. 'She is ill. Very ill. If we move her she will die.'

Ramdas shrugged. Save yourself from worrying. Take her to the river or the chasm and hurry it up.

Wanita sat frowning for a while, her thoughts confused, though she said nothing to Ramdas. They were fine people. The Nathan man did good. He helped the tribals. She didn't feel able to kill him.

Ramdas eyed her sleepily. 'Come,' he said, and held out his arms. 'Let's rest a little. Nothing can happen in the night. The one who ran away has probably got lost in the hills or even been eaten by a jackal.' He laughed.

Wanita glared at the fire, her mind whirling.

'Come, my lovely,' he whispered, but she appeared not to bear.

'You like the white man?' he asked after a while.

She shrugged. Nathan did appear gentle and understanding. And he was handsome. Thoughtfully, she stoked the embers with a stick.

Ramdas came closer to her and caressed her rigid arm. 'You do fancy him, eh?' His hand brushed her cheek. She frowned impatiently as he nuzzled her neck.

'But I am your lover.' He grinned up at her lazily and moved even closer. Wanita glanced anxiously towards the men; one of them had turned on to his side and was snoring like a grandfather.

'They are asleep,' whispered Ramdas, his hand playing with her breast.

'Mmmm?' he said, still fondling.

She drew back and glanced over to the guard beside the hut who nodded to her.

Wanita stood up abruptly. She was holding the gun and bent to lift up the blanket she had been sitting on. She looked down at Ramdas and lifted her head. 'Come,' she commanded.

177

He sighed with satisfaction. Heaving himself up, carrying a gun and a blanket, he followed his leader until they were out of sight of the hut and the dying fire.

In the kitchen of the mission it would soon be three o'clock: the time when the most devoted Travellers at Kundi awoke to greet their particular dawn. The exhausted Kalidas had eaten and drunk, and told the horrified Michael and Francis his story. They could hear him now in the wash room, splashing as he removed the grime of the last three days. Father Francis had decided to leave Antony sleeping, but he appeared now, rumpled, a *lunghi* round his waist, torso bare.

'What's happening?' he asked, bewildered.

Francis poured him some tea and explained briefly that Kalidas had escaped and the other three remained imprisoned by dacoits. Antony listened in amazement, then stood up abruptly.

'What are you doing?' asked Francis.

'I promised that I would phone the Peter man at the ashram.'

'So early?'

'He said whenever we had any kind of news.' Antony turned to look at Kalidas, who entered the dining-room, freshly washed and barbered, dressed in clothes lent by Michael. He grinned down sheepishly at the jeans which he had had to turn up by several inches. Antony greeted the young man warmly, and Francis pottered about until he found a first aid box. He told Kalidas to sit, bathed his head with antiseptic and dressed it with a large pink plaster.

'I'm surprised they don't make elastoplast in the right colour here,' said Michael.

'Maybe you should patent the idea,' said Francis.

'Brown elastoplast for Indian nationals?'

'Of all colours and castes – we could call it Elastocaste,' Francis giggled.

Antony told Kalidas that he was about to phone Kundi and asked if he would like to come with him. Kalidas nodded and they went out together.

'I thought you had a phone here?' said Michael.

Francis nodded. 'We do, but at this time of night the

178

operator will be asleep and they will have to wake her up in order to be connected.'

'Ah.' Michael nodded, then looked at Father Francis closely. 'We must have a plan of campaign. What do you suggest we do?'

Francis sat for a while, frowning. 'It is not easy. I don't really want to tell the police; they are not a reliable bunch here. I also feel that there's an element of urgency.'

'Exactly. The dacoits sound as if they may well panic now that Kalidas has escaped. They'll be expecting a police posse, therefore Jenni and the others are in imminent danger. If they do panic, heaven knows what might happen.'

'I agree. We must act quickly.'

'But we're unarmed. They've got four guns that we know of. We only have the one Kalidas took – that is if he can find it – and I presume that there wasn't a lot of ammunition with it?'

'He said he took about ten cartridges.' The little brother looked up at Michael. 'I am a man of peace, but sometimes I must confess I believe in being pragmatic.'

'I am not a man of peace in the sense that you are, but I am a pacifist at heart. Nevertheless I agree with pragmatism and even violence in extreme cases, and this is obviously an extreme case.'

Francis sighed heavily and gazed into his empty tea cup. 'Michael, can you handle a gun?'

'I can as it happens. I used to shoot clay pigeons a long time ago.'

'Clay pigeons?' Francis paused. 'It's not quite the same as an armed man or woman.'

'The mechanics are the same.'

Francis's eyes were large and sad. 'Unfortunately it is not mechanics I am talking about.'

'I appreciate that, but this all seems rather theoretical anyway.'

Francis looked at him thoughtfully. 'Perhaps.'

Michael watched him keenly but the plump face was inscrutable.

Antony and Kalidas came back after some time to say that the operator was trying to put a lightning call through to Kundi. They went into the adjoining room where the mission telephone was kept in a wooden box. Eventually Antony came to tell the others that he had got through to Kundi and had even spoken to the guru who sounded very disturbed.

'Did they have any suggestions?' asked Francis.

'No.' She said she wanted to go to try to reason with the dacoits, but she would like to speak to you first.'

'Ah.' He got up. 'She is waiting?'

Antony nodded and Father Francis scuttled away. Michael was impressed by how quickly he could move when pushed.

'What does Kalidas think we should do?' asked Michael.

Antony spoke to the driver, then translated his answer.

'He thinks we should go as quickly as possible. Immediately. To surprise them.'

'Unarmed?'

'He says that we can find his gun, and use it to frighten them, that they can be surprised if we are quick and make some sort of diversion with noise. At least two of the men were very drunk when he left and one of them was out for the count. They'll be extremely hungover. That only leaves the woman who is very aggressive but sometimes listens to Nathan, the big man who sounds pretty violent, and the little boy.'

Michael stood up. 'I'm game, but I'd like a cricket bat or something to wave if nothing more.'

Francis returned. He had spoken to Maya but they hadn't yet formed a plan. Michael told him that they all three were ready to leave at once. He asked if there was a reliable vehicle and how near it would take them to the hideout.

'Our Mahindra four-wheel drive vehicle can handle very rough roads.'

Kalidas drew a plan of the encampment.

'Right.' Michael took control. 'I suggest that we attack from four different places. They seem to be in a sort of natural amphitheatre of small hills, so if we come at them from here and over here.' Kalidas nodded and showed them where he thought there were trees and bushes.

'OK, let's get dressed quickly. I'll meet you outside.'

Michael went to his room and was surprised to find Francis at his heels. 'Please,' said the priest very quietly, 'when you are ready, will you be kind enough to come to my room? It's across the yard, through the main doorway and the first door on the left.' He giggled a little nervously. 'Knock and it shall be opened.'

Puzzled, Michael nodded and went to find comfortable garments and a pair of training shoes. He dressed as fast as he could, tying the knots of his laces with deliberate care, thinking all the time of Jenni. Jenni in danger and Nadine ill – critically so from the sound of it. The whole business sounded highly dangerous, but how wise was it to presume that they must use violence? It could so easily end in a stupid bloodbath if they did. They should try to parley first.

He put out the light after checking his room and at the last moment pocketed the Swiss Army knife Jenni had given him during their first ecstatic months together. Since then he must have used it once a day; it was a useful object to have on an expedition like this. When he got outside he saw by the feeble electric light that Kalidas was already waiting for them by the vehicle. Antony had gone to warn the third brother, who was to stay behind and alert the various authorities of what was happening if he hadn't heard from them by the following evening.

Still curious, Michael went quickly across the yard and knocked as instructed on Francis's bedroom door. He answered at once and ushered Michael in to his cell-like room which was as plainly furnished as a monk's bedroom should be, except that it was cluttered and obscured with papers and over-spilling files heaped higgledy-piggledy everywhere. Francis was wearing gym shoes, old jeans and a too tight tee-shirt, topped by a jacket which had obviously once been part of the suit he used in court. On top of all this he wore his brown shawl, wrapped round him like a huge scarf. He was flushed with excitement and looked more than a little comical.

'Michael, I have to tell you I have reached a decision.'

Michael eyed him curiously.

Francis sat down on his unmade bed and wiped his brow with an aged hanky. 'I do not find it easy.'

Michael glanced at his watch. It was almost a quarter to three; they must get going if they were to strike at dawn. They had said it was a two-hour drive and then more into the hills.

'I told you that we have experienced some violence in the past – difficulties with beatings and threats?'

181

Michael nodded. Maybe the guy was simply scared, and no wonder. He was obviously a bit out of his depth playing commandos. Michael could sympathise.

'I want to show you something,' said Francis, getting up. 'These were put here rather against my better judgment by some friends of the mission after all the violence started.' He watched as the priest knelt awkwardly on the floor by a wooden cupboard built into the wall. He pulled open the door and proceeded to fiddle about with the wooden base of its interior, prodding the cracks between planks with a biro which promptly snapped.

'Let me help.' Michael joined him. 'Perhaps you could use this?' Pleased to find a use for it, he handed the priest the Swiss Army knife.

'Quite perfect. Thank you.'

Whatever situation he was in, Francis managed to maintain an endearing formality. He eased out a couple of boards at least and sat back.

'There we are.' He handed back the knife to Michael and reached in beneath the floor. Michael watched in amazement as Francis took out one, two, then three cotton-wrapped packages which turned out to contain rifles; all – from the look of them – well-oiled and useable. Then he reached further into the hole and brought out a plastic bag of cartridges.

'Right,' he said brightly. 'Now I think we're ready.'

At Kundi a lot was happening. The old man Pradip was still fast asleep, dreaming of tigers and blue-eyed British generals in dress uniform, when he was woken by the sound of voices and the half-familiar thrum of an engine. Puzzled, he climbed off his string bed, pulled on his ancient tweed jacket, slipped his piebald feet into worn leather slippers and shuffled out to discover what was happening in the main courtyard. It was all lit up, and he was amazed to see the guru Maya – fully dressed and shawled against the early morning chill – standing there beside the ashram bus. The driver was already in the vehicle which was half-filled with sleepy Yellow People. Peter was writing down names on a clip-board list, checking each devotee as he or she climbed on to the bus where a bony woman with a flat rush basket was handing out food packages.

182

The guru Maya was talking to the people as they stood waiting to climb up the steps of the bus.

'Think of it, my friends, as a practical exercise in gentle power. It is a wonderful opportunity to make real what we believe. We must be like shining beacons for the world, and today we will act together to show how strong and powerful a group of people who share a spiritual reality can be.'

She was radiant like a goddess. Pradip, not fully under-standing the words but feeling the enormous strength of her, stared in wonder and watched as the bus filled up almost to bursting.

'That's it,' he heard the Peter man say, 'with the mini bus and this lot we will be seventy.'

'Good.' She nodded then gazed at the Travellers on the bus, touched her hand to the gold dot in the centre of her forehead and beamed lovingly at them, right palm lifted. The passengers on the bus returned the double gesture, their faces openly adoring. As the doors were slammed shut, a strange singing started up from within the vehicle. Pradip's skin prickled as he listened. He had often heard chanting before at Kundi, it was an everyday event, but this morning he found the noise the Travellers made both eerie and moving and wished he could join in. The vehicle revved up and two strong young men went to pull open the heavy wooden gates of the palace as the minibus bearing the guru and eight or nine other exalted Liberated Ones – immaculately white-garbed and gold-dotted even at this unearthly hour – closely followed by the crammed bus, everybody singing, drove down the hill towards the black lake and beyond.

'Why not?'

Still locked in the hut, the frustrated Jenni looked towards the shadowy bulk that was Nathan. They were at this point both kneeling, facing each other like people in a Japanese ritual, but no longer with any part of their bodies touching. His embrace had felt so sweet, so intimate and right; best of all it had been manifestly obvious that he wanted her as much as she wanted him. But that was just before the awful moment when he had drawn away from her.

'I'm sorry, Jenni.'

183

She felt his hand on her cheek again which this time made her angry.

'Please don't do that. Don't start it all over again. *I'm* not a bloody celibate!'

'You told me not long ago you would like to be.'

Damn him! She still felt incredibly aroused. Why did he ever start this hopeless business? She clenched her hands and tried to control her breathing which, to her chagrin, was displaying a strong tendency to burst into sobs, but she had played that scene once and look where it had led.

'Maybe I did feel that way for a few days when I was at Kundi.'

'What happened to the thought?' he asked gently.

She made a noise that was half laugh, half sob, but definitely bitter, and hoped that he couldn't see her wiping her nose on her sleeve. 'I suppose if I'm honest I started to get interested in you. But when you found me yelling – remember? – I'd already decided that it wasn't for me.'

'I'm fond of you too, Jenni. You are a strong intelligent woman. Brave too.'

'But you don't fancy me?' She was laughing and crying now, uncontrollably.

'It's not as simple as that.' His voice was pained. 'You know very well that I do find you attractive. I guess it must have been obvious.'

'It was rather.' Jenni said at last. She was aware that she sounded almost like her mother. Prim and non-committal, expecting nothing.

'Look, I've been like this for a long time. I used to be a normal hot-blooded American boy. I had affairs, ended up with a wife. I loved sex, enjoyed my orgasms.'

'And now you prefer spiritual ones?'

'Spiritual orgasms?' He laughed a little. 'That's a good phrase. Yeah, I do. They can be just as exciting.'

She looked at him steadily, trying to make out his eyes. 'So what happened to you? How can you cut off from your sexuality? It's unnatural.'

'For me it's right. I have my relationship with my God and my spiritual journey to make. That is now – and has been for several years – by far the most important thing in my life. I

184

have a voluntary association with something higher than me, an aspiration to be a better, purer human being.'

'I think you could apply some of that to me too, but I don't negate my physicality. I know that I need to find a balance in my life.'

'Exactly. Celibacy helps me to keep in balance, in a state of communication with my spiritual being.'

'No regrets?'

'None. It's a choice I've willingly made.'

He was, she felt, a little too emphatic.

'You still haven't told me what happened to make you become so immersed in the whole Kundi doctrine?'

'It's just made total sense to me. I felt happy and found my spiritual life became more important than sex or individual love. Now I am free to love the whole world – liberated.'

'God, Nathan, sometimes you speak in pop song clichés. "I have no regrets." "I love the world."' She sang to him now: '"I got de whole wide world in my hands".'

'Excuse me, lady, but you were the one who asked if I had no regrets. Be fair.'

This time she had the grace to laugh. It was easier than crying, and she liked him too much to go on being angry.

'I love you, Jenni. You are a soul with whom I feel an incredible connection, a deep affinity, just as I do with Nadine and Maya. You are my beloved friends. I also particularly love or have an affection for certain people I work with, but I don't any more want to have a single bonded relationship.'

She decided to go right in. 'What happened to your marriage, Nathan?'

There was a long sigh and he didn't answer.

'Don't you want to talk about it?'

'Not really. It seems irrelevant now. It was a long time ago. We were extremely happy for a while.'

'I presume you divorced?'

His breathing was surprisingly loud and spasmodic, but his voice was quiet. 'No, we didn't.'

Jenni didn't say anything. She sat for a while puzzling over possible storylines for the demise – without the finality of divorce – of Nathan's marriage, but didn't get very far.

Finally, he spoke. 'Do you think when you get home you will meditate at all?'

'*If* I get home you mean. And don't change the subject, Nathan. I used to meditate sometimes before I came to India anyway, so I expect I shall, but I won't wear yellow or a dot, nor will I be celibate and teetotal – that is if I can find a lover I like. It's easier said than done.'

Nathan would have liked to tell her that he felt they might well have been lovers in a previous incarnation, but didn't think she would accept that idea too readily.

Instead he asked: 'You don't have a man in your life?'

Damn him, why did that particular question make her want to cry?

'You don't seem to keen to talk about that one,' observed Nathan. This time when he reached out and touched her on the arm, she knew with a pang that it was as a friend.

They both turned simultaneously at a grunt from Nadine.

'Jenni,' she called faintly. 'I don't feel good.'

Jenni jumped up and went to her. Nadine was very hot, her face, hardly visible in the feeble moonlight, clenched in pain.

'Where does it hurt?' asked Nathan, leaning over her.

'All over.' She gestured and they saw her hand move in front of her. 'My chest – I think I need another pill.'

'OK.' Jenni scrabbled for the water bottle on the floor.

'Take some of this first.' She helped Nadine to drink the muddy liquid, then gave her a pill and bathed her gently as she lay back to allow it to take effect.

'It's helping,' said Nadine after a while. Then she murmured, 'I wish we had some music,' and seemed to fall asleep.

Nathan was leaning over her. 'Her breathing is getting steadier.'

'What on earth are we going to do?'

They both went and looked out into the night. The fire was glowing and the man they called Rambo was sitting staring towards the hut. He looked pretty fed up, sitting there smoking, his rifle across his knees.

'I guess we just have to sit it out. Let's hope Kalidas gets help.'

'I hope he'll bring a doctor if he does. Nadine's very weak – her ankles and fingers are swollen.'

'Any idea what that means?'

'Not really. It's called oedema, and I think it's bad. Heart or blood pressure. My sister-in-law had it when she was pregnant. They whipped her into hospital very fast.'

Nathan sighed. 'I don't think I can sleep yet, I'm wide awake. How about you?'

She could think of a good way to help them both towards sleep but refrained from pressing the point. Remembering the feeling of his body against her own, Jenni sighed too.

'Come and sit.' Nathan looked towards her. She could see his eyes now. 'Where were we?' he asked as Jenni came near him under the window, huddling herself inside a blanket.

'You were about to tell me about your marriage.'

'And you were about to tell me about the man who hurt you so much.'

She was astonished by his perceptiveness but didn't tell him so. Instead she by-passed the challenge for a while. She would prefer him to go first. She had a feeling it might take quite a while; there was obviously a lot more there than just a broken marriage. She could still smell old pain on him, despite Kundi and all that spirituality.

'Nathan, you know what you were asking me – about meditating and spiritual beliefs?'

'Yeah.'

'Well, I've been thinking about all that for the last couple of days and I confess that I became very involved and emotional at Kundi. I got high on the whole thing, and for a few days – that elevated, shining attitude to a better way of being that the Travellers have, is highly infectious – I almost wanted to stay there forever.'

He grunted.

'Well, now I think it was because I was in a bad way. I was upset and tired – unhappy for many different reasons, too many to go into – possibly near to crack-up. I was extremely vulnerable. Kundi was like balm to my hurt mind. It made life suddenly seem possible and even simple. But I really believe it was a cop-out. A flirtation with God. Too simplistic.'

'I can promise you that being a Traveller is no way simple.'

'I appreciate that, but it seemed to offer me a grid, a pattern

187

to live by. It does that for those who decide to go on the Journey, doesn't it?'

'Yeah, I guess so, that makes sense.'

'And I found that very seductive – so seductive that I even started imagining completely changing my lifestyle.'

'Well, plenty of people do. Maybe you still will.'

'No, Nathan. I know I won't. That day on the picnic I realised who I was and what I was. I returned to myself.'

'That's the day I met you screaming in the wilderness, huh?'

'Yes.'

'Well, all I can say is that if that's the real you, it looked pretty wild.'

'I can be quite wild. It's part of me, a precious part of me, and I don't want to lose it. It has to do with my creativity. It's the same for Nadine.'

'Why do you think you'd lose it?'

'Because many of the Travellers I met seemed to have a blandness, a denial of reality as I know it. And the way they mouth the jargon . . . quite honestly I felt they were damping down the creative part of themselves. Perhaps because they were afraid of it. But I know that I can't abdicate from my passions, nor do I want to.'

'"Let passion rule, copulation thrive", you mean?'

'Don't tease me, Nathan. I think you know what I mean. But what I started to try to tell you at the beginning of all this harangue was that I decided a couple of days ago that what I actually am is an agnostic mystic. There now, how does that sound?'

'Agnostic mysticism. Sounds quite good. I think maybe we could still find a good few areas in common.'

They sat for a while, talked out, aching with hunger. There had been no food since breakfast. Then Nathan asked Jenni if she could sing.

'I love singing. Won't it disturb Nadine?'

'She said she wanted music, didn't she?'

'OK, Let's sing.'

Outside the hut, by the dying camp-fire, the sleepy guard whose drunken companions were still slumbering, listened bemusedly to the man's and the woman's voice working

188

through the repertoire of all the songs they knew. Papageno's song from The Magic Flute, Cole Porter, a couple of violin concertos, negro spirituals and childhood funnies. The tribal man grinned; it was good noise, utterly strange to him, but he smiled and jiggled in time to one or two of them, and when he heard gentle laughter from the two in the hut, he presumed they were arguing about what to sing next. Beside him little Ravi stirred in his sleep, twitching like a dog and murmuring excitedly as he dreamed. The tribal man, who was a benign enough fellow, covered the boy where his blanket had fallen off and patted the thin little back affectionately.

'My voice is going,' croaked Jenni after a couple of hours.

'Mine too. We should try to sleep. Anything could happen tomorrow.'

'Oh God, Nathan, do you think we'll come out of this alive?'

'I don't know. Are you afraid?'

'I feel afraid of losing Nadine more than anything.' She spoke in a whisper. 'Are you afraid?'

He shook his head. 'I once nearly died. I'd been very sick.'

'What was it like?'

'Wonderful. I could see a long tunnel ending in amazing shining light. I really wanted to go there. I knew it would be lovely – no worries.'

'Sweetness and light.' Jenni shivered. 'Sounds horrible. Me, I like it here.'

'Truly it wasn't horrible,' Nathan assured her. 'It changed my whole view of life.'

'You're not frightened of dying?'

'Not after that experience.'

'I'm certainly not ready to go yet.'

'Jenni, I think Kalidas will find help.'

'Unless they shift us, or decide to dispose of us.'

'Well. Let's hope he makes it soon.'

They sat in silence for a while. Nadine was asleep but breathing heavily.

'I know it doesn't help to say it, but I am so hungry,' said Jenni.

'I'm starving. They'll have to feed us in the morning when Wanita's calmed down a bit.'

They sat in silence for a long time.

'How do you know all the harmonies for all those songs? It was lovely,' asked Jenni at last.

'Like I said, music was my profession.'

'Of course! That explains it! What did you play?'

'Sax.'

'You never play now?'

'I don't have a sax any more.'

'Why?'

'Somebody beat it to death.'

'Come again?'

'Somebody killed it. Smashed it up.'

'Who? How?'

'It's a long story,' said Nathan. 'Lie down there and I'll tell you.'

Eighteen

Wanita woke with a start. She knew at once that Ramdas had gone, had run away and left her alone with this awful mess. It was still dark but there was a dawn glow just visible above the line of blue hills beyond the encampment. She turned and groped amongst the tangled blankets for a minute till she found the embroidered bag where she'd put the money. It was empty of course.

Of course! Madwoman that she was, she should have realised. She knew he was a piece of shit, the dirtiest filthiest piece of shit she could imagine. Ramdas the braggart, the strutter. The lover. She crouched on the ground, huddled in a blanket, cursing her own weakness.

In a terrible, inevitable way she had expected him to betray her long before this. But he was a good-looking traitor, strong too. He had pleasured her and she him until the world seemed upside down and dancing. She felt the stones on the ground hard on her forehead as she beat her head against them moaning quietly. She was still folded up, rocking slowly backwards and forwards, when some time later the most reliable of the four guards came up and stood near her.

'Wanita,' he called urgently. She heard his voice but could only just make out his dark shape against the sky.

'What is it, Manoj?' she asked wearily.

'It is the old woman. She is very sick. They are asking you to come.'

She didn't ask if Ramdas was there. There seemed no point. Anyway, if the old woman was sick, dying even, what

191

did it matter now? The old woman was lucky: she might soon be out of it.

'Are we nearly there?' asked Michael.

Antony was driving the mission Mahindra. 'Kalidas says it will take twenty minutes more. We turn off the main road in a minute – if we don't get stopped by some other bandits – then we drive for another three or four miles up the track, after which we walk for about half a mile.'

'OK.' Michael tried to relax. None of the four in the car was very chatty; they were almost silent until after several miles Kalidas leant forward, tapped Antony on the shoulder and said something in Gujarati. Antony nodded and a minute later when Kalidas spoke again, turned left up a narrower road and stopped the vehicle. Kalidas, after a quick look round, leapt out, went over to a dry stone wall and crouched down behind it. He emerged holding a gun and a bundle of cartridges, climbed back in and handed the cartridges to Francis. Then, carefully, he emptied out the gun and handed it to the priest who, bemused, asked if he didn't want to keep it. Kalidas shook his head and gestured no. The Jesuit, moved, patted the young man on the back.

'What's going on?' asked Michael.

Bashful, Kalidas pointed to himself. 'I like Gandhi. Not kill.'

'Ah.' Michael understood. He turned to Francis. 'Can you ask him if he will at least wave the gun? It would look a bit more effective.'

'He has said he will do that as long as it is empty,' Francis assured him. 'He is a fine boy. He is feeling unhappy about the man he has already hit.' The little priest was sitting forward clutching the dashboard as Antony started up the engine once more. 'I only hope they won't hear us coming.'

'Me too, but it sounds far enough away to be OK.'

Francis was gnawing his knuckle nervously.

'Shouldn't we have brought a doctor with us?' Michael asked suddenly. 'If Nadine is as ill as Kalidas says, we might need one.'

'I am trained in simple first aid and basic medicine,' said Francis. He felt in the glove compartment and pulled out a

192

tattered book. 'I have used this book often and studied it well. So has Antony.'

Using his lighter to see by, Michael peered at the book which was called *Where There Is No Doctor*. It looked pretty comprehensive.

In a part of the Chittokundi Valley where the big river runs parallel and close to the main road, a tribal farmer called Tulsiram had been up all night with one of his goats which had at last given birth safely. Tulsiram felt cheerful as he walked the few hundred yards back towards his little hut, up on the hillside in a grove of coconut palms which he could see now silhouetted against the dawn. He would do *puja* and light incense when he reached the house to thank the Mother Goddess for her kindness in watching over the animal and allowing her to produce her young ones safely.

Usually it was quiet in this part of the valley at night, except for an occasional long-distance lorry, but during his vigil which had concluded in success – fine twin goats – Tulsiram had witnessed two unusual sights that had made the night appear particularly auspicious. The first thing he had seen had been a turbaned horseman who looked like a warrior, riding along the road as if all the evil spirits of the world were after him. And a few minutes ago he had seen an even stranger sight: a small bus – followed closely by a big one – had driven past. In itself an unremarkable happening, but the luxury bus was filled with people wearing yellow. He could see clearly because the vehicle was lit up on the inside, and the passengers – Westerners mostly, as far as he could make out – were all singing. It was a strange chanting noise which he felt sure must be religious, it filled the air so hauntingly.

He stood to watch them past, mouth and eyes open in wonder. They smiled and waved to him, and many of them saluted him strangely. The smaller bus contained people in white who looked like gods or angels, and when he glimpsed a woman's face with great burning eyes like the Mother Goddess herself, he could have sworn that there was a light shining from her forehead.

Tulsarim had never seen anything like it in all his forty-eight years (he was an old man) and almost wondered now that it was silent but for the early morning trilling and cooing of waking birds if perhaps he had dreamed up the two busloads of singing yogis.

At a sign from Kalidas, Antony stopped the vehicle in a hollow by some sparse trees near a trickle of water.

'OK.' Michael, like the other three, had got out and stood watching as Francis carefully withdrew the three guns from the blanket in the back of the machine. 'Let's just do a final check and organise the ammunition.'

They all nodded and examined their weapons, Francis looking particularly serious.

Somewhat embarrassed, Kalidas stood awkwardly holding his.

'Ask him if he wants to change his mind,' said Michael.

Antony did so, and Kalidas shook his head, but promised he would wave the weapon convincingly.

'It means he is unprotected,' said Michael. 'I don't know if we should take him.'

Kalidas frowned. 'I come,' he said firmly.

'We can only pray that we don't actually have to use them, and if we do we must only try to frighten them, I presume?' said Francis anxiously.

'It depends,' said Michael. 'They sound to me like they mean business. We can but hope.'

'We will deploy so that we come at them from all sides, you said?' Francis obsessively removed and wiped his spectacles, which made his uncovered eyes look very vulnerable.

'I think that's probably best, but if you have a better idea . . .'

'Not at all, not at all. I simply worry about what we do if we can't see each other. For instance if one us is hidden behind the hut. We might shoot one of our own party.'

'True.' Michael frowned. 'But it would be best to come at them from behind the hut, it would give us some protection.' He took Kalidas's drawing out of his pocket and they all looked at it again and agreed as before to split up. Kalidas said something as Antony translated.

'He says that we can almost certainly all see the encampment from some boulders up here.' He pointed to the drawing. 'It is halfway round the encircling hill – which is only a little one, perhaps fifty feet high. As you said, like an amphitheatre.'

'OK.' Michael nodded. 'Let's go to the boulders so we can look down at it together. I think Kalidas should cause a diversion from here – ' he jabbed at the image again – 'and then we'll rush them.'

'Er, Michael,' Francis tapped on the arm.

'Yes?'

'I don't want to undermine your leadership,' he said mildly, 'but should we not synchronise watches?'

Jenni and Nathan had fallen asleep at last, but not until he had told her about the saxophone, though it hadn't really been about a sax, it had been a much worse story than the mere wrecking of a cherished musical instrument. She had listened horrified, knowing that he needed the protection of the darkness. She felt sure he had told nobody fully about it until now. It had made her feel much better about the sex – no longer personally rejected – though more than ever she felt that she would like to comfort him and show him that he could function normally and be ordinary again. Before they slept, she asked:

'Was the Indian guy who was so good to you in New York the same Ram who now works in London – the quiet efficient one who brought our group to Kundi?'

'The same.'

'Small world.'

'Yeah. Goodnight, Jenni.'

She knew he was asleep, and had hardly drifted off herself when she was woken by Nadine. In extremis.

She was vomiting again. Jenni guessed it was about two in the morning – Ramdas had removed all their watches early on. This time it all happened too fast to get Nadine outside, and anyway when Nathan summoned Rambo from the bonfire he spoke very fast and said he had been told to keep them locked up. Jenni wiped Nadine's burning body down as best she could. She was delirious, her fingers and wrists now as swollen as her ankles.

'We'll have to undo her bracelet,' said Nathan. He started

to fumble with the catch. It was hard to make out its workings in the tiny glimmer of light which filtered into the hut. Nadine tried feebly to resist him, but at last he managed to pull out the long silver pin which slotted through a series of clasps and remove the heavy silver cylinder.

'It needed to come off,' he said. 'Feel her wrist now.'

Jenni did so, her fingers, aware of the fast irregular pulse, travelled along the harsh ridges where the silver had cut into the swelling flesh.

'She'll forgive us.' She laid the bracelet down by the bed. 'Ugh. This place stinks.'

'It will stink more soon if they don't let us out.'

'Where the hell is Wanita?'

'They went off hours ago.'

'The horses too?'

'No. She and Ramdas. Into the sunset together sort of thing.'

'It must have been the weather,' murmured Jenni.

Nathan felt a great longing to embrace her once more. Telling her his story had been such a relief to him that he felt quite light-headed. Up till now he thought it had all been untangled. 'clarified' as Maya would say, but tonight had shown him that the sediment remained, ready to be stirred up to obscure his clarity. Only now he was beginning to wonder if that particular brand of enlightenment was still what he really wanted. More than once, when following Maya's teachings on the Journey, he had felt that the state of being a Liberated One was not really all he had hoped it would be. Always there seemed to be higher summits to attain, more complex knots to untangle.

Nadine had settled again. Jenni, after cleaning her as best she could and covering her tenderly, was sitting on the heaped rags of Kalidas's bed next to Nadine, ready to help her the instant she was needed. She watched as Nathan stood up and crossed purposefully over to the window.

'You have such practical plumbing you men,' she said enviously. 'I'll have to go in the corner. It's going to be unbearable here.'

Nathan fixed his clothes. 'Ours is useful in circumstances like these but your plumbing is capable of much cleverer tricks.'

196

'Vagina envy, eh?'

'It makes a change from the other one, but it's just as strong I think.'

'Maybe you're right.'

'Goodnight again,' Nathan settled into his nest.

'Goodnight, Nathan.'

Jenni remained sitting, wide awake. Her mind was full of violent images – Nathan's story for a start. That plus her own frustration, rage, and now this. Distractedly, she reached for the silver bracelet and sat fondling it. She hadn't told Nathan what it was she thought she had seen on Nadine's swollen inner wrist. It had been too dark to be really certain, and maybe she had imagined it, but if the blue marks were what she thought they were, this was obviously not the first time in her life that Nadine had been a prisoner.

The sky was blazing pink and gold by the time the Sapat-dongri group finally reached the boulders which gave them a view of the camp. They could just make out the shape of the hut and could see three sleeping figures by the remains of the fire. A fourth man was awake and walking around. They watched as he went over to the hut where he stood talking to the people inside.

Michael, watching intently, almost imagined that he could hear Jenni's voice, but it was too far away. The fellow gesticulated with his rifle and pointed. He seemed angry. Then, after a pause, he seemed to shrug and went to wake the men by the fire. They scrabbled up, clutching for their weapons, but one of them who was unsteady on his feet, had no gun. He tried to stand but sat down again suddenly. Kalidas grinned a little at this, and Francis asked him something at which he nodded self-consciously.

'He's glad he didn't actually kill him with the paintbox,' Father Francis whispered, and Michael watched nervously because he looked as though he was about to have the giggles. He worried about Francis as a man of action: the fellow was so good-natured, but he was also clumsy. Michael had feared on the way up the hill that he might trip over his gun, so eager had he been to reach the observation point.

All three dacoits were standing up now and the fat one was gesticulating.

197

'Where are the others?' Antony voiced what they were all wondering. They watched carefully as the first man, who had obviously been on duty, went off up the slope behind the hut.

'We could run down now and overpower them now,' hissed Francis.

'I don't think it's safe. Let's wait to see what that guy's doing. Maybe Wanita and the big bloke are up there.'

Nervously, they watched. Moments later, they saw a girl, also armed, striding down towards the hut, closely followed by the man who had gone to fetch her.

'Wanita,' whispered Kalidas. 'Ramdas not there.' He said something else and Francis whispered that Ramdas's horse was also missing.

They watched Wanita go to the hut and speak through the window. She had a powerful voice: the sound if not the content carried well. They saw her gesture to the dacoit who went to unbolt the door. It was tantalisingly impossible at this distance to discern who was inside the hut, but they saw the man and Wanita, guns at the ready, enter and shut the door behind them. The other men stood outside, one watching the hut, the others warily ranging the surrounding countryside.

'Right.' Michael nodded to the others. He thrust out his watch and they checked again for synchronicity. 'Let's deploy. We'll give it till a quarter to six, then Kalidas will throw the boulder. Keep your heads down – and good luck!'

Wanita slammed into the hut, followed by the guard. She didn't trust the prisoners at all now that the driver had escaped. She looked down at Jenni, kneeling by the old woman who was obviously very ill. When Nathan came towards Wanita, she at once gestured to him to stay with his back to the wall, hands on head.

'What do you want?' she demanded.

She looked manic today, plait awry, eyes staring. Frightening.

Nathan, talking quietly, said that the old woman was much sicker and growing weaker fast. Not for the first time he suggested that Wanita allow him to go to fetch medical help, leaving the young woman as a hostage, so that the old one could be taken to hospital. Otherwise, he said earnestly, he was certain she would die, and then where would Wanita be?

198

She listened, her mind a confusion of terror and longing. She wished that she, like Ramdas, could simply leap on a horse and escape, but he had taken every rupee, and how far would a woman get alone? She would be caught in no time. Even if she reached her uncle's village or the city and tried to get work the police would find her. Anyway, there were no jobs for an illiterate Adivasi like herself, nothing except prostitution which was not a possibility for a leader of her people.

Nathan persisted. He repeated that he was willing to get legal help for Wanita if only she would let them go. Wanita had heard of the Jesuit man at Sapatdongri who helped tribal people in legal matters. In fact her own uncle, who had got horribly into debt paying for his daughter's dowry had been helped by the lawyer priest.

Food, Nathan was now saying. We have had no food for twenty-four hours. We too will soon be sick.

Ha! she thought. Maybe they should just be left to die in the hut. That way she wouldn't have to shoot them. She wasn't too sure that she could actually do that.

And water, Wanita. Nathan was holding the empty bottle upside down. Did he think she was stupid that she couldn't see it was empty?

Manoj returned with a cotton sack which Wanita took and emptied on the bed. It contained bananas.

'Eat.' She pointed imperiously.

Jenni felt like a monkey in a cage.

Nadine's breathing was harsh. Jenni begged to be allowed to go to her.

'No!' yelled Wanita. 'Stay there!' She threatened convincingly with the weapon. Then she ordered Manoj to go for water.

He went out after looking doubtfully at the prisoners. Wanita stood pointing the gun and gestured to Jenni to stand up with her hands on her head. The old woman looked beyond help anyway, so it barely mattered whether or not the young one sat stroking her arm. Anyway, what was a white woman doing with a tattoo on her wrist like that? It wasn't brown like the henna patterns Wanita and her sisters put on the palms of their hands. That she might have understood but it was like a tribal tattoo. She was definitely a very odd old woman.

199

Nineteen

Among the seventy Spiritual Travellers who were getting off the bus which was parked near the Jesuits' vehicle there was a Scotsman. Like his companions – apart from the Enlightened Ones who had travelled in the mini-bus, now also disgorging its passengers – the man (a lapsed poet) knew little of what this was all about. His ego having not quite yet been eroded by his many courses of intensive meditation at the Glasgow School for Spiritual Travel, he wore a bright yellow balmoral and a matching kilt of the McLeod tartan. Adrenalised, he joined in the spirit of the dawn by singing to his companions to the tune of 'The Campbells are Coming': 'The Yogis are coming, hoorah, hoorah.'

Peter came over to him. 'Brother Hector, we need to maintain silence for the next bit, if you don't mind.'

'Sorry, brother, no harm meant,' the Scotsman apologised.

'No problem brother. Contain the light.'

Abstractedly, Peter patted the man's shoulder and continued to check the names on his clipboard.

'OK, people.' He addressed the group. 'We are going to walk up the hill for almost a mile. The road is clearly marked with boulders, you'll see them every few yards. Keep between them. March as quietly as possible, six abreast – brothers in the first five rows, sisters following.'

Obediently, the Travellers shuffled into lines.

'Maya and I will lead with the other Liberated Ones. We will then stop and make a line and then we will all Connect together, still in total silence, until we reach the top of the hill which has three palm trees on the summit.'

'It all sounds very strange to me,' muttered the Scotsman to his neighbour, but the latter was staring raptly at his spiritual leader who, poised majestically beside Peter, was gazing intensely from face to face of her assembled followers.

'I'd follow Maya anywhere,' said the neighbour fervently. He was a quiet little man, a successful accountant back home in Leeds. 'Anywhere.' He was almost in a state of bliss.

'We are going now.' It was Maya speaking. 'Keep Connected in gentle power as we walk, but don't make any noise whatsoever until we give the signal.' She smiled lovingly at her assembled followers who fervently murmured 'Peace – Connect – Contain the Light' as they returned her salute.

'I still wish I knew what on earth this was all about,' said the Scot.

'We'll soon find out.' The accountant's eyes were shining. 'I think it's all marvellous.' Proudly he wrapped his shawl round his skinny shoulders.

'OK. That's fine.' Peter, a general in white, checked his troops. 'Let's go.'

He turned to Maya who nodded, and the small army of Travellers led by the group of Liberated Ones set off up the hillside.

'What an unholy dawn,' whispered the Scotsman as they walked.

'Shhh.' said his neighbour. 'Peace – Connect.'

Kalidas, lying behind the hut on a small bluff a few feet above the well, watched intently as the shadowy figure of Manoj came to fetch water. Kalidas couldn't see any of the others and glanced restively at his watch. He was well hidden, but could just make out the turban of the dacoit as the man lay down his weapon and bent to fill a crock with water. Poised ready to fling his rock at the hut, Kalidas was finding his breathing hard to control and feared that Manoj would hear him.

Michael, on the other side of the encampment, stared hypnotically towards where he knew Kalidas to be waiting though he couldn't see him. Wanita had not yet emerged from the hut but he thought he could hear voices. A horse whinnied which made the watchers almost jump out of their skins. Twice a turbaned man had come out of the hut, once wearily going over to a tree near the horses to fetch something. Michael couldn't see him at all now because he was on the other side of the hollow. Michael thought of Jenni but was unable to find comfort in payer; begging favours from God was against his religion. Then, to his surprise, he thought of his wife Nella and her lover – originally his trusted friend.

Father Francis was having trouble with his spectacles again. They were continually steaming up and making his vision go swimmy. He could not remember when time had ever passed more slowly. He tried to focus on his watch but the second-hand seemed paralysed. He wiped his lenses with a hanky and mumbled an act of contrition under his breath: 'Oh my God, I am sorry I have sinned against Thee, and I resolve not to sin again.'

Brother Antony did not have such holy thoughts. Instead, he remembered his earthly father and mother in their small house in Bilbao, in north-east Spain, and was moved by the image. The memory of a girl – now married with three children – also came to mind. He had admired her for a season, and now felt momentarily bereft.

In the hut Jenni tried to eat a banana as Wanita, waving the gun more and more wildly, had ordered, but was unable to swallow. She felt ill and afraid, frightened of this crazy girl and frightened for Nadine, who was now an awful grey colour, shivering violently.

Gagging, Jenni looked despairingly at Nathan who was standing in a state of surrender, hands on head as Wanita had ordered.

Overcome by his impotence, he suddenly spoke with great fierceness to her. It was obvious that he was demanding that Jenni be allowed to go to Nadine.

'OK,' Wanita yelled. 'Let her go! Let her try to help. What difference could it possibly make?'

Jenni ran across the floor to support her friend who was gasping, her breath frothing a little. Her skin felt cold and clammy. Almost dead, thought Jenni frantically.

'Need to sit up . . .' gasped Nadine.

Anguished, Nathan made to move but Wanita shouted at him to stay still.

Desperately, Jenni reached for the rags she had slept on and piled them behind Nadine.

Nathan roared. He must be allowed to help, to honour this ill woman. For humanity's sake, Wanita must allow it!

Go then, she yelled. Help her. She watched, breathless with tension, as Nathan grabbed more blankets, rushed to the *charpoy* and helped to lift Nadine into a sitting position.

'I'm sure she needs oxygen,' said Jenni hopelessly.

Nathan started to reply but was interrupted by a sudden hellish clattering on the roof-tiles. At virtually the same moment an extraordinary noise rose up outside. It was a sustained vibration at first, a huge thrumming which filled the air mysteriously. Jenni, horribly shaken by the racket on the roof, had no idea what it was, but Nathan knew at once. Wanita, wide-eyed with terror, ran to the doorway, convinced that evil spirits had at last come to finish the nightmare.

Nadine knew too. Her eyes fluttered open, and she smiled like a child.

'It is Maya,' she said. 'Maya has come.'

Kalidas had thrown the rock on to the roof – and almost as a continuation of the gesture – jumped on to the turbaned head beneath him. Then, for the second time in less than twelve hours, he betrayed his Gandhian convictions by doing violence to another human being, only this time he used a rifle-butt. He tied up the groaning man with his own turban, and ran round to the side of the hut to see what was happening. There, to his astonished gaze, on the curved ridge of hillside opposite him, stretched a human chain of singing people. In the centre was a group of leaders in white, Maya in the very middle, flanked by Peter and Ram. On either side (the chain must be nearly a hundred yards long) were the yellow-dressed Travellers, singing their various one note open-mouthed 'Aaaahhhhs' with all their hearts and all their might. The noise reverberated through the air and swelled up to the sky just at the moment that the sun reared like a lion, fierce and dazzling, over the dark hills of the horizon, gilding the ecstatic faces of the Travellers and filling the air with light.

Ravi, asleep by the bonfire, head covered by a blanket, was on his feet yelling with fright before he knew anything. Like an ocean of sound in his familiar little valley, he heard the surge of song and looked in wonder to the crest of the hill. An army of shining people was walking towards him with linked hands. He gazed at them, and the thought that they must be gods, coupled with the fact that they were inexorably coming to get him, possessed him with terror.

'Wanita!' he called hopelessly, and ran screaming towards the hut.

The hungover guards gazed fearfully at the extraordinary sight of the singers, coming nearer and nearer, their noise vibrating and growing louder and stranger with each step. Stan, the thin man, bruised from Kalidas's thump with the paintbox, was sure his time had come. He hurled his rifle towards the people whom he knew could not be human, but the weapon bounced and lay before them with no effect. Still they kept on coming. Like the boy he yelled then prayed aloud and ran off towards the hills, still praying. His eyes were so wild that he saw nothing, so it was a relatively easy task for Brother Antony to put out a long leg and trip him up.

'You are a devil! An evilness!' the man cursed as Antony secured his hands.

As the dacoit Nathan called Rambo turned towards the invading singers, he heard Wanita scream 'Kill them!' Obediently, he veered towards the woman in the centre of the ethereal chain and raised his gun.

Father Francis saw the man take aim. He blinked. The humming swelled and the prisoners in the hut jumped as priest and dacoit fired simultaneously.

'Oh my God!' said Jenni. 'What's happening?'

Wanita screamed so much louder than usual that Jenni – still holding Nadine – thought the bandit leader had been hit.

'Ravi, Ravi!' wailed Wanita, and Jenni saw her rush out through the doorway.

Nathan ran too. He saw Ravi lying bleeding, hit by Father Francis's bullet which had grazed the arm of the tribal man before hitting the panic-stricken boy. Nathan, running out behind Wanita, saw her take aim at the advancing Travellers, who were still coming on either side despite some sort of

204

fracas which was taking place amongst the Liberated Ones. He saw blood on white and realised that someone was hit. There were more shots, and Wanita pulled the trigger just as Nathan felled her with a rugby tackle.

Rambo was standing bewildered, his arm stinging, his mind whirling. He had shot their leader but it seemed to have made no difference. The golden people – for so they were in the brilliance of the dawn – had barely quivered. The chain had parted only for a moment and the noise had swelled in a great moan, then they had continued walking downwards like immortals, still making their music. There was no doubt about it, they were coming straight at him. Like his friend, he thought that evil spirits had come to destroy him. He gasped, took one more terrified glance at the singers and fled.

Father Francis was lying sprawled on the ground. Antony and Kalidas had tied up the second guard and Kalidas was carrying the bleeding body of the boy into the hut whilst Nathan was trying to deal non-violently with the truly violent she-cat of a dacoit.

Rambo, running, could hardly believe his luck; he still expected a shot with every step, but knew he was quite far away by now because the noise of singing had receded. He slowed down a very little, then became aware of footsteps other than his own and half-turned, suddenly numb with fear.

'Hi there!' said Peter, blond ex-lifeguard and onetime football hero of his high school.

The man swore and stopped, pointing his gun at Peter, but he found himself grabbed by the waist and whirled about like a dancing dervish until he didn't know what was sky or earth. He shouted to all the gods he could think of and tried to trip up the young giant with the rifle. They fell with a clatter, all entangled. Round and round they rolled. The blond man was laughing hideously, singing an exultant one-note chant. It was all too much for the dacoit. Forced to let go of his gun, he capitulated and lay sobbing on his back. Peter, his legs scissored excruciatingly round the man's middle, broke the gun above his chest, removed its cartridges and hurled them aside. Between his legs, Rambo tried to squirm round but Peter gripped him with massive white-clad thighs until he begged him to stop. He did so at last, and the two lay panting together. Then, deviously, the dacoit produced a knife, long, sharp and murderous, and instantly the two were once more scuffling like mad dogs.

The young American was overwhelmed by the unaccustomed rage and desire to kill which blinded everything in him except for a basic animal will to survive. The tribal man likewise, only it was not such a strange sensation for him. He had not been living a meditative life for five long years. This time when Peter sang again it was a battle cry he remembered from the football field from years ago.

The adrenalin roared. He hardly felt the blade cut him, and was oblivious of the blood which flowed. His only reality was the desire to exterminate this creature whom he believed had killed Maya and who now threatened his own survival.

Kalidas entered the hut carrying Ravi. Nadine, propped up by Jenni, was still breathing shallowly. A minute ago, when all the shooting had happened, Jenni had thought she was lost.

'Kalidas, you're here!' Jenni lit up then moaned, 'Oh God! Not him, not Ravi.'

She watched as Kalidas tended to the boy, and handed him some torn cotton. 'Is it bad?' she asked.

Kalidas shook his head in the subtle Indian way and smiled. 'Ravi not bad.' He frowned. 'Maya bad.' He moved his head again, worried.

There was more shooting and Jenni could still hear the singing, but had no idea what was actually happening. There were gasps and thumps outside the hut but it was impossible to guess who was doing what to whom. All she did know was that it was a madhouse and it would be a miracle if any of them survived.

Michael's battle with the dacoits was not particularly heroic, it all happened too fast. He saw Maya fall, blood streaming, and was horrified. When he saw the boy shot and Father Francis collapse, his killing instincts evaporated. Francis fell when the dacoit woman fired and at almost the same instant Michael fired a couple of token shots after the man who was running away, but he was too quick and too far off for the bullets to hit him. Michael saw that the tall man he guessed to be Nathan had felled Wanita and turned to run to the stricken priest. There was still no sign of Jenni. Where the hell was she?

People in white were kneeling by the barely conscious Maya, who was bleeding from a chest wound – a lot of blood. Michael was amazed to see that the majority of her followers were still walking on down the hill towards the hut, singing away with linked hands. It was a most impressive sight. Brave or dotty, depending how you viewed it. One of the dacoits, doubled up in the dust at the bottom of the hill, gibbering with fear, had thrown away his gun. The man was in a hysterical world of his own so Michael deemed it safe to ignore him for the moment and ran back up to see to Francis. The Jesuit was on his back, spectacles squint, hair awry, out for the count. Michael knelt and examined him all over, expecting to find a wound, but there was none.

Father Francis's breathing was stertorous, then it stopped.

Intently, Michael felt for his wrist, and to his relief the little man's eyes fluttered open.

'Hi,' said Michael quietly. 'How are you doing?'

Francis moaned.

'I thought they'd got you,' said Michael, 'but I actually think you're OK.'

'Oh.' Francis struggled to sit up. 'I shot that poor child. May God forgive me. Did I kill him? What's happening?'

'I don't know. He was certainly hit. The rest is bedlam, but I think we're winning. Except that the guru lady is badly wounded.'

He tried to sit up. 'I think I fainted.'

Suddenly there was a shout, a loud report, and Michael yelled and lay back, felled by a shot from the gibbering Ollie Hardy in the valley below. Francis gawped as blood gushed from the Irishman's leg, then reached shakily for his gun.

'Father, forgive me,' he murmured. He aimed for a space two feet to the side of the tribal man and squeezed the trigger just as the fellow threw away his weapon for a second time and hurled himself to the ground, screaming.

Nathan and Antony were both scratched from the dacoit leader's clawing hands, but Wanita was under physical control at last, though demanding loudly to be allowed to see Ravi's body.

'OK.' Nathan stood up wearily. He was holding his gun again. He clasped Antony's arm. 'I'm glad you came, my friend.' He sighed and looked down at Wanita. 'I think we'd better tie her up. Take her into the hut so she can see the boy. I've told her that he's alive but she doesn't believe me.'

Kalidas came out of the hut and Nathan hugged him. Kalidas, pleased, looked down at the raging Wanita.

'Shall I do it?' he offered, smiling a little.

'Please do,' said Antony. 'You are very good at it. I'll see to the ones in the hut and fetch water.'

Kalidas set about tying up Wanita, using her own *odni* cloth, pulling so tightly on the long strip of brilliantly coloured cotton that she winced. He felt sorry for her: she was like so many of the girls he had grown up with, only wilder. She obviously didn't like this game at all, and looked ready to bite.

'OK?' asked Nathan.

'OK.' Kalidas, smiled broadly.

Nathan set off at a trot towards the hill and encountered the chain of Travellers. They had come to a stop and were standing quietly, encircling half of the natural amphitheatre. Nathan paused and surveyed them, touching his forehead and raising his palm. They returned the gesture, then they all went back to gazing up towards their wounded guru who was lying immobile, tended by half a dozen Liberated Ones.

Nathan reached the summit and greeted Ram, not with the usual salute but with a long warm hug.

'Gentle peace isn't in it for some people, I guess.'

'It is their Karma,' Ram said factually.

'Some Karma. How is she?'

'She is very weak. Can we take her down to the hut?'

'Sure. Antony is cleaning it up, it got pretty nasty in there.'

Nathan came to where Maya was lying and the others parted to let him kneel beside her.

'How is it, Maya?' he asked gently, touching her arm, but she barely seemed to recognise him.

He looked up as the group of people round Maya parted to make way for someone, and was overjoyed to see Father

208

Francis. Beyond the priest, doubled up on the ground, was a man Nathan had never seen before. One of his legs was bleeding badly and he was in obvious agony as a couple of girls tended to him.

'I have brought the first aid box,' said Francis breathlessly. As they bent to kneel by Maya, Nathan glanced curiously at the injured newcomer, who was obviously not a yogi.

'This looks pretty bad,' said Francis quietly.

Nathan nodded bleakly.

Seeing them, Michael tried to rise above his own pain. He could tell that this was a fine man, special. He must speak to him.

'You must be Nathan,' he gasped weakly, groaning as a girl in white tried to stem the flow of blood. 'My name is Michael O'Brien. I came to find Jenni – please can you tell me how she is?'

Irrational though he knew it to be, for he realised at once who the man was, Nathan felt a sensation of loss surge through him like a current. He looked at Michael, and a memory of how it had been with Jenni in his arms persisted in his head and flickered through his body.

'Jenni is OK, but Nadine I'm afraid is very ill. We fear for her life.'

Francis, helped by a nursing sister from Cardiff, was working on Maya, trying to staunch the blood. He looked up, 'This wound is very deep, I don't know what internal injuries there are. We must get her into the shade.'

Ram, also kneeling beside him, his hand held softly on Maya's arm, suddenly looked up, his eyes anxious. 'Where is Peter?' he asked. 'He should be with us.'

'He ran after one of the men,' said somebody.

'I hope he's OK,' murmured Ram.

Francis looked up at last. 'The boy – I must see to him too – and poor Michael. Oh dear . . .' Flustered, he stood up and went to examine Michael, leaving Maya with the nurse.

'Antony and Kalidas are with Ravi,' said Nathan.

Francis groaned. 'I must go down to him. That poor child.' He looked very distressed. Briefly he examined Michael's leg and frowned. It was really bad, and like Maya, he was losing far too much blood.

209

'Poor you,' he murmured. 'I will give you an injection for the pain.'

He did so quickly, then looked up. 'Ram is right. We must now carry Maya down to the hut – Michael too. But how do we do it?'

'Shawls,' said Ram, and the others looked at him blankly. 'A couple of shawls on top of each other like a hammock. I think it will work.'

Gently, the followers of Maya lifted her on to two white shawls which were laid down unquestioningly one on top of the other. Ram and Nathan took the front corners and Francis and another man took the back two.

'We need another couple of people in the middle to keep her level,' said Nathan, and two other Travellers came to help. Despite his discomfort, one of them, Michael noted hazily, was a Scotsman wearing all the gear.

The Scotsman was very upset. 'Oh God,' he murmured. 'She mustn't die, it isn't possible.'

'It's all possible,' said Michael hollowly.

The Scotsman eyed him sideways. And where did he fit into this strange scheme of things, he wondered aloud. He didn't look as though he belonged to either camp.

Michael looked at him hazily as Maya was lifted on to the improvised hammock. 'You could say,' he drawled, sounding very Irish, 'that I am a camp follower of sorts, and now they've kneecapped me, the buggers.' Then he lost consciousness.

Jenni managed to sip some water at last. The relief of knowing that they were free and Ravi's shoulder wound only superficial was almost overwhelming. Wanita was allowed to sit beside Ravi while Antony attended to his wound. She looked surprisingly small and miserable, and though her wrists were bound, she managed to hold Ravi's hand as he tried bravely not to cry.

Nadine, still breathing badly, seemed to be asleep. She hadn't spoken for ages, not since the singing had started and she had announced that Maya had come. Jenni went to peer out of the hut at the Yellow People who were sitting watching their recumbent guru. There were too many people round her to make out what was actually happening, though it looked as though somebody else was injured too. Suddenly feeble with exhaustion, Jenni went over to sit against the wall of the hut opposite the doorway. She had closed her eyes and almost drifted away when Antony shook her awake:

'Jenni,' he looked at her earnestly, 'I am going to fetch the Mahindra and the police. Please will you take the gun and keep watch just in case she does anything. You know.' He indicated the pale Wanita.

'OK.' Smiling tiredly, Jenni took the weapon almost as a token gesture, watched dully by Wanita from where she sat on the floor beside Ravi.

The fourth bandit, Jenni's Ollie Hardy, was still weeping outside the hut. He remained there, oblivious to the two Travellers – one male, one female – who sat humming quietly on either side of him as he grovelled in the dust, calling dramatically on his ancestors and tribal deities. The male Traveller had confiscated the man's abandoned gun and held it across his knees as he hummed. Stan Laurel was unharmed, lying with his head in his hands some yards away.

Peter squatted down by the body of the dacoit and stared at the man's eyes which were open as they had been when he had entreated Peter not to kill him. Peter looked at his own guilty hands, bloody as Macbeth's, and shuddered before starting to weep. He had become a Traveller because he hated violence, hated the American way of life with its in-built crudity and consumerism, and here he was in a desert place in India – a murderer. He prodded the body once more, just in case the man wasn't really dead, but the lined brown face grinned up at him in a frozen rictus of terror.

'Oh, Maya, what have I done?' he moaned. 'Maya, Maya . . .' He keened and hid his face in his bloody hands. He was sitting like this when they came and found him, alone and weeping in the wilderness, two vultures circling expectantly above.

Jenni, dozing, jerked into consciousness and automatically clutched at the rifle when she heard people enter the hut. The

211

light from outside was very bright and she was dazzled at first. Then she saw that it was Maya, obviously very badly wounded, being carried in. There were lots of people outside trying to crowd the entrance, and a Scotsman's voice was telling them to please sit quietly in a circle round the hut and try to *Connect* for heaven's and Maya's sakes.

Men came in and laid Maya – her face ivory-white – on the *charpoy* beside Nadine's. Wanita, terrified that she had killed the plump man with spectacles, was amazed to see that he was perfectly well and helping to carry the wounded woman – a woman whom Wanita had observed with interest and some envy was a true leader of men. Jenni's grip on the gun tightened as Wanita shuffled over on her bottom to squat in the far corner and stare anxiously at the incomers. Ravi, sleepy from Antony's injection, had been lying quietly miserable, but he grinned when he saw Nathan come in, and called eagerly to him. As the boy's face lit up, so did Father Francis's, thrilled to see that the child was alive.

A second lot of newcomers came into the hut and laid down a wounded Westerner right in front of Jenni. She was still forcing herself to watch Wanita so was only dimly aware when the man groaned and tried to sit up. She looked at him wearily when he murmured something incoherently and his shadow fell across her lap.

'Jen,' he said weakly. 'Hello, my love.'

Shocked, she stared at the drawn face. Gasping, Michael reached across to touch Jenni's hands which to her felt paralysed.

'Thank God I've found you at last,' he croaked.

Twenty

Nathan let go of his corner of Maya's woollen hammock and helped Ram to ease her on to the bed. Painfully aware of Jenni sitting opposite him against the wall, he stood aside to allow Francis to set to work. Then he Michael being carried in and laid down close to Jenni and watched as the Irishman leaned across to her. The expression on her face made him want to run to her, but instead he busied himself with the immediate problem.

Francis seemed to know exactly what to do. Quickly and efficiently he gave Maya a painkilling injection. 'Now,' he said firmly, 'I want the scissors please, Nathan.'

Nathan handed him scissors from the first aid box and the priest, breathing heavily, set about cutting open the front of Maya's long-sleeved cotton top.

'Keep the room clear except for those involved or hurt, please,' he said. 'I need to examine the extent of the injury.'

Nathan glanced across and saw Jenni, very white, shaking her head bewilderedly at Michael and then himself. He smiled faintly at her and checked on Nadine, whose colour was still poor. Her eyes were shut but at least she was still alive.

'More dressing, please.' Francis jabbed the scissors towards a wad of sterile pads. He had almost finished cutting away Maya's clothes, but had genteely covered her exposed bosom. The bullet had entered the side of her chest. She was now lying facing Nadine.

Jenni was coming back to reality. She looked wearily at Michael.

'I can't really believe this,' she said. 'I'm truly sorry you're hurt. It looks terrible . . .'

He tried tentatively to take her hands, to stroke her fingers. 'No.' She pulled away.

Momentarily numb to his injury, Michael wanted to embrace her, to touch her funny short hair which was strange to him, but she was still looking completely dazed. Nathan caught Jenni's eye for a moment and gave her a sad little half-smile.

She pulled away abruptly from Michael and stood up.

What was Michael doing here anyway? she wondered. Was she hallucinating? Then she remembered Nadine. She must go to her.

'Here.' Abruptly, she handed Kalidas the gun and pointed to Wanita. 'Please take this.'

'Ok.' He nodded.

She want to sit with her friend whose eyes fluttered open. Nadine asked feebly for water. Jenni helped her to drink, which she did with difficulty. Then Nadine's gaze wavered across to settle on the bed next to her.

'Oh my God!' she groaned, and stared in shock at Maya's devastated body.

Francis had almost finished, but there was still a lot of blood about. Obviously aware of what was happening, Maya groaned deeply as the Jesuit carefully wiped and bandaged.

Nadine was still staring. 'My poor girl – *ma pauvre petite*,' she murmured softly, her voice full of pain.

The watchers saw the guru's dark slanting eyes open.

Francis took Maya's hand and asked quietly how she felt.

'Body bad, soul good,' she murmured succinctly, and turned to Nadine. The two gazed at each other.

Maya managed to speak at last: 'I knew – I had to come.'

Slowly, Nadine reached towards Maya. The circle of watchers saw the women's fingers touch. The emotion generated by their hands clasping was almost tactile. Both Nathan and Jenni saw the line of blue numerals at the same instant. As they stared at the tattooed inner wrists of Nadine and the guru, Jenni felt Nathan hold her arm. Of course. She nodded. No wonder the pair of them looked so alike. Simultaneously there were rapturous smiles on the two faces which were now so obviously similar.

214

'*Maman*,' said Maya, and her eyes closed.

'Maya,' murmured Nadine and collapsed back on to her pillow of rags and blankets.

Jenni felt tears falling. She groaned and leaned back weakly against Nathan who held her firmly to him.

'She has left us,' he said. And he too wept.

Michael's sense of desolation was complete when, surfacing from pain, he saw Jenni and Nathan together. But he also wondered if he was imagining things. He blinked and looked across the hut again. He could have sworn that there was a golden light above the guru's bed.

Outside the hut, the Travellers were sitting in a circle meditating. There was a feeling of great tranquillity in the air when at virtually the same moment all the members of the group began to hum together; as they did so, first a few, then all of them looked up. In front of them, in the hollow, a few dry leaves and sticks stirred in a sudden small whirlwind. As they watched, the wind grew unexpectedly and swirled, whirling the objects round and up with a fierceness which matched the brilliant glow which seemed to fill the whole amphitheatre.

The watchers stared in awe and continued to sing as the whirlwind travelled upwards. Then the door of the hut opened and Ram emerged. He looked at the Travellers, his sad eyes seeming to embrace every singing soul, and each one of them knew without words what had happened.

In Ahmedabad in the house with the flat roof the woman had been waiting. She had already fed several lots of uneaten *chapatis* to a neighbour's goats and her almond sweetmeats now sat half-eaten and soggy in the kitchen under a poster which stated glibly EQUALITY IS A GOOD GAME TO PLAY. The poster showed a boy and a pig-tailed girl, both smiling, dressed in football gear, holding a large football between them.

Exhausted from two sleepless nights, the woman was woken soon after dawn by a loud battering on the door. Half-awake, she stumblingly took the end of her *odni*, wound it round her head to shield her face and went to the door. She

215

found two policemen standing there. Thin, uneasy, his uniform crumpled, the younger of the two was carrying her husband's briefcase.

The woman recognised this at once and stared at the men in terror. When one of them asked if she knew her husband carried a gun she said no, vehemently. Embarrassed, he nodded and spoke quietly to her. Moments later, the woman's neighbours were woken by a terrible wailing, and those who had been watching as neighbours do, saw the policemen on the doorstep nod to the weeping woman, remove their caps, enter the house with her and close the door behind them.

When they emerged some time later, the woman was left sitting alone on a low sofa clutching the briefcase in a tight embrace, rocking from side to side in wordless misery.

Tulsiram, the tribal farmer who lived near the Chitto river and had been up all night helping to deliver twin goats, saw three more strange sights after he had returned home bewildered by those of the early morning. Later in the day, when the sun was past its height, he had gone out in search of a goat which had strayed from the flock. A friend had reported seeing vultures wheeling further up in the hills so he had come looking in case his goat was dead. Here he encountered the first of the three strange sights: he met with two men dressed in yellow, one of whom wore an unusual hat – yellow, with ribbons down the back, a chequered headband, yellow and white, and a yellow pom-pom. They were carrying what was obviously the corpse of a tribal man whose eyes stared at the sky from his jolting head as they held on to his splayed arms and legs and walked down the incline towards the point where the track from the main road petered out. Tulsiram crouched down behind a clump of boulders as they passed and waited until they were beyond the next ridge before continuing. Soon after this he met two men in white garments – an Indian of about forty, with an air of great authority, and a yellow-haired younger white one who had bloody hands and clothes. The Indian man was leading the latter gently by the arm, murmuring comforting words to him. The bloodstained one, who was stumbling and weeping, seemed almost blind with grief.

216

Tulsiram did not approach them either; the happening was too unusual and the men were strangers in the district. He walked on until he came to the spot where the vultures had been circling and realised from the blood and signs of scuffling on the dry earth that this was where the fight must have taken place. Looking round he found an abandoned rifle, its barrel embedded in sand. The weapon was bent as though it had been thrown there. He also found a knife and presumed from its state that it must have been used by the weeping man. Tulsiram stared at the knife and wondered for a moment if he should take it as it had a fine sharp blade, but decided it might get him into trouble and left the place hurriedly. He knew now of course what the vultures had been waiting for.

Tulsiram found the lost animal at last, a youngster, bleating faintly from a small cliff top. He was carrying the small creature home when he saw the eeriest sight of all. First of all he looked up to the sky and then he gasped, for ahead of him, above the small circular valley where his now-dead friend Devilal – father of runaway Wanita – had lived, he saw a strange orange light. He could tell from the swirling of leaves and bushes that there was a whirlwind by the hut, which was not in itself unusual, but the orange light was like nothing he could remember and he grew more than a little afraid. He stared wonderingly towards it and superstitiously hoped it meant good luck. Then, as he came to the ridge of the hill, he sank down astonished beneath a small fig tree to observe what was happening.

By late-afternoon Tulsiram saw that a funeral pyre had been built. For a while he wondered if it might be for the dead man he had seen earlier, but he was soon certain from the demeanour of the many people who were circled round the pyre that it could not be. The mourners were nearly all dressed in yellow except for a few in jeans and some – who looked like *sahibs* – in white. The body on top of the pyre was covered with a white cloth. He guessed from the shape that it was female, but the unusual demeanour of the people and the strange whirlwind made the event seem very special.

He watched as a wounded white man was lifted out and laid on a *charpoy*, then he saw Ravi, also bandaged, being carried

217

out of the hut in the arms of a youngish tribal fellow in jeans, that were too big for him. The latter was standing with a bespectacled man in a jacket, a white woman and a tall man who had curly hair and brown skin though he didn't look Indian. The woman was weeping, as were many of the mourners. Tulsiram realised with the sudden jarring of recognition that the tall man was the same *Bagwan* who had come in a white vehicle to Tulsiram's village more than once to help the tribal people, and had even arranged to take Tulsiram's son to the mission hospital when he was nearly dead with the red fever. He watched, moved, as the man took a blazing torch and with great ceremony handed it to the same authoritative Indian man whom Tulsiram had seen earlier leading the bloodstained one by the hand. The Indian nodded and, flaming torch held high, proceeded to walk firmly round the funeral pyre the traditional five times. The mourners threw garlands of frangipangi and marigolds on to the bier – flowers which Tulsiram learned later came from the gardens of his village. Then he saw that the *Bagwan* with the curly hair was looking at the crying memsahib with great intensity. He also noticed with interest that the wounded white man watching them from the ground looked sad and alone.

The Indian man finished his circling of the pyre and stood still. Tulsiram watched in awe as he set fire to the brushwood heaped high beneath the corpse. In moments the flames were flaring and spreading until the whole thing was enveloped in fire and smoke.

When the ring of people started to make noise, it was not the weeping and wailing that Tulsiram was used to. At the funerals he attended people made much clamorous lamentation, but this was different. It was very controlled and also very affecting. Holding the little goat, Tulsiram bowed his greying head for he felt certain now that all this must surely signify the passing of a great soul.

His eyes were closed and as the noise increased his body seemed to vibrate, as did the entire landscape. He became aware that the thrumming noise he could hear now was not a human one. Astonished, Tulsiram and the circle of singing Travellers turned to gaze upwards and saw a helicopter heading straight for the funeral pyre like a gigantic evil insect.

218

'Who on earth do you think they are?' whispered the Scotsman in the yellow Balmoral to the man next to him.

'Police, I expect. This is all going to be hell to explain. There'll be two murder charges and only one body,' said the accountant from Leeds, then continued to hum louder than ever.

The mourners stared as the helicopter dropped so low that they thought it was going to land.

From the ground Nathan and Jenni looked up at the whirling blades of the helicopter as it hovered above the still-flaming pyre.

'What do you reckon?' asked Jenni as the machine swooped upwards and flew northwards away from them.

'It's very unusual to see a helicopter here,' said Nathan.' I'm sure it's the police – Antony went for them.'

'Maybe they're looking for you, Jen,' called Michael hoarsely, and Jenni shivered.

Twenty-One

At the Sapatdongri hospital near the mission, where the survivors of the kidnap had spent several days recovering from exhaustion and dehydration, Brother Antony arrived with clothes for Jenni.

'I hope I've got the right ones, it was lucky you left some behind when you set off on tour,' he said, handing them over.

When she had dressed she asked the sister-in-charge if she might visit Michael who she knew to be on the other side of the building. The doctors had told her that Michael's leg required more surgery and that he would have to be taken to a bigger hospital for this. Her feelings were mixed as she pushed open the door to find him sitting reading on his bed.

'How are you?' she asked quietly, aware that she still found him remarkably good-looking despite his present pallor.

He grimaced. 'Nearly legless, but you've seen me that way before.'

Always the repartee with Michael. That had been much of the original attraction. 'It's awful. I'm so sorry . . .'

He shrugged. 'It's happened. I can hardly take it in. Could have been much worse. I'm lucky, really. I'll probably have a limp, but at least I'll be able to walk.'

'How long till you can go home?'

'It will take a few weeks. I've got to be moved to Ahmedabad for more surgery.'

'How will they move you?'

He winced. 'That I'm not looking forward to. Luxury private ambulance, but the roads are so rough . . . I'm frankly dreading it, but thank God for BUPA.'

220

'And then?'

'A couple of weeks at least, then maybe I could fly home. I'll need to rehabilitate, learn to use crutches for a while.' He paused. 'I – er – had hoped to get to Udaipur.'

'To the Lake Palace?'

He nodded. 'We always said we'd go there sometime.' He tilted his head sideways in the way she had loved for so long. Looking at him, Jenni felt strangely sad. It would be so easy, especially because he was injured, to reach across and touch him, to respond to the physical pull. It was hard for a moment not to.

There was a long silence.

'You wouldn't have come, would you?' he said at last.

Sadly she shook her head. 'You know that this year there's no water left at Udaipur – because of the drought – the lake's actually empty.'

'Ah.' He nodded almost formally and looked away. It seemed symbolic, the empty lake. He looked at her again. 'I still love you, Jen.'

She couldn't answer.

He looked at her. 'I'm sorry for the silence.'

Jenni shrugged.

'I'm free now too. Honest. I've moved out into a flat.'

'Free.' She tasted the word. 'Liberated?'

He nodded.

'What made you finally make the break? What about Nella?'

'Nella's all right.' He said it too quickly.

'What do you mean, all right?'

'She's got somebody.'

'Ah. You mean she left you?'

Michael's expression hardened for a moment. 'Call it mutual.'

They were silent, then he reached for her. 'Jen, I'm sorry I took so long.' He tried to make eye-contact again. 'Please can't we try again? I know this has been a horrendous few days for you.'

His touch was insistent. She remembered the let-downs, the silences, the broken promises. Her always being second best.

He was still trying. 'We could relax and try to find each other again. It's only a year and a half since France.'

221

She pulled away, tears not far off.

He tried to make her smile, saying it was only the leg that was out of commission, but she didn't react.

She shook her head. 'I'm sorry. I guess you're too late. You left me sitting there for too long. 'She frowned. 'The kidnap, the funeral, it's been too much . . .' A knock on the door interrupted her.

Michael looked at her, worried. 'Jen – about Ahmedabad. You'll come with me, won't you?'

Jenni felt icy cold. She hugged herself and vacantly examined the texture of his bedlinen.

'Just for the journey, and to be with me when they operate?'

Time seemed to go into slow motion. Jenni felt paralysed by warring feelings.

'I . . .'

There was a second, louder knock on the door.

'Damn!' Michael looked at her. 'Are you OK?'

She shrugged.

'Come in!' he called.

A bony nurse bustled in with a jug of water. 'You have another visitor, Mr O'Brien.'

Michael looked towards the door and saw that Nathan was standing there. Speak of the devil.

Nathan, wearing jeans and a striped shirt, looked well and rested. To the dazed Jenni, he seemed beautiful.

'Am I disturbing you?'

'No, not at all,' said Michael.

'No whites?' asked Jenni, surprised.

'I felt like a bit of normality.' He came over to shake hands with Michael almost formally. 'How are you? Stronger, I hope? It's really tough about the leg. I'm truly sorry. You're a real hero.'

'I'll survive.' Michael smiled grimly.

'It must be terribly painful . . .'

'From time to time it's almost unbearable, but they've got very good medication.'

Nathan nodded, then turned to look closely at Jenni. 'And you? It's good to see you up and about. How do you feel?'

'I'm good.' She nodded. 'How is the boy?'

222

Nathan laughed. 'He's amazing. Playing Boxes on his temperature chart at six a.m. He's never been so well looked after for years.'

'Any news of Wanita?'

'She's been taken to Ahmedabad prison and will probably await trial there for months, or so Father Francis says. He's going to handle her case. Peter is awaiting trial there too.'

'So Ravi is alone in the world now?'

Nathan nodded. 'He does have an uncle who is married with no children – Francis knows them. They are simple people: the man is jobless and landless.'

'Could they take him?'

'They would, but I have a better idea.'

'He's so bright,' said Jenni. 'He must have an education.'

'I know. I've decided to try to adopt him. He can go to a Gandhian centre for his schooling and live with me.'

'But with all your field trips, how would it work?'

'Kalidas says he and his wife can help look after him. That way he would have continuity with his tribal roots, plus he'd be educated.'

'And loved.'

Nathan nodded.

'Brilliant.' Jenni imagined Nathan bringing Ravi to London, the three of them going to concerts and the zoo. 'I'd like to help in any way I can. It's a great idea.'

'Hey,' said Nathan at last, 'I almost forgot why I came in the first place. The doctors have finished next door. D'you want to come and see the patient?'

Jenni nodded and looked at Michael. Shall we take you in the wheelchair?'

Michael nodded, then groaned as they helped him out of bed.

'You OK?' asked Jenni, taking the handle. Sweating, Michael muttered, 'Got to keep moving.'

Nathan went out and they followed him expectantly down the corridor, Jenni wheeling Michael.

They found Nadine sitting up in bed drawing.

'Ah!' She beamed and held out her arms. 'My beloveds.'

Jenni could hardly believe what she saw. 'Are you sure you're allowed to work?'

Nadine shrugged. 'I was bored with just lying doing nothing. I have to stay in bed too much – ugh!' She grimaced.

Jenni sat on the bed and touched her wonderingly. 'I thought we had lost you, you know.'

'Me too.' Nadine looked up at her.

'I'm so sorry about Maya. I had no inkling . . .'

All of a sudden Nadine's expression was very bleak and Jenni saw that Nathan too, had tears in his eyes. They had both really loved the dead woman. She also noticed that Nadine was wearing the silver bracelet again. The tattooed numbers might never have been.

'I'm really sorry.' Jenni stroked her hand.

Nadine shrugged and looked away. Jenni waited. After a while Nadine gestured helplessly. 'It's life. Rather me than her, but what can you do?'

'I had absolutely no idea about you two . . .'

'Nobody knew. Maya herself only knew a few years ago.'

Jenni and the two men sat quietly.

'Can you tell us?'

'How we escaped the prison camp is too long a story to tell now. One day.'

'But you did?'

'Yes.' She nodded into the distance. 'We escaped. Maya was three years old. I was twenty-three.'

'Was she Mordecai's child,' asked Jenni, 'the man you told me about?'

There was a long silence then Nadine nodded. 'Mordecai didn't escape,' she said at last. 'The Germans killed him. I was crazy for almost five years. My sister and her husband took the child to the States with them and she was very happy there, so we left it like that.' She shrugged again. 'My work I could cope with, but not a small child. It was my loss in the end.'

'But you didn't really lose her?'

'No.' Her eyes were distant. 'Perhaps not. We loved each other in our own ways, but I was not exactly a perfect mother.'

'Only you, Nadine,' Jenni's voice was fond. 'Only you could be a guru's mother.'

Nadine smiled her ironic life-affirming smile, then she turned to Nathan.

'And you, Nathan. How are you?'

He embraced her. 'Glad that you're still with us.'

Nadine smiled and lay back. 'Will you take Maya's place at Kundi now?'

'No.' Nathan was firm. 'I shall still go there but less often. I guess I'm changing – have changed.' He glanced shyly at Jenni. 'Ram will be the leader of the Spiritual Travellers now. The movement will continue, I am sure, as Maya always said it must.'

'Ah.' Nadine nodded, moved. Then she grinned. 'It seems I'm not dead yet. But I have learned one important thing from you, Nathan, one very important thing you taught me on the journey.'

'You have? What's that?'

They craned forward to listen, expecting some profound philosophy to have emerged from all the suffering. Nadine was obviously tiring visibly. She had, they knew, undergone a slight heart-attack when they were imprisoned by the dacoits. Her eyes were very blue as she looked at Nathan.

'I know that camels really do pee backwards.'

Even Michael was still laughing when they left her. Nathan said goodbye and Michael and Jenni were once more alone.

'What a woman,' said Michael, settling with relief back on to his bed. 'I've never met anyone like her.' He looked up at Jenni and wished that he was on his feet and could simply put his arms round her shoulders. Touch had always been their best language.

'Just a few days away together – I can show you much of Rajasthan,' Nathan had suggested tentatively. 'Nadine says she's OK to be left. She's happy here, drawing and resting and talking to Father Francis and the hospital sisters.'

'She falls in love with every place she visits, that one.' Jenni smiled fondly.

'Well?' said Nathan. 'Just four or five days. I have a couple of places to visit, and I've hired a vehicle. Jaipur is very lovely, and we'd get there in a day. Would you like to come?'

She was certainly tempted. She frowned. 'But I've decided

to go home, and I feel I ought to accompany Michael . . .'
Their eyes met. 'Can I think about it?'
'Sure.' Nathan smiled and her insides leapt.

Later, Jenni told Nadine.
 'And you said no?'
 'I said I had decided to go back to work.'
 'Work?'
 'Work is important.'
 'Sure. But you have more than proved yourself in that area.
You are the best. But what about you yourself?'
 'What do you mean?' Jenni bristled.
 'You know what I mean. I mean love. Life. Intimacy. Basic
needs.'
 'Are you telling me to go?'
Nadine frowned. 'Only you can decide that.'
 'I have decided one thing for sure, though.'
 'What's that?'
 'I really want to give him something.'
 'Like what?'
 'I'd like to buy him a saxophone. He used to play one.'
Nadine nodded. 'And the idea of the trip?'
Jenni was silent.
 'You scared?'
 'Maybe.'
 'Of what?'
 'Hurting. Being hurt.'
 'So you avoid the chance of some happiness. Some loving.
Or even just some fun. You need those things, Jenni. You
deserve them. Friendship matters too, even more than work.
I think it is the most important thing.'
 'Would you go if you were me?'
 'Impossible question. But if it was me, yes, I'd go. He is
irresistible, an outstanding person. It is wonderful that he is
reaching out to you. Nature is powerful. Enjoy!'

'Jen.'
 She looked him in the eye at last.
 'It's Nathan. You like him, don't you?'

She didn't answer at first. 'Sure I like him.' She paused. 'But it's not like that. He's a celibate anyway.'

Michael laughed hollowly. 'I'm sure that won't be too much of a challenge for you.'

She sighed, then sadly heard herself say, 'The point is, Michael, I don't love you any more.'

He drew back his hand. There was a long silence; Jenni, aware of Michael's pain, physical and mental, irrationally longed to comfort him, but a still small voice prevented her. Instead she stood quietly, breathing slowly.

He made a last appeal. 'And Ahmedabad – coming with me?'

'I'll have to think about it, Michael,' she said at last huskily. 'I haven't really decided what I'm doing yet. I'm actually due to fly back next week.'

He nodded and turned to stare out of the window where he displayed a sudden mesmeric interest in the view.

They both jumped when there was a knock on the door. Jenni turned towards it, agonised, and called for them please to wait. She looked at Michael and their eyes locked. His were wet.

'I'm sorry but it really is over. It has been for me ever since I said it was.' She was crying too now.

He looked very sad and his eyes stared bleakly across the room until he nodded at last in weary acknowledgement of what she had said.

'Will you be OK?' she asked feebly.

A hollow laugh. 'I seem to have no option. I'll survive, don't worry about me, Jen. You've made your decision, I'm not your problem.'

She closed her eyes fiercely.

'I need a cigarette,' said Michael. Clumsily, he scrabbled for the pack and dropped it.

'I'll get it.' Jenni bent down, picked up the pack from under the bed, extracted a cigarette and lit one for him.

'Thanks.' He touched her arm briefly. 'Thanks for it all, my love. We were happy for quite a few seasons, weren't we?' He inhaled and looked at her.

She nodded.

'It's a hard bloody life sometimes, Jen.'

The visitor this time was an ebullient Father Francis, newly returned from Ahmedabad where he had visited Wanita in prison.

'She is still aggressive and very frightened, as you would expect,' he told them. 'But the authorities agree in principle that Nathan can adopt the boy. Wanita understands that she will be locked up for a long time.

'By the way, I brought you the London edition of *The Times*. I thought you might like to see it.'

'Ah, thank you.' Michael lit up.

'I couldn't concentrate on it, it all seems too far away.' Jenni handed the paper across to Michael who eagerly set about reading.

'Hey,' he said minutes later when Jenni and the priest were chatting together, 'listen to this!'

He declaimed: '"Yesterday the London Confederation of National Media Awards announced that freelance television journalist Jenni Bartlett had won the Journalist of the Year Award for her outstanding investigative report in the programme British Made which was transmitted on BBC2 last Wednesday."'

'How marvellous!' Father Francis's eyes were enormous. 'You are truly famous!'

Jenni couldn't believe it, but listened amazed as Michael continued to read aloud: '"The controversial winning programme, originally scheduled to be shown in December, was recently the subject of Parliamentary questioning and an injunction against the BBC. After the decision by the Board of Governors to prevent transmission there was a general strike of BBC television journalists which lasted for a week until the embargo was lifted. Miss Bartlett, who is believed to be on holiday in India, was not present to receive her award. It was accepted on her behalf by her producer Mr Roger Norton."'

Jenni gasped and they gazed at her.

'Jenni, that's wonderful. You clever woman, you. And it's a fifteen thousand pound prize.'

Michael was genuinely moved. 'There's real affirmation for you, Jen. The best sort, from your colleagues. It's marvellous.'

228

Jenni couldn't speak for a moment; her eyes were once more full of tears. 'Yes, it's wonderful. I am vindicated, and it confirms what I must do. I've got to keep working. There are areas I want to explore . . .'

Frowning, Michael reached for a cigarette.

'I'm going to do a programme that will consciousness and fund raise. That's where I want to put my working energies from now on.'

'Jen, give yourself a break.'

'I've just done that. Now I need to get back to work. I need to go home first but I'll be back here soon. There's so much to be done.'

'Oh Lord.' Michael, bravely joking, his heart trampled flat, looked at the fascinated Father Francis. 'What do you do with a woman like that?'

'Don't ask me,' said Francis cheerfully. 'I'm a celibate, remember?'

Twenty-Two

He had thought for a long time about asking her. He knew that he wanted to spend time with her, get to know her in a relaxed state. He wasn't sure what would happen, or even what he wanted to happen, only that he kept thinking about her, being with her, touching her. He was scared. But Jenni was so easy to talk to, to be with. She had an innate truthfulness, a rare integrity. And she made him laugh. This morning he had looked at himself in a mirror and for a change had felt good about what he saw. In the bright striped shirt the reflected man looked more like the musician he used to know. Maybe – he had grinned at his image – maybe he would even find himself a sax or a santoor to play. he would like to fly that way again too.

Nathan was resting under a banana palm in the garden of the mission hospital when he sensed Ram's approach. They hadn't seen each other since the day of Maya's cremation, and he was at once aware that Ram was laden with grief. Nathan himself was still mourning the loss of Maya, who had been his dear friend as well as guide and mentor, and their hug of greeting was an emotional one.

'Hi, Buddy. How is it at Kundi without her?'

Ram sat beside him and shook his head. 'The joy has gone. The daily routine of life continues as normal but the very centre, the hub of our small universe, is missing. I don't know what will happen now.'

'But you will continue?'

'Of course. We must. I must. But I am not Maya.'

'We'll always miss her.'

230

Ram nodded, his eyes wet. He couldn't articulate. Then he stared at Nathan's shirt and looked away. The colours were a mute witness to Nathan's state of mind regarding Kundi.

'What news of Peter?'

Ram looked at the ground, pain in his face.

'Have they let you talk to him?'

'I went to the prison this morning. I have come straight from there to here.'

'You got to see him?'

Ram nodded heavily.

'How is he?'

Ram shook his head. 'He seemed so young today. Just a kid, but all the world was weighing on his shoulders.'

Nathan nodded.

'He could have been my son; sometimes I felt like his father. He tried so hard to change himself . . .'

'He did grow up a lot; he became very responsible and aware. Maya trusted him, considered him Liberated. Is that devalued now by what has happened?'

'I don't know any more. Who knows what he will have to undergo to amend for the murder? I am afraid his Journey will be endless.'

'What's going to happen to him?'

The lawyer thinks that with luck he may be released after trial; Father Francis is advising. They will claim that he killed in self-defence.'

'So he could be free before too long?'

Ram shrugged. 'It's possible.'

'Maybe Maya will set him right, wherever she is.'

'Maybe.' Ram shrugged. 'He gave me a letter for you. I have it here.'

Nathan took the cheap flimsy paper and was moved as he read the childishly formed words written in blue biro.

'Dear Nathan,

I realise that I cannot live alongside other Travellers any more with my guilt and with no Maya to help me along. I feel too bad and miss her too much. I will go *senyassin* if I am ever let out of here, and disappear. I am sorry that I have to leave you all but can see no other way out. I have tried to escape the violence in my life but it seems it was inside of me all the time. I need to earn peace in my soul.

Please tell my parents what has happened, I enclose their address in Florida, and forgive me for failing you all. I have betrayed Maya's trust and wish I could end my life here now, but I know I cannot do that thing.

Contain the light, Brother. You really know how to do it.

Peter'

The two were silent as they imagined the golden-haired young man, filled with grief and self-reproach, wandering alone throughout India with only a begging-bowl and the clothes he stood up in.

'Poor guy. What else could he do, really?'

Ram nodded sadly and Nathan put his hand on his shoulder. The two of them sat side by side, grieving in silence for a long time.

In the end Jenni had hugged Michael. A loving hug, just before he set off. To do them both justice it was a pretty tearful farewell; not a lot of script, but plenty of emotion. Michael remembered her face as he was driven away. She had looked very fragile and up to the last moment he had still felt hope, but there had been a finality in her goodbye despite the tears.

'When does Maggie arrive.'

'Nella said she was leaving yesterday. I'll see her tomorrow – Gordon's brother in the embassy at Delhi has arranged for her to stay near the hospital with friends of his.'

'That'll be nice.'

He nodded. 'She's a good kid, Maggie. I think Nella will come out just after the op and I'll go home with her.'

'That sounds civilised.'

Michael's eyes were weary. 'She is. Deeply so.'

'I'll see you in London,' Jenni promised. 'Take care.'

'Sure. We'll keep in touch. Ring me when you're back.' He had even managed a wan smile as the ambulance man fiddled with his wheelchair.

'Get strong soon. You're a survivor.' She touched his shoulder but did not hug him again as he palpably yearned for her to do.

232

He looked at her. 'And you take care. You know I'm always there if you need me.'

She had looked at him without accusation, the answer implicit in her silence.

'Good luck, Jen. Don't get too carried away.'

She bristled. 'What do you mean?'

'The exotic setting, the good-looking guy . . . holiday romance.'

'Thanks a bunch.'

'I'll see you, Jen.'

'Of course. I'll ring you when I'm back. I trust you'll be on your feet by then.'

She followed him in the wheelchair to where his private luxury ambulance was waiting for him. Obviously in pain, he was lifted in. A reliable-looking nurse was to accompany him.

'Have you taken your medication, Mr O'Brien?' she asked as she carefully placed a cage over the injured leg and covered him with a sheet.

'I'm groggy already.'

'That's the best way to be on that road. Don't you worry, you'll be fine now.'

Jenni stood watching for a long time after the ambulance had driven off. She was aware of an equal sense of relief and sorrow, and an image of Michael's eyes gazing bleakly at her as the door was slammed shut stayed with her until she became aware of Ravi calling. Ravi, still bandaged, his arm in a sling, for whom she had decided to share financial responsibility with Nathan. The child grinned at her and spoke a newly learned English sentence: 'Jenniben, will you play Boxes with me, pliss?'

In the morning Kalidas came with Ravi to see Nathan and Jenni off. They had brought garlands for the travellers – bright flowers interwoven with threads of silver tinsel. Ravi ran towards Nathan who knelt down and the child leapt into his arms still holding the rope of flowers. Nathan could smell its heady sweetness as he set the boy on his shoulders. Kalidas shyly handed the other garland to Jenni and helped her to put it round her neck before she climbed into the hired jeep. Nathan bent his head to allow the boy to put the garland round his neck, and hugged him goodbye. Ravi, suddenly sad, stood close to Kalidas who put an arm round his shoulders as Nathan started up the engine.

'We'll be back soon,' Nathan promised him. 'Then you can come home with me.'

Jenni, unexpectedly shy, produced incense and busied herself with lighting it as Ravi and Kalidas waved and called tenderly in farewell.

'One, two, three, four, five, goodbyee!' Ravi shouted.

As they drove through the mission gates, Nathan turned to Jenni and asked quietly: 'Are you ready for the next step in the journey?'

She inhaled the smells of blossom and incense and looked out at the landscape, the beauty and the squalor, and nodded.

He smiled, laid his hand for a moment on top of hers, and they were on their way.